Thrown Under The Bus

ALSO BY STEVE PARKER

DETECTIVES PATERSON AND CLOCKS
Book 1: Their Last Words
Book 2: The Lost Children
Book 3: The Burning Men
Book 4: You Can't Hide
Book 5: Their Dying Breath
Book 6: Child Behind The Wall
Book 7: His Mother's Bones
Book 8: Dead On Delivery
Book 9: Slaughtered As They Slept
Book 10: Thrown Under The Bus

STANDALONE
Jack Knife

# THROWN UNDER THE BUS

## STEVE PARKER

*Detectives Paterson & Clocks Series Book 10*

JOFFE BOOKS

Joffe Books, London
www.joffebooks.com

First published in Great Britain in 2024

Cover art by Nebojša Zorić

ISBN: 978-1-83526-836-0

*For Caz.*

*From the very beginning. Thank you for letting me get on with it.*

*'Sometimes, you have to do wrong, to do right'*
*Johnny Clocks*

# CHAPTER 1

With a steaming cup of coffee in hand, Chris Striker sat upright in his chair, eyes fixated on the 5'x5' HD screen directly in front of him. As the duty officer in charge of London's Traffic Management System, his days were consumed by the thirty-two screens before him, pressing buttons and solving problems to keep the traffic flowing smoothly. It was no easy task, even at the best of times. Every day brought a new set of challenges — a two-car collision on the Hammersmith fly-over causing a massive two-mile tailback; a lorry shedding its load on Blackheath Common due to careless driving, leaving commuters in a four-mile queue. These all too common occurrences would send most people into a frenzy, but for Striker and his team, they were just part of their daily routine, problems to be sorted.

This morning, though, something on one of the screens told him his day, along with that of tens of thousands of commuters, was about to get seriously fucked up.

A dark-haired woman in her mid-thirties stood on the pavement of the southern approach of Tower Bridge, looking to her right as if waiting for a safe moment to cross. But this woman kept glancing at her phone in between watching the

1

road, and that concerned Striker. Something wasn't right here, he could feel it. He sat forward and punched a button marked 'MD' on his console: code for Southwark Police Station.

'Good morning, Mike Delta,' he said into his headset. 'This is Christopher Striker, duty officer from Met LTMS. I have a dark-haired female in a bright-red coat standing on the east pavement of the southern Tower Bridge exit road exhibiting NNB. Can you send the nearest unit you have to check on her, please?'

A female voice answered. 'Met LTMS, from Mike Delta. I'm not familiar with NNB. Please clarify.'

'My apologies, Mike Delta. "Not normal behaviour." She appears to be agitated about something. Constantly glancing at her phone and the traffic.'

'Thank you, LTMS. Will do. Standby, please.'

\* \* \*

Lucy Sharp punched a button and relayed the message over the airwaves. 'Any units close to Tower Bridge. Message from Traffic Control. Southern approach. Dark-haired female wearing a red coat appears to be agitated about something. LTMS officer has concerns.'

Mike One, the borough's fast response car, was first to respond. 'Mike One. Two minutes.'

'Mike Delta Four Five, leaving the nick now. Two uniforms on foot, also leaving now.'

'Mike One and Four Five, thank you.' She clicked off one button and pushed another. 'Met LTMS, I have units assigned. ETA two minutes.'

\* \* \*

'Thank you, Mike Delta.' Striker killed the call and went back to his screen. The woman in the red coat was still there, still agitated, still checking her phone.

A red light blinked rapidly on Striker's console. He pushed a button on his headset. 'Go ahead, Sean.'

'Sir. I have a man on the west side of London Bridge. He's standing near the kerb and keeps looking at his phone. Dunno what he's up to but he's making me nervous.'

Striker looked away from his screen to Sean's. It was a similar scenario to the woman in red. He was now decidedly worried. 'I've got one as well. Call Mike Delta. They know about mine. Marry them up.' He cut the call and stood up. On his screen, the woman appeared even more agitated. There was no more time for button punching. This would be managed the old-fashioned way. He clapped his hands. 'Everybody, listen up!'

'Sir . . .' Sophie Lane, Striker's 2IC, sat close to where he stood.

'Not now, Soph. I think we have a problem brewing.'

'Me too. I've got a woman standing outside the mosque in the Old Kent Road. Looks very edgy. Keeps eyeballing her phone and the traffic.'

'The mosque? What the . . .' He turned to look at the screens.

'And me,' said another operator, Baz Lemon.

'Location, Baz?'

'Southwark Bridge.'

'All right everybody, confirm. Are these folks all looking at their phones?'

All three nodded. Striker looked at the large digital clock that hung on the wall: 08:28

'Shit!' he muttered to himself. 'Okay, listen up, all! We might have some form of terrorist situation here. Sophie, get back to Mike Delta. Patch them through to the room.'

Sophie hit the button on her console. 'Mike Delta from Met LTMS, receiving?'

Lucy Sharp's voice boomed into the room from the speaker system. 'Yeah, LTMS. Units have been despatched to all locations. Mike One approaching Tower Bridge now.'

3

Striker's eyes remained glued to the screen as he watched the woman in the red coat move across the frame, her back turned toward the camera. She made her way to the balustrade, her movements graceful yet determined. With a flick of her wrist, she tossed her phone into the River Thames before turning and walking back toward the road. Almost on cue, Mike One pulled up onto the northern approach road, its presence looming large in the scene. Two uniformed officers exited quickly and strode purposefully toward the woman. The radio operator raised his hand to halt the traffic, allowing them to navigate through the chaotic flow of cars and trucks. Striker watched the two officers approach her. One held his arms wide, nonthreatening.

* * *

PC John Hardiman, a twenty-year veteran, wasn't happy about this scenario based on a five-second appraisal and a ton of experience. He'd been to more than his fair share of distraught people in his time but the look of sheer anguish on this woman's face troubled him.

'Hello, love. How you doing, there? Got a call to say that there was a lady in distress and by the look of things, I'd say I've found you. What's happened?'

The woman placed a hand on her chest. Her face was etched with grief and tears. 'Please . . . I didn't do it . . . I didn't . . . Please . . . I love my family . . . Tell them it wasn't me . . .'

Watching the scene unfold, Striker grew agitated. It would now be clear to everyone that something was off about this. He made his judgement call and tapped his mic. 'Mike Delta! Stand them down! Stand them down, now!'

'Mike One. Stand down! Stand down!' Lucy Sharp's voice matched Striker's in its urgency.

On the screen, both men stopped in their tracks.

'Get them out of there, Mike Delta. Possible terrorist situation.' Striker looked across at Sophie's screen then at Baz's.

'Shit!' said Baz.

Four incidents couldn't be managed in time. Something was about to happen. Striker knew it. He watched the crew of Mike One carefully. In the top right-hand corner of his screen, the woman lowered her head.

'Mike One!' said Lucy Sharp. 'Back away from the woman! Possible terror suspect. All other units attending scene, approach with extreme caution. Four Five, block traffic movement along Tooley Street. Mike One, block traffic movement north and south. Any units assist with building evacs, acknowledge?'

No reply. No one left.

Striker looked at the clock: 08:29. 'Christ! Someone get on to the terrorist squad. We need units at all four locati—'

At 08:30 the woman, whose name was Jeanette Colney, stepped in front of a lorry. Striker watched in horror as she was punched forward a good twenty feet before the lorry went over her, unable to stop its massive bulk. He swung his eyes to another screen.

Oliver Hayes stepped in front of a bus.

Matt Sullivan stepped in front of a car.

Susan Banks stepped in front of a fire engine on a blue-light run.

The traffic management room fell silent as they watched four people die. Baz Lemon shook his head in disbelief.

'TMS . . .' Lucy Sharp's voice boomed into the silent room. 'Mike One is reporting that the female stepped in front of a lorry. Most likely fatal. Ambulance is on way. Can you confirm?'

Striker took a deep breath. 'That's confirmed, Mike Delta. You'll also be getting calls about another three fatals on your ground. Mike Delta, standby. I'll call you on the landline in a moment.'

Sophie Lane dropped heavily into her chair, her face white. 'What the fuck was that all about? What the hell just happened?'

Christopher Striker said nothing. He'd done exactly what Jack Forrest had asked of him.

# CHAPTER 2

*03:30 — Five hours earlier*

Lyndsey Clocks carefully opened the front door of her home and laid her kit bag gently on the floor, trying not to wake up her husband. He wasn't expecting her home until later that day but, having finished her latest 'job' early, Lyndsey had managed to grab an earlier flight and wanted to surprise him. She closed the door softly behind her, the metallic click of the latch barely audible in the stillness of the early morning, and unzipped her Gore-Tex jacket, wet from the heavy rain that had been falling since she arrived at Gatwick.

Inside, the air was heavy with the scent of home, mingled with the faint aroma of freshly brewed coffee lingering from the night before. The floorboards creaked beneath her as she stepped forward, the sensation sending a thrill shiver up her spine. Her husband, Johnny Clocks, was sound asleep upstairs.

She shrugged off her sodden jacket, droplets of rain cascading from its surface and pooling on the polished wood floor. A torrential downpour had accompanied her journey from the airport. She shivered slightly, the cool air sending goosebumps racing across her arms.

She had been away for the best part of four weeks on this latest trip, and she worried that these constant excursions were putting too much of a strain on their fledgling marriage. An ex-inspector with the Metropolitan Police Firearms branch, SCO19, she had been recruited into a 'security' job that required her to use her considerable abilities with firearms wherever the need arose. That need had arisen a bit more than she had expected when she signed up.

Her plan was simple: creep upstairs, get undressed, slip into bed next to her husband and wake him up in the nicest possible way. But one thing she had learned from bitter experience was that it was true what they said about the best laid plans of mice and men. She bent down to lay her jacket neatly atop her kit bag. In that moment, a flash of lightning illuminated the living room ahead of her, casting stark, fleeting shadows across the space. She stood stock still as the silhouetted figure of a man moved from left to right across her patio in what she instantly recognised to be full combat kit. He wore a protective helmet of some kind and there was no mistaking the outline of a Heckler and Koch MP5SF machine gun held at his shoulder. A second man followed the first, then a third. She'd known this was coming, but it was sooner than she'd expected.

Her heart thumped against her chest and her nerves jangled. Her training told her these men were going to come through the front door, where she stood. She reckoned on two minutes at the most before they forced entry. The hallway was tall and wide and the double front doors swung inward. She duck-walked her way behind one of the doors, scooping up her kit bag as she went. Kneeling, she unzipped the bag and removed a small metal case containing her weapon of choice: a Glock 34 pistol. She removed the gun and the two seventeen-shot-capacity magazines housed in the case, jammed one into the bottom of the Glock and the other into her belt. She searched her jacket for her phone and hit 1 on the speed dial. She could make out the phone ringing faintly upstairs.

Two rings.

Four rings.

'C'mon, John,' she whispered. 'Pick up! Pick up! Pick up!'

'Lynds . . .' Her husband's voice was thick with sleep.

'John! Listen! I'm downstairs. We're about to be hit. Get ready!'

'Lynds . . . what the—'

'Move, John!' She hung up and strained to hear any sound, however slight, outside. The faint scrape of boot against gravel told her the wolf was at the door. Lyndsey Clocks stood, raised her gun in front of her face, closed her eyes and took a deep breath.

* * *

Clocks was up and running. He stumbled across the carpet and stubbed his toe on a chair. 'Oh, you motherfu—' He fought to stay quiet despite the bolt of pain that shot through his toe. He grabbed a pair of jogging bottoms off the back of the offending chair and hopped about on his feet as he pulled them on. No time for shoes. A quick dash across the bedroom and he was at the gun safe kept hidden in a double wardrobe. Thirty seconds later his Glock 19 was loaded and ready. He heard a loud bang as the first blow of the 'Bosher', a small metal battering ram, hit the door. He grabbed a T-shirt off its hanger and pulled it on as he ran out into the hallway.

Lyndsey had chosen the right door to stand behind. As it flew inward toward her, she shoulder-barged the door coming at her and met its force with her full bodyweight going in the opposite direction. She glimpsed the barrel of the MP5 for a second before the gunman banged up against the wall and lost his footing. The man behind him pushed forward and the first gunman stumbled into the hallway, lost his footing and crashed to the floor. She heard Johnny Clocks hurrying down the stairs, two at a time.

'John! Careful!' she shouted to him. He kept coming. Fast. The fallen gunman scrabbled to pick himself up but, as he got to his knees, Clocks kneed him in the chin, sending him backward.

'Armed police! Armed police!' The man behind shouted as he tried to navigate a way over his fallen colleague. As he raised a foot to force his way in, Lyndsey slammed herself against the door again, knocking him against the wall. He lost his footing completely, fell backward and out of the hall. Lyndsey ran toward Clocks.

A loud bang and the tinkling sound of glass on wood startled them both. She saw it first. Three more gunmen had smashed their way in through the garden patio doors. All three had weapons raised and advanced toward them.

'Armed police! Armed police! Stand still! Stand fucking still!'

Clocks and Lyndsey were caught in the hallway with nowhere to go. They both knew it. They stood back to back, Lyndsey watching the front door, Clocks watching the back.

'Drop your weapons! Do it! Do it now!' The lead gunman was very much no-nonsense and looked prepared to shoot if necessary.

'Fuck yerself, Noddy!' Clocks shouted back. 'Drop yours!'

'Put the gun down or I will shoot!'

'You put your gun down or I'll shoot!' Clocks was deadly serious.

'John . . .' Lyndsey's voice was calm and controlled. 'Put your gun down.'

'Nope!' Clocks fixed his eyes on the gunman giving orders.

'John . . . we're outnumbered. Heavily. Don't be silly.'

'Not bein' silly, luv.'

'Last chance,' said the gunman. 'Drop the weapon!'

Clocks shrugged and fired his gun twice. Both shots hit the man in his chest and punched him backward as his armour plate absorbed the bullets but not the impact. Lyndsey reacted. She whirled around, fired one shot which hit the second gunman in the leg, swivelled and caught the third gunman in the chest with her second shot. All three were down. She spun again. The gunman at the door. He was going to fire. She fired two shots into the wall near to his head, forcing him back out. 'John! Upstairs!'

Clocks ignored her and made his way toward the front door.

'John! What're you doing?'

'Givin' out free education.' He raised his gun.

'John! No!'

He stopped and looked at her. His eyes widened. Behind Lyndsey and coming through the broken windows were another six gunmen.

'Freeze!' shouted the gunman. 'Drop your weapons and get on your knees! Do it!'

'Ah, bollocks!' Clocks said. 'We're done.'

Lyndsey turned and dropped her gun. She got to her knees and put her hands behind her head.

Clocks dropped his gun but wasn't getting on his knees, not for anyone.

The incoming troop of six quickly surrounded them and kicked away their guns. One of them shouted at Clocks. 'I said on your knees!'

Clocks managed a smile but that faded rapidly when he was hit in the ribs from behind. He staggered forward before collapsing onto one knee.

'Motherfucker!' he said. 'That's a bit on the cowardly side, innit?' The officer pulled him up.

One man stepped behind Lyndsey and slapped on a handcuff behind her head before forcing down her free hand and cuffing her fully. He pulled her roughly to her feet.

'Hey! Hey!' Clocks tried to push past the officer that had him. 'Take yer fuckin' 'and's off of 'er!'

The officer with him pulled him backwards, trying to drag him away. Clocks spun and shoved him with both hands, sending him sprawling. He ran toward him and jumped, swinging his fists wildly. He stopped when he felt the barrel of a gun on his neck.

'Get off and stand up,' said a male voice.

Clocks did. He turned to face this new gunman.

Another officer cuffed Clocks behind his back.

'All right. You got us. Well done. Only took, what . . . eight, nine of yer? Someone, somewhere's gonna be double prouda their boys. What's this all about, then?'

An officer strode in through the front door. Male, mid-forties, polished to within an inch of his life even though he was in full combat gear. Probably never seen a day of action in his life. Upwardly mobile. His shoulder insignia told Clocks he was a superintendent. 'Get medical aid for Officer Street. He appears to be bleeding from the leg.' He gestured toward the other two officers that had been shot. 'And for these two.'

Clocks rounded on him. 'Oi! What's all this about, then?'

'They told me you'd be a handful, Mr Clocks. I apologise but I wasn't expecting your good lady wife to be present. Gave us quite a run for our money for a minute or two, the pair of you.'

'Well, I'm a grumpy ol' bastard when I'm woken up in the middle of the night by a bunch of tossers dressed up like the bleedin' SAS an' wavin' machine guns around. You know how it is.'

'Fortunately, I can only imagine. I'm Superintendent Shark.'

'Well, whatever it is you want, make it snappy,' said Clocks with a grin.

Shark chuckled. 'They said you had an interesting sense of humour too. Good to see it hasn't failed you.'

'Well, I try an' laugh me way through life, mate. Makes it a bit more bearable. So, come on then, let's 'ave it, Jaws. What've I done to warrant this little lot?'

'It appears that you've murdered someone, Mr Clocks.'

Clocks nodded. 'Oh yeah, 'course I 'ave. Do it all the time. Go on then, anyone I know or just a rando?'

'Oh, you know him. One Mr Thomas "Tommy" Gunn. Remember him? One of your team.'

11

Clocks's mouth dropped. 'What? Tommy? You serious?'

'Take a look around, Mr Clocks. These officers are not here to wish you a happy birthday, are they?'

'Bloody 'ope not. They're three months early an' the jelly's not set. Fuck's 'appened to Tommy, then?'

'He was gunned down by a motorcyclist while crossing the road outside Scotland Yard.'

'What? Jesus!'

'Seems he had gone to make a formal complaint about you and Mr Paterson and your somewhat . . . how shall I put it? Unruly behaviour. He believed you both killed one David Steers, the rather unpleasant man who murdered several children, some police officers and blew up a school bus full of teenage girls.'

'Oh, did 'e now? Well, I can tell you, mate, that's all bollocks. We never killed Steers.'

'Nobody's seen him since you chased him.'

'Oooh, wait. Let me think. Got it. Must have gone into 'iding. Who'da though that, eh? A killer 'iding. Never 'eard of such a thing in all me life. Anyway, what's that gotta do with Tommy bein' killed, then?'

'It's rather obvious really. You both killed Steers. He knew about it and was going to have you both arrested. You got wind of it and had him killed. One of you on the motorbike, perhaps?'

'Perhaps, my bollocks. Nothin' to do with us, mate.'

'Sir. Show some respect to the rank.'

'Yeah, whatever. So, I take it you're going over to arrest my guv'nor, then?'

Superintendent Shark looked at his watch. 'Underway as we speak. This was a double door-knock operation.'

Clocks chuckled. 'Oh, gawd. Well, fuck their luck, then.'

# CHAPTER 3

The urgent chiming of an alarm brought Ray Paterson out of his meditation. Unable to sleep yet again, he'd treated himself to a hard, two-hour training session in his home gym and was topping it off with a meditation before showering. In just a pair of sweatpants, a T-shirt and training shoes, he sat cross-legged on the floor, feeling the drops of sweat trickle down his muscular torso. He opened his eyes and stood straight up. He knew this sound. A perimeter alarm had been triggered.

He ran from the gym into his basement man-cave, snatched up the remote and switched on his TV. The screen divided instantly into four smaller screens.

Movement in the top two screens caught his eye. Two teams of heavily armed gunmen were swarming across his lawn. They'd be at the house in under fifteen seconds. He pressed another button on the remote and listened carefully as heavy metal shutters began to descend on all possible entryways into his home. That would buy him time to arm himself and prepare to meet his attackers if they hadn't come with heavy equipment. They had.

Another alarm went off. Two of the gunmen were hammering large metal spikes into the gulley of the shutters that would cover his patio windows, one each side. They wouldn't hold for long, but it would be long enough for a team to breach.

He grimaced. These boys were prepared and professional. He zoomed in on one of the men holding a small club hammer. His arm patch bore the legend 'POLICE'. Turning away from the screen, Paterson ran back toward the gym, turning off lights as he went. The loud crash of glass told him they had breached successfully. His strategic mind kicked into overdrive as he moved. From what he'd seen of the team at the windows, he'd have to take out two initially and hoover up the rest as he went. Shouldn't be a problem. He had the advantage of home turf and a small handheld taser tucked away in his gym. If nothing else, Ray Paterson was always prepared for trouble.

He figured he had two to three minutes before anyone found the gym in the basement of the house. He checked the taser for a full charge and, with practised grace, reached for his trusty bo staff, a six-foot-long stick crafted from strong oak and polished to a smooth finish. This versatile weapon served as both a shield and a sword in the art of martial combat, its weight and length perfectly balanced for precise movements. Paterson had spent countless hours training with this staff, winning many competitions with it. With each step, he felt its familiar weight in his hand, ready to defend or attack at a moment's notice. He could hear the usual shouts of 'armed police!' and the heavy tramping of boots across his wooden floors throughout the house. Wherever they went, SCO19 were not a subtle presence. The other team would be coming in now. Ten in total. Four would likely peel off upstairs. Four would search the ground floor and two would go for the basement. Standard procedure.

He laid the bo staff across the toes of one foot, held the taser in his hand and breathed deeply, clearing his mind for the coming battle and allowing his eyes to adjust to the darkness.

\* \* \*

Johnny Clocks, hands cuffed behind his back and flanked by two SCO19 officers, strolled across his lawn seemingly unperturbed by the night's events. Slightly behind him was Superintendent Shark.

'So, come on then, Jaws. Why the 'eavy mob? You didn't 'ave to go smashin' up me gaffe, did yer? Could've just knocked at a sensible time an' I'd 'ave let you in. Could've nicked us at the office if you wanted. Why not just do that?'

'Orders.'

'Orders? From who?'

'From above.'

'Really? God? God finally signed off on us, did 'e?'

'Not God. Think bigger.'

Clocks shrugged. 'Bigger than God? Blimey. Er, Taylor Swift?'

'All in good time, Mr Clocks. All in good time.'

Clocks stepped into the waiting police car, Superintendent Shark's hand in place between his head and the door frame.

'Mind your head, Mr Clocks.'

Clocks looked up at him, a grin on his face. 'Mind yours, guv.' The two men glared at each other before Clocks sat down and squirmed around, trying to get comfortable in the seat. He looked up at Shark. 'Just sayin'.'

Shark slammed the door and walked back toward the house. Lyndsey was standing outside.

'Are you all right, Lyndsey?' said Shark.

'Will be when these cuffs are off.'

'What? Oh, yes! Sorry!' He fumbled in his trouser pocket for the key.

'Leave it until the car goes.' She watched the car begin to pull away, before turning her back to him. As the car drove out of sight, Shark unlocked the cuffs and slipped them into his pocket. Lyndsey rubbed her wrists and nodded. 'Didn't expect to see you out of the office. How've you been?'

'All right. Team's not the same since you left the service. Pity you did, but . . . you always did your own thing, didn't you?'

She smirked.

'Look,' Shark said, 'I don't know what this is all about. We were just told to bring your husband and Paterson in — to go mob-handed and use force if necessary. I hoped we wouldn't have to, but in fairness, he shot at the officers. Hit one in the chest.'

'He got lucky. If I know John, he was aiming for his head. Couldn't hit the floor if he fell over.'

'Small comfort.'

'Will Mick be all right? Tell him I'm sorry about his leg.'

'We'll get him off to hospital. I hear it's not too serious. You didn't hit anything vital.'

She nodded. 'Good. Pete's chest?'

'As bruised as his ego. He'll forgive you and, knowing him, he'll be wanting to know how the hell you learned to do those things. Certainly a step up from us. I'm sorry how this went down, Lynds.'

'Don't be. You had orders. You carried them out. I knew this was coming, so I'm not surprised. No hard feelings.'

Superintendent Shark chuckled. 'About cuffing you . . .'

'S'all right. Did the right thing. Had to look proper, didn't it?'

'Do you think he bought it? That you've been nicked too?'

'Hope so.'

'Lynds. Wanna tell me what is about?'

'Nah. Just recruiting, is all. Look, you take care, guv. Say hello to everyone for me and make sure you get the bloody glaziers in to patch my house up a bit quick.'

* * *

Paterson heard them coming down the stairs and along the hallway. He saw torches flashing wildly about under the door. Two of them.

A voice shouted, 'Door!' and the footfall stopped. He breathed slowly. The doorknob rattled. He knew what would

16

happen next. One was going to kick it open, the other would enter — fast. He counted silently. *One . . . Two . . . Thr—*

The door flew inwards to shouts of 'Armed police! Armed police!'

He let the first one in. The man moved fast toward the left-hand side of the room. The second man entered, moved right and straight into Paterson. He jammed the taser onto the man's chin; his thin black nylon mask offered no protection. The man grunted, stiffened and fell backward. Paterson dropped the taser, raised his knee fast and took the bo staff off his foot. He snapped on the room light and topped it all off with a forward roll into the middle of the room.

The remaining gunman shouted as a brilliant flash of light exploded inside his night vision googles, temporarily blinding him. Confused, he moved from his position toward the last sound his colleague had made. Paterson struck. He brought the bo staff down hard, hitting the man across the hand that held the machine gun's front grip. The man howled with pain as a bone snapped and he immediately let go of the gun.

Paterson drove his elbow into the side of the man's face, knocking him up against the wall. As the man stumbled, Paterson kicked his legs out from under him and sent him crashing to the ground. He drove his knee three times into the man's face in quick succession. Satisfied that he was no longer a problem, Paterson walked off and retrieved his taser.

Placing his bo staff on the ground, he knelt in front of the man who had fallen. The man reached weakly for his gun, but Paterson stopped him. 'Ah, ah . . . Good effort, buddy, but no banana.' Paterson tased him on the side of the neck, got up, grabbed the bo staff and set off to hunt the others.

He made his way upstairs quietly. At the top, he had a decision to make. Left or right. The decision was made for him as a lone gunman stepped into view. Paterson flattened himself against the wall and waited until the man drew level with him, crouched down quickly and jammed the taser into the man's leg. As the gunman jerked, Paterson struck out with his forearm and smashed it into the man's face. He crashed to the ground as Paterson ran through to the living room.

Two gunmen were waiting for him, weapons raised and pointed straight at him. 'Armed police! Armed police! Drop your weapon!' Paterson sighed. His plan was to have gotten these two out of the way before starting on the upstairs cadre, who he heard running downstairs. Now there were seven.

'Evening all,' he said to the two in front of him. 'Take it easy. You got me. You got me.' He began to raise his hands and threw the taser toward them, high, exposing their throats as they watched it sail toward them. He thrust the bo staff forward and hit one in the throat before swiping it sideways and hitting the other in the neck. Both men staggered about. Paterson launched himself at the man on his right. He swept the man's legs from under him and sent him crashing onto his back. Once down, Paterson grabbed the man's armoured vest, pulled him up toward him and punched him several times rapidly in the face. The man to his left, desperately clutching at his throat, was a problem. Paterson didn't want to render him unconscious. With his throat closing up, he would die if he did. The noise on the stairs grew louder as the three officers came hurtling down to join the fight. Paterson shoved his man backward onto the sofa.

'Stay!' he said. 'And breathe slowly. You'll be fine. Just calm yourself.'

Paterson turned away from him. He was in trouble and he knew it. Then luck intervened. The fourth man to search the ground floor ran through from the dining room and got between the three on the stairs. Paterson launched himself at him, knocking him backward and into the front officer on the stairs. The momentum of the two behind pushed the man forward. With nowhere to go, they lost their balance and tumbled over each other, landing in a heap at Paterson's feet. Easy meat. He grabbed the ridge of the top man's steel helmet and pulled him half up before driving his fist into this chin. Paterson let him go and dropped the man onto the two officers scrabbling to get up. They collapsed again under the dead weight of the unconscious officer.

'That's enough, Paterson!'

Paterson spun to see a man in plain clothes standing a good fifteen feet away and pointing a gun directly at him. He was a brick shithouse of a man — at least six foot two, with arms like tree trunks, hands like shovels, a barrel chest and a bulging stomach, which told Paterson he was all weight lifting and no cardio.

He couldn't possibly close the gap before the man pulled the trigger. 'I will shoot if you make me, so don't make me.'

'And you would be?' said Paterson.

'Inspector Bagg. SCO19.'

Paterson sniffed. He'd heard a thing or two about Bagg. 'If you trained this lot, I'd suggest a change of career. No offence.'

'Offence taken,' said Bagg.

'Why're you here?' said Paterson.

'To arrest you.'

'For?'

'Murder.'

Paterson frowned. 'Of?'

'Tommy Gunn.'

'Tommy?'

'Yep. Shot dead in the street, just outside Scotland Yard. But you'd know that, wouldn't you?'

'Actually, no. I wouldn't.' He half turned his head. Behind him, the fallen officers were picking themselves up. He back-kicked one, sending him tumbling into the crowd and knocking them into a heap again.

'I said *enough*, Paterson! Get on your knees!'

Paterson smirked. 'Fuck off. I don't kneel for anyone, except maybe the King when he knights me, but I'd have to think about that.'

'I said get on your knees!'

19

'And I said fuck off! Come and make me, big boy.'

'I'd snap you like a fucking twig.'

'Think so? You can always drop the gun and give it a try, fatty. Assuming you can waddle over here on those terribly misshapen stumps you call legs, of course. Up to you.'

Paterson could see the man's face change. Just a bit more . . .

'Tell you what, fat boy, when you eventually wobble your way over here, you can have a couple of swings, see how you get on, yeah? Fancy that? Go on. You know you do.'

Bagg had had enough. He holstered his sidearm and rolled up his sleeves, making a show of it. 'I'll pull your fucking head off, Paterson!'

Bagg charged forward, head down. No skill. No finesse. And no vision. An ungainly rhino in Paterson's house of pain.

As Bagg closed the gap between them, Paterson stepped deftly aside and watched as he charged headfirst into his own team, scattering them like skittles. He clattered to the floor with them. Paterson shook his head and watched as they scrabbled about. Two of his team helped Bagg to his feet. He could see the rage on Bagg's face. Humiliation.

'Up you get, fatty. Haven't got all day.'

Bagg squared up to Paterson and began to circle. Rhino hadn't worked so he was going for boxing — of sorts.

Bagg thumbed his nose as he put his hands up in front of his face. Behind him, battered and bruised, his team decided to sit this one out and watch how events unfolded. Paterson had heard that Bagg was a bully and not popular with his colleagues. At least two of them looked as if they were hoping he'd get his arse handed to him.

'C'mon then, posh boy. Let's see what you've got.'

'In my accounts, you mean? Oh, lots. I doubt you could count it. It's waaaay past ten.'

'You're a funny fucker, ain't you? You won't be taking the piss in a minute.' Bagg turned to what was left of his team. 'He's mine, all right? Stay out of this.'

They all nodded. More than happy to let him get on with it. One went over to his colleague on the sofa, still struggling to breathe.

Paterson smiled. He'd already worked out at least a dozen ways to bring this lump down. It all depended on what Bagg did next. Bagg lumbered forward, left hand extended, ready to throw a right. He swung. Paterson ducked, stood up and back-handed him in the face. A stinging slap.

Bagg wiped blood from his lip. Paterson goaded him, beckoning him forward. The man went for it, the slap having enraged him even further. As he charged forward, Paterson leaned back out of reach, kicked forward and hit Bagg on the leading knee. His leg straightened out behind him as his momentum carried him forward. With his leg gone, he fell forward, breaking his sudden fall with his hands. Paterson stepped over him, grabbed him by the hair and slammed his face into the floor. Blood squirted out across the polished floorboards. Paterson raised Bagg's head and slammed it down again.

'Oi! Enough!' said one of Bagg's team. Paterson raised the man's head again before a bolt of searing pain shot through his body, tensing his muscles and pitching him forward onto his face.

The man behind him holding the two-coil taser kept the trigger pressed until Paterson was safely in handcuffs.

Bagg stirred and tried to raise himself up. Every move looked painful to the watching officers. One tried to help him up, but he shook him off. 'Fuck off! Leave me alone.'

He pulled himself into a crouch position, glared at Paterson, wiped the blood from his nose and then looked at the red mess on the floor. He was sure to develop two black eyes over the coming days. Paterson had seen to that.

'Take the taser off. He's secure.' Bagg looked up at the officer holding the taser.

'Sir?'

'He's not going anywhere, is he? Disengage. Now!'

'Sir?'

'What?'

'Your nose.'

'Broken?'

'I reckon.'

Bagg sighed. 'Serves me right.' He turned to Paterson. 'Turns out you're the one my dad was talking about when he said there's always someone better than you.'

Still face down, Paterson smiled up at him. 'I guess. Don't feel too bad. Happens to us all.'

Bagg nodded. 'You're all right, Paterson. Fearless fucker, ain'tcha? Still, you're nicked.' He pulled himself upright and wobbled on his legs for a second or two before heading toward the front door. 'Pick him up and caution him.'

Both officers hauled Paterson to his feet.

'Shot me in the back,' said Paterson. 'Bad form, mate.'

'Didn't leave me any choice,' said the taser man.

'Could've pulled me off of him. Would've been the manly thing to do.'

The officer nodded. 'Fuck that, guv. I've seen what you can do.'

\* \* \*

Clocks squirmed about in the back seat. 'What nick we goin' to?'

The big SCO19 officer next to him looked ahead and didn't answer.

'Oi! Tree trunk! I asked you a question. Where we goin'? What nick?'

'You don't need to worry about that, guv.'

'I'm not worried, son. Just makin' small talk to while away the minutes I get to spend in your company. You seem a nice enough chap. Not bright, but pleasant enough.'

The officer looked across at Clocks. 'Not bright?'

'Nothing personal, but no. Not overly.'

'Well, I'm not the one in handcuffs having been nicked for murder. I'd say that makes me a bit brighter than you. Sir.'

22

Clocks sniffed before answering. 'Touché, my son. Touché. I can't argue with that, can I?'

'You can, but there's no point.'

'I can see this is going to be a pleasant ride.'

'It doesn't have to be *un*pleasant.'

'No, it don't. What would make it more pleasant then, Officer Tree Trunk?'

'If you shut the fuck up.'

'Duly noted. Oi! Driver chappie!'

The driver half turned his head. 'Go on.'

'Tree Trunk's gone on a brain cell strike an' run out of words, so p'raps you could tell me what nick we're goin' to.'

'I could. Yes.'

'But, judging by your tone, I get the impression you won't, right?'

'Right.'

'Why all the secrecy?'

'Dunno. It's a secret.'

'Oh, fuck me. I'm stuck in a car with Cannon and Ball.'

'Who?'

Clocks looked at the driver. Thirty at the most. He shook his head. 'Don't matter, mate. Before your time. Okay, riddle me this, boys . . . Is Superintendent Paterson goin' to the same place?'

'Does it matter?'

'Does to me. Be nice to talk to someone with a bit of a brain.'

'It won't work,' said Tree Trunk.

'What won't work? Your brain?'

'You insulting us.'

'I'm not insultin' you. I'm just pointin' out the fact that 'avin' been in your company for a few minutes, I can see that at least one of you was dropped on yer nut when you was a kid. You, most likely. And yer mate probably got put on the thick table at school. Just sayin'.'

'Well, thanks for pointing that out,' said the driver. 'But as my colleague mentioned, we're not going for it. They won't work, all these silly little insults. We've been briefed about you.'

'Briefed?'

'Briefed. We were told you were a cocky gobshite with an attitude problem that would likely try to wind us up for your own amusement and, so far, that does appear to be the case.'

'Ah. Well, dunno who put your briefin' together but they seem to 'ave got me personality down cold. What else do you know about me?'

'Borderline psychopath. Drink problem. Violent. Anti-authority — which is a bit odd given the job you do. Wind-up merchant. Xenophobic. Stroppy. Childlike . . . Want me to go on?'

'No, no, no. That'll do yer. But I do wanna know 'ow you got 'old of me Tinder profile, though. An' I'm a bit disappointed you missed out the bit that says, "Loves dogs, walkin' in the rain, readin' poetry an' starin' at rainbows all day long." Did you do that on purpose to make me look bad?'

'No. I think Tinder must have removed it,' said Tree Trunk.

'Dirty bastards,' said Clocks. 'That's me scuppered for a bunk-up, then.'

# CHAPTER 4

Paterson was sitting in the back of a marked police van with four SCO19 officers for company. Inspector Bagg was taking no chances. Paterson smiled at the officer sitting opposite, staring at him. 'These cuffs are a bit tight, mate. Can you loosen them a notch for me, please?' The officer stared at him. 'Please?'

'Sorry, sir,' said the officer sitting next to him. 'We won't be long. Just sit still.'

Paterson turned to him. 'Okay. How long will we be? Do you know?'

The officer looked at his wristwatch, trying to make out the dial in the gloom of the van. 'Twenty minutes or so.'

'Twenty minutes? They're cutting off my circulation.'

The officer looked hesitant, then went for the key on his belt.

'Leave it!' The officer sitting opposite Paterson was still staring.

'I'm in pain,' said Paterson.

'Un-fucking-lucky.'

Paterson raised his head before nodding a few times. He understood. This one had a problem with him. 'I'm still your senior officer, so show some respect.'

'Don't have any respect for killers and certainly not for a cop who kills cops.'

'I get that, but do you know for certain that I killed a cop? Or are you just going off what you've been told in your briefing?'

The officer narrowed his eyes.

'Y'see? It's dangerous to make assumptions about people. You need facts—'

'I've got all the facts I need.'

'You think you have, but you haven't. Not by a long shot. But I can see you're not in the mood to negotiate, so that's fine.' Paterson leaned forward. 'But know this. When I'm out of these cuffs, I'll break your fucking arms.'

The officer lurched forward, grabbed Paterson by the throat and slammed him backward onto the wall of the van before pushing his face into him. 'You think so, do you? You think you'll break my arms, do you? I don't give a fuck about your rank, mate. Any time you wanna go, we'll go.'

Paterson, his throat seriously constricted, managed to speak out. 'Have a quick count-up of all your pals back at my house. You really think you'll be a problem for me?'

'Oh, I'll know I'll be a problem for you, tough boy. First chance we get, me and you.'

Paterson's eyes were watering.

'Bill. Let him go,' said the officer next to him.

The man ignored him.

'Bill! Let him go. He's a fucking superintendent!'

Bill snorted and let Paterson go, pushing his head against the van once more.

Paterson coughed a few times, grinned at his attacker then turned to the man next to him. 'Which nick we going to?'

'Nick?'

'Yeah. Nick. Which one?'

His attacker chimed in. 'You're not going to the nick, pal. Nowhere near one.'

# CHAPTER 5

Striker stepped out of the CCTV room and sat himself in a toilet cubicle. With his head in his hands, his mind wandered back to the day he'd met Jack Forrest, the day that changed his life completely.

\* \* \*

Striker walked along the hallway of his little flat as the doorbell rang for a third, more insistent, time. It was unusual for him to get any visitors, let alone one whose frame filled the frosted glass panel in his front door. The sight of it unnerved him slightly but, he reasoned, nobody was out to harm him anymore.

He opened the door and was met by a six-foot-nine man who looked as though his hobby was breaking things with his muscles. He instantly regretted opening the door, but to shut it abruptly might just piss off this hulking carcass. 'Hello?' Striker could hear the nervousness in his own voice.

The man smiled at him. 'Christopher Striker?' He sounded pleasant and not at all like a man of his size should.

'That's me. How can I help you?' He kept his weight behind the half-opened door in a gesture that would be entirely redundant should the man want to let himself in. Still, it was the thought that counted.

'My name is Jack Forrest and I'm with the Foreign Office.' He held up a card just long enough for Striker to see the photo of the man and a logo in the corner but not long enough to read it all properly. Forrest slipped the card back into his pocket. 'May I come in? I have something I need to talk to you about. It won't take long.'

Striker panicked. Something about those last few words made him feel like he was about to be snapped in two, yet the man's gaze had a kind of hypnotic power over him. He knew that saying no wouldn't mean a thing to this man.

'Yes. Of course.' He stood aside as he opened the door fully. That Forrest had to duck to get under the door frame didn't go unnoticed. He walked past Striker looking from left to right as he made his way along the short hallway.

'At the end, turn left. Make yourself comfortable.'

'Thank you,' said Forrest.

'Can I get you a tea?' said Striker.

Forrest turned and smiled. 'Thank you. That would be lovely. Left, you say?'

'That's it. I'll pop the kettle on and be with you in a sec.'

'Thank you.' Forrest wandered off, leaving Striker in the kitchen.

\* \* \*

The living room was impeccable, every item placed carefully in its designated spot. It had the sense of order and discipline that one would expect from an ex-serviceman. However, it lacked personality and felt bare and stark. The curtains were drawn halfway, as if trying to hide something from the outside world. Despite the lack of natural light, the small space felt cozy and inviting. A well-thumbed Jack Reacher novel lay on the coffee table. Forrest couldn't help but smile at the simple pleasures found in this room. Although it could use some sprucing up, it served its purpose as a comfortable sanctuary for its occupant. Striker poked his head into the room with a gentle question: 'Do you take sugar?'

'Not for me, thanks.' He smiled at Striker. 'Sweet enough.'

'Won't be a minute.' Forrest looked out of the window into the street far below. Until a little while ago, he'd never set foot in Surrey Quays before, although he'd heard about it. Fashionable place to be these days. The whole of the docks had been refurbished many years before and replaced with expensive flats and a few houses dotted about in rows of six. Striker's block was still rooted in the past — an old council estate where the echoes of better days clung to the peeling paint and crumbling concrete. The stairwells carried the stale scent of damp, and the corridors were dimly lit, as if trying to hide the signs of neglect. This wasn't a sleek, modernised flat that the gentrification around the corner possessed, but a relic of a bygone era — an embarrassment tucked among the flashier, more expensive flats. Its stubborn resistance to the tide of change only made its dilapidation more pronounced, a stark contrast to the polished facades surrounding it.

A few miles away was the former office of the Mayor of London, a strange dome-shaped glass building that looked as if it was on the wonk. Much like the staff inside used to be, he mused. Tower Bridge, that magnificent feat of Victorian engineering, spanned North and South London. Forrest remembered as a kid reading about Tower Bridge and had seen some ancient photographs of it being constructed. One fact had always stuck in his memory. For years, he had carried it around as if it were a prized possession, often pulling it out of his mind for others to admire. Before the bridge was controlled by electronics, the bascules were operated by water. As unfathomable as it seemed, the addition or subtraction of a mere pint of water could cause them to open and close. Whether or not this was true, he couldn't swear to it, but it had always fascinated him that the Victorians could build something so precisely, so delicately balanced, yet so sturdy and reliable.

Striker came in holding a tray with two mugs of tea and an open packet of digestives. He placed it on the table as Forrest nodded his thanks and retook his seat.

'Yours is the one on the left. Help yourself to biscuits.'

'Thank you.' Forrest picked up his mug and sank back into the armchair.

'What is it that I can do for you, Mr . . . I'm sorry. What was your name again?'

'Jack. Jack Forrest.'

'Wow! For a minute I thought you were going to say your name was Reacher.'

'I get that a lot.'

'You know, 'cos you're so . . .' Striker gestured a large shape in the air with his hands.

'I get that a lot too. Nope. Plain old Jack Forrest.'

'Yes, yes. I'm sorry. Sorry . . . rude of me.'

Forrest gave him a big grin. 'No, no. Don't worry about it. I'm used to it. To be honest, I think I should ask Lee Child for royalties. What d'you think?'

'I think you should too.' Both men chuckled.

'Listen, Mr Striker—'

'Christopher. Chris. Please.'

'Chris. Call me Jack. Chris, the reason I'm here is . . . well, it's a bit of a delicate matter, but my bosses wanted me to speak to you to see if you would be willing to help us.'

\* \* \*

Striker, his mug to his lips, stopped what he was doing. 'Help you?' While he was making the tea in the kitchen, Striker had run a number of reasons for Forrest's visit through his head. Helping him and his bosses hadn't been one of them.

'Umm-hmm.' Forrest sipped at his tea.

'I don't quite understand. How can I be of help to you? I'm a bit of . . . a nobody really. Ex-army. Now a CCTV operator.'

'Well . . .' Forrest cradled the mug in his lap. 'As I said, it's a bit of a delicate matter. You see, it involves your partner.'

30

Striker tensed up. Of course it was him. He was the important one.

'I know that you've been seeing him for some time now but — and I am sorry to tell you this — he's not what he seems.'

Striker frowned. 'What d'you mean? I don't understand.'

'You've been together . . . what? Two years?'

'Something like that.'

'Well, I need you to know a couple of things about him. Let me get this out there first. He will never leave his wife and children, if that's what you're hoping for.'

'Excuse me? How dare you . . .' Striker felt like he'd just been slapped. He started to stand up but before he got even halfway, Forrest waved him back down.

'Please, Chris. I appreciate you're upset. A stranger turns up on your doorstep and tells you that you're being used. I get it. It's not nice, but it is important that I tell you this.'

'Hold on,' said Striker. 'What do you know about our relationship? How do you know I'm not using him?'

Forrest sighed. 'Please, Chris. I only have to look around. Do you really think someone like him would leave his family and ruin his life and reputation to come and live in a two-bedroom flat on the arsehole side of Rotherhithe'

'What? That's . . . that's bloody rude!'

'I know. I'm sorry. I didn't mean to offend, but at the same time, it's the truth, isn't it?'

Striker shook his head. He knew it was true. In fact, he often wondered how the relationship had lasted this long.

'Look,' said Forrest. 'He's using you for sex, nothing more. And you're not the only one.' He let that comment hang there.

Striker went rigid with shock and he felt the hot blood flooding into his cheeks.

'He's . . . shall we say, a bit of a boy. Likes to get it where and when he can and, to be honest, you're not that high on his list of priorities.'

'That's not true. He loves me, he told me.'

'Did he?' Forrest chortled. 'Well, I love you too. Except I don't. And he doesn't. Some blokes will say anything to get

31

their end away, and you, Chris Striker, are just the end away. Sorry.'

'Mr Forrest. Jack. I don't mean to be rude, but I think it's time you left. I don't know why you came here, what your purpose was, but if it was to tell me the man I love is cheating on me, well, I don't understand why you would do that. So thank you for being so rude. You can leave.'

Forrest put down his mug. 'As I said, Chris, I'm sorry. I really am. But there's more.'

Striker looked at him with contempt. Whatever it was he wanted to tell him, he would have none of it. 'No thank you. We're done here.'

'You were discharged from the army after court martial, correct?'

Striker felt himself crumple slightly. Not this again. He said nothing.

'Cowardice in the face of enemy fire. Left your colleagues to face a number of hostile insurgents alone.'

Striker didn't need reminding. The quiet times allowed him plenty of time for that.

'For that, you were sentenced to three years inside. And after serving your sentence you were dismissed. During that time, you were diagnosed with PTSD and associated anxiety and night terrors. A mental breakdown for all intents and purposes, yes?'

Striker just stared at the man without answering.

'It was shortly after your discharge from the army that you bumped into your lover and, being of unsound mind — and, let's not forget, poor judgement — got yourself embroiled in a relationship with him. Now, I read your file from back to front, and apart from that one incident, from where I sit, you were a good man who made a bad mistake and have been suffering for it ever since. Is that about right?'

Striker wiped at his right eye as a tear formed in the corner. 'You weren't there. Not one of those pricks that prosecuted me were there. The shock, the fear, the confusion, the fucking heat, the smell of burning flesh, the smell of blood. I lost my shit, I'll admit that, but if I could go back — if I could just go back — things would be different, I swear. That wasn't me. It wasn't. You read my file. You know that wasn't me.'

'Hey . . . hey . . .' Forrest's voice was calmer, quieter. 'It's okay. It's okay. I'm not judging you, Chris. I'm not. Fuck! No, I wasn't there. I wasn't in your situation. I mean, I'm a big lump but I'm sure I would have been bricking it too.'

Striker looked across at him, searched Forrest's face for any hint of insincerity. He didn't find any. 'Thank you,' he said.

'I know you served queen and country bravely before that incident and that you're a loyal soldier. That's why I've come to give you an opportunity. A chance to redeem yourself. A second chance, if you like.'

Striker was utterly confused.

'Look,' said Forrest. 'You want to help your country, yes?'

Striker nodded. 'Of course.'

'You want to put right the mistakes you've made in the field?'

Striker nodded.

'Okay, good. I'm going to tell you something about your other half, as it were, that you are going to want to do something about.'

'And what's that?' said Striker. 'I'll talk to him about our relationship. Find out what he's playing at.'

'Oh, it's not about your relationship. That's not why I'm here. I can tell you what he's playing at, Chris. Treason.'

Striker felt the room spin slightly. His partner could be a bastard, he knew that. He hadn't known he was being strung along like a piece of fuck meat, didn't know a lot of things about him really, but treason? What the hell had he been doing?

\* \* \*

33

Forrest told him everything. He emphasised certain points, left out some details, slotted in others. Lies to help the story. Lies to push Striker's loyalty to breaking point and he kept on. For the next twenty minutes, Jack Forrest poured poison into Christopher Striker's heart and mind until he finally agreed to help Forrest kill the man he loved.

# CHAPTER 6

Striker sat back in his chair and closed his eyes. In just twenty minutes, a stranger, a monster of a man had stepped into his life and torn it up for arse paper. And his past had come back to haunt him. It always did.

After leaving the army, it had taken him a while to settle back into civilian life having served six years. Things were different for him now. Gone were the regimens and routines that he needed to get him through the day, as was the camaraderie that made even the direst situation seem bearable. To this day, his internal struggle tore at his brain, scratching around inside his mind with clawed fingers, picking that day over and over again.

The day itself had been nothing special. He'd been on routine patrol in the Land Rover just as he had done dozens of times before, laughing and joking with the rest of his unit. The sun was high, the vehicle was hot, the boys all smelled of sweat. Nothing unusual there. Until the IED went off and upended the vehicle. The screams of his friends in the front told him that they'd lost feet as a minimum, whole legs more likely. Their life was done for, those that survived.

The deafening crash of metal against the ground shook him to his core, followed by shouts and clamouring from outside. His unit had scattered and were preparing for a fight, but he couldn't focus on that right now. He was trapped inside the overturned vehicle, surrounded by chaos. The fear surged within him. His eyes strained to make out the form next to him, his best friend, Laurie Peters. But it wasn't Laurie anymore. The left side of his body was mangled beyond recognition, bones jutting out like shattered glass, blood oozing from every orifice. The metallic smell of blood filled Striker's nostrils, overwhelming and nauseating. In a moment of blind panic, he screamed and clawed at the roof above him, desperate to escape the gruesome scene before him. But the door was jammed shut, trapping them both in this hellish nightmare.

'No, no, no, no, no!' Striker shouted. 'Let me out, let me out! Please! Let me out!'

Two sharp thumps on the bodywork stopped him short. 'Chris! It's Jimmy Boy. Stay calm, mate! We'll get you out.'

'Jimmy? Jimmy Boy? Jimmy! Lemme out, lemme out!'

'Calm yourself, bruv. I'll get you.'

Striker became aware that Jimmy Boy was joined by another. To this day he didn't know who it was. He heard them shouting but it was garbled in his head.

'Come on! Come on!' Striker screamed and kicked out, his foot thumping against the unyielding door. He stopped the second he heard the familiar *pock-pock* of bullets hitting metal. He was under fire. Panic rising, he reached for his side-arm and wrenched it out of the holster strapped to his leg. He had trouble gripping it before realising his hand was wet with blood. He dropped the gun onto his chest and wiped his hand frantically on his trousers, taking off enough of his own blood to pick the gun up and hold it firmly. 'Jimmy Boy! Lemme out! Come on, you fucker!'

The door shrieked and buckled under Jimmy Boy's desperate pull, the metal hinges groaning in protest. Striker added his own brute strength, booting it until a hinge snapped and the door flew open with a resounding crash. He stumbled out into the blistering heat, scrambling on all fours from the scorching metal to the burning sand. He squinted against the blinding sun, struggling to make sense of the chaos around him. A hand suddenly yanked at his collar, pulling him upright. He stood dazed, taking in the carnage around him. Three out of four vehicles had been obliterated, flames and thick black smoke billowing from their twisted frames. Gunfire erupted once again and Jimmy Boy fired back from behind their overturned Land Rover, his back pressed firmly against its charred metal surface.

'Ragheads!' Jimmy Boy shouted. 'Ten, eleven and one o'clock! Return fire! Return fire!'

Striker looked out into the desert and saw his worst nightmare. Taliban fighters were running toward them. How many, he didn't know, but he told the court martial there were at least twenty and that was probably in the ballpark. He raised his gun, pointed it toward a fighter but never pulled the trigger. He turned and ran, putting the Land Rover and Jimmy Boy between him and the fighters. He kept running, his feet heavy, sucked down by the soft sand as he tried to get away from the carnage behind him. Shots whizzed past and some bit into the desert as he pushed on, struggling over the dunes in his desperation. As his legs burned with the strain of scrabbling over the sand, the ground shook beneath Striker's feet as explosions ripped through the air, sending shockwaves and shrapnel flying. He could hear the screams of the enemy mixed with the deafening sound of rotor blades approaching. With a burst of adrenaline, he pushed himself to keep running, not daring to look back until he collapsed from exhaustion. Hot sand seared his skin as he lay face down, gasping for air. But when he finally mustered the courage to turn over, he was met with the sight of a circling American Black Hawk helicopter overhead.

The enemy was quickly taken care of with a few sidewinder missiles and the .50 cal machine gun in the helicopter. As American troops rushed out to help the wounded, Striker lay there trying to process everything that had happened. But his mind felt like it was about to explode, images flashing before him and the smell of fear still lingering in his senses.

Then it hit him. He had run away. Shame and regret washed over him as he realised he had abandoned his fellow soldiers in their time of need. Mortified at what he'd done, he stumbled his way back down the dunes toward the battlefield, tears in his eyes when he saw his dead friends. An American soldier saw him coming and raised his weapon, pointing it straight at him.

'It's okay, it's okay. British. It's my unit. Thank God you're here. Oh, thank God.' He stumbled and was caught by another American.

'Jeez! You okay, pal?'

'Yes, yes, thank you. Thank you.'

The helicopter pilot walked across to where he stood with the two Americans.

'All right, buddy? For a second there, I didn't think you could run any faster.'

Striker felt his stomach lurch and almost threw up. 'I . . . I . . . It was, was so . . . I . . . panicked . . .'

The pilot snorted his contempt. 'You ran away, soldier. I saw it. Ran like a prairie dog with a firecracker up its ass.'

'I didn't . . . I'm sorry . . . I couldn't think straight . . .'

'Striker!'

He felt his stomach lurch again, harder this time at the sound of Jimmy Boy's voice. 'You fucking bottleless bastard!' He was heading fast toward Striker, his face etched with fury.

'Jimmy, I'm sorry . . .'

'Fuck your sorries, you fucking coward!'

Striker held his hands up.

An American soldier hit him in the back of his leg with the butt of his M4 rifle and dropped Striker to one knee. 'Don't want you runnin' off again now, do we, boy? Seems to me you owe your friend here an explanation.'

And then Jimmy Boy was on him. The first punch broke Striker's jaw. An injury that would require it to be wired up for three months. As he collapsed in the sand, he felt the heavy thumps of Jimmy Boy's boots hit him in the chest, in the stomach. He felt his friend stamp on his knees, determined to cripple him and finally, before the lights went out, he felt his head being stamped into the sand.

# CHAPTER 7

'Where are we, then?' said Clocks, looking out of the car's window. 'Is this a safe office? I've 'eard about 'em.'

'You're spot on, guv,' said Tree Trunk. 'Can see why they made you a DI.'

Clocks let the snarky comment ride. 'What're we doin', then? What's the story?'

'No idea. We were just told to bring you here. That's all we know.'

'Hmm. Seems odd.'

'Perhaps they've got a new holding centre for cop-killing cops.'

Clocks nodded. 'Oh yeah. It might be, mightn't it? Didn't think of that.'

'You'll know soon enough,' said the driver. He took a right and pulled up at the security gate.

An elderly man with an electronic tablet stepped out of his little hut and approached the car. 'Morning.'

'Morning,' said the driver. 'Special delivery.' He nodded to the back of the car.

The gateman looked startled when he saw Clocks in the back. He crouched lower. 'Er . . . Hello, Clocksy. You all right?'

'All right, Alfie? What you doin' 'ere, then?'

'Got a transfer. Gettin' on a bit now and this is closer to home for me.'

'Ah, good on yer, mate. You deserve a break.'

'What're you doing here?

'Oh, y'know me. In trouble again. Ol' Tick and Tock 'ere picked me up a while back and wanted to give me a tour of the place. I told 'em I've been 'ere before, but you know what the kids are like these days. Can't tell 'em anything, can yer? Wife okay?'

'Yeah, thanks. Lyndsey?'

Clocks's mind flashed back to the house. No point upsetting the old boy. 'Yeah, sound as a pound, mate. Thanks for askin'.'

'Any chance we could get in, please?' said the driver. 'I'm sure you two can catch up later.'

Alfie turned to the driver and gave him a drop-dead look, no doubt unhappy that his friend Clocks was in the back instead of the front of a police car. 'Catch you later, Clocksy. Be careful.' He walked back to his hut, pressed a button on his console and opened the electronic gates. He nodded to Clocks as the car sailed past him into the underground car park.

Finding a spot near the lifts, the driver backed in and switched off the engine. He sat still, looking toward the entrance.

'What we waitin' for?' said Clocks.

'Your other half?'

'What? Lyndsey? Me missis? She bein' brought 'ere too?'

'Not Lyndsey, no. But, yeah, your missis. The other one. Paterson.'

'Oh, him. Okay, then. Listen, you sure this isn't some sort of prank? It's not the commissioner's birthday, is it? I'm not gonna get out of this car and see a bunch of strippers wigglin' it all about, am I?'

'In an underground garage?'

'Well, it's been an odd night.'

'You can't say strippers anymore,' said Tree Trunk.

41

'Don't surprise me. I went to see a strip show a few weeks ago. Fuckin' shit it was, 'cos of all this "woke" bollocks. Some bird came out dressed in a pair of jeans and a thick woolly jumper and just stood there. No wigglin' about for 'er. Nothin'. Not a carrot. She kept rantin' on about 'ow we were doin' violence to 'er and everyone in general by keepin' people with wombs suppressed an' that those people with wombs were objects of men's dirty desires. She went right off when me mate Barry shouted, "Show us yer tits, Treacle!" Oooh! She was not 'appy at all.'

'I'm not surprised,' said Tree Trunk.

'No? Why's that?'

'It's insulting. This is the twenty-first century, not the eighties. We're all a lot more enlightened now.'

'Barry's not enlightened. Not at all. An' I think she 'ad the 'ump 'cos she only had a coupla little 'uns. They're generally all miserable, ain't they? A bit like short men.'

'You're a heathen,' said Tree Trunk.

'You're not the first to say that,' said Clocks. His attention was taken by the arrival of a police van. He watched it intently as it pulled up opposite him. The driver jumped out and walked around the back. His own driver got out and opened up his door. Tree Trunk got out and walked around. Clocks got out at the same time as Paterson stepped into view, flanked by officers. Twenty feet apart, the pair of them smiled at each other.

'Morning, John,' said Paterson. 'How's it going?'

'Morning, Ray. It's all copacetic, thank you.'

'Copacetic?'

'Yep.'

'Where'd you learn that from?'

'Got a new *Word of the Day* app on me phone.'

'Ah. Explains that. D'you know what it means?'

'I did, but I've forgotten.'

'It means everything is in good order.'

'That's it! Yep. It's all in good order.'

'When you two fuckwits are quite finished, you've got somewhere to be,' said Superintendent Shark.

'Oh, sorry. Ray, this is Mr Shark, my arresting officer. From a distance. Wouldn't come near me 'imself. Bottled out. His friends call him Jaws.'

'I didn't bottle out and no one calls me Jaws,' said Shark. 'Only you call me Jaws and you only started that earlier on.'

'Gotta watch 'im, Ray. Can be a bit snappy.'

Paterson grinned. 'I'd introduce you to my arresting officer but he's being treated at Guy's Hospital for facial injuries.'

Clocks nodded slowly. 'Ooooh . . .'

'C'mon, you two,' said an officer. 'Move your arses.'

Paterson and Clocks were pushed into one of the lifts. 'We goin' up?' said Clocks.

'Well, we're in the basement, Clocks,' Shark said. 'So no one's goin' down, are they?'

Clocks shrugged. 'Story of my life, that is.'

# CHAPTER 8

As soon as the lift doors slid open with a muted mechanical hiss, Paterson and Clocks were ushered into a sprawling, almost endlessly long corridor. The stark white walls stretched out on either side, converging into a single point marked by what appeared to be a solitary door at the farthest end. The air was thick with anticipation and the sterile scent of polished linoleum.

Superintendent Shark led the way, and three armed officers walked behind Paterson and Clocks.

'Who do you think's waiting for us behind the door, John?' said Paterson.

'James Bond. Must be with all this weird shit goin' on.'

'James Bond? You wish.'

'Ha! I've told you this before, James Bond wishes he was me, matey. Proper geezer, me.'

'I thought Daniel Craig was the best Bond ever,' said Paterson, ignoring him.

'Agreed,' said Clocks. 'Breathed new life into the character, I thought.'

'Will you two shut up and take things seriously?' said Shark. 'You've both been nicked for murder, for Chrissakes!'

'No point lettin' it ruin the day, is there?' said Clocks. 'Besides, it's all a load of ol' bollocks. Tommy's death's got nothin' to do with us. Just a misunderstandin' for which we will sue the arse out of the Met as soon as we're released.'

Superintendent Shark rapped on the door.

'Come,' said a male voice from within.

Shark opened the door and they all walked in. Seated behind a large desk was the Commissioner of Police, Sam Morne. Paterson and Clocks had time for him. He treated them with courtesy and respect and stood aside when necessary. He'd let them do the job they were paid for.

Seated in the corner of the room, Paterson spotted a woman in her forties. She had a thin face, dark sunken eyes and close-cut hair. She was sharply dressed in a well-cut suit and heels. Paterson knew authority when he saw it and this woman radiated it.

'Hello, boys,' Morne said. 'Pleasant journey?'

'A bit uncomfortable, to be honest, guv,' said Clocks, turning his body sideways. 'Bleedin' 'andcuffs stuck 'alfway up me back.'

'Officers,' said Morne. 'Release them both. Why are they still in cuffs anyway, Mr Shark?'

'These are violent men, sir. Three of my officers were shot during the arrest by this one,' he nodded at Clocks. 'And this one, Paterson, has put about seven men in hospital.'

'Oi!' said Clocks. 'Get it right, Jaws. I shot one. Me missis shot the other two tryin' to defend me from you an' yer two-bob army.' Clocks rubbed his wrists as an officer moved on to Paterson.

The officer pulled Paterson about and made the removal of the cuffs as uncomfortable as possible. Paterson stayed silent until the man had finished. Then he turned around to recognise his attacker in the van, the one called Bill. He flashed his eyebrows at Paterson.

Paterson grinned. 'Hello, Bill. Good to see you again.' He headbutted Bill straight on the nose. The officer staggered backward as pandemonium broke out in the office.

Clocks spun and threw a right hand into the jaw of one of the gunmen, sending him crashing up against a full-length filing cabinet. The man slumped to the floor, unconscious. Paterson shifted his body weight and sent a high kick crashing into the head of the only gunman standing. He dropped like a stone.

'Enough!' Morne jumped up from his seat.

Superintendent Shark stood, mouth wide open, as he watched another three of his officers be despatched.

Paterson hadn't finished with his tormentor. 'Not so fucking clever now, are you? Get up! You wanted a row with me, eh? Then get the fuck up and let's see how you get on!'

'Paterson, pack it up!' said Morne.

The officer, his face smothered in blood, his nose clearly shattered, tried to pick himself up. Morne strode out from behind his desk and stood between Paterson and the officer. He stared at Paterson. 'Ray, no! Just . . . no!'

Paterson was breathing steadily, unaffected by his sudden assault on the man. He looked at Morne and gave a small nod. 'Sir.'

'The fuck was that all about?' said Morne as Paterson turned his back on the fallen man.

'Sorry, sir. He started showing off in the van when I was cuffed up. Got into my personal space a bit too much for my liking, so I just levelled the score a bit. Nothing to worry about.'

'You . . . you're nicked . . .' said the officer, trying to sit upright.

'Shut up, you muppet!' said Clocks, waving his hand around. 'Got any ice, guv?' he said to Morne. 'I might 'ave broken a bone.' He looked across at Paterson. 'Nice headbutt, Ray. Impressive. I didn't realise you'd been practicing my style of fighting. See? Much better than all that kung fu arm-waving shit you do.'

'I don't wave my arms about,' said Paterson. 'That's on the telly. Not real life.'

'I . . . what just happened?' said Shark. 'I've never seen anything like this. Aren't you going to call security, sir?'

Sam Morne chuckled. 'What? And rack up more casualties? I don't think so. Look, you've done your job, Mr Shark, and I thank you. If you could take him with you as he's the only one awake, I'd be grateful.' He indicated Bill.

'What?'

'Don't worry about the other two. When they wake up, I'll send them back down to you. Wait . . . On second thoughts, I'll call security. They can drag them outside and call an ambulance if need be. I have a duty of care, don't I?' He picked up his desk phone and punched a button.

'This can't be happening,' said Shark. 'These men are out of control. They have to be cuffed again.'

Johnny Clocks held out his arms and exposed both wrists. 'You wanna put 'em on me then, Jaws?'

'Er . . .'

'No? Thought not. Now, do as the big boss says an' toddle off back to yer little 'idey 'ole. There's a good egg.'

Morne shook his head. Paterson and Clocks had been in his office less than two minutes, and he had two men out cold, one with a broken nose and a superintendent who was both shocked and bewildered at what he'd just witnessed.

'Mr Shark. Thank you for all your efforts in today's exercise. Suffice to say, this little episode remains within these walls, understand?'

Superintendent Shark shook his head. 'No, sir. I really don't. I was tasked to bring these men in and to go in hard and fast and bring them to you for evaluation. I was not expecting my officers to be shot, beaten and end up in hospital. I certainly wasn't expecting the violence to continue in your office and for you to take such a casual stance toward it. So, no. I don't understand. Perhaps you would explain?'

'I understand your concern, Mr Shark, but I don't have the time or the inclination to explain everything now. If you'd be so good as to show yourself out, I'll be in touch.' Three security guards burst into the office, startling Shark. Morne indicated that it was time for Shark to leave, and he barged his way past the security men.

'Sir?' said one of them to Morne.

'Nothing to worry about, boys. Things got a bit heated for a moment or two. All sorted now. I'd be grateful if you could remove these chaps for me and get them some medical aid. Thank you.'

'Need me to help you up?' said Paterson to Bill.

'Fuck off!' Bill stood himself up, swaying on his feet.

Paterson grinned. 'Fuck off, *sir*,' he said.

Bill staggered out of the office as the security team began removing the two unconscious officers.

'Couldn't get us a bag of ice, could yer, mate?' Clocks showed the guard his knuckles.

The man nodded. 'Yeah, course.'

'Take a seat, gents,' said Morne. 'Well, it's been an interesting morning all round, hasn't it?'

'Couple of questions, Sam,' said Paterson.

'I thought there might be.' Morne settled back into his leather chair. 'Go on.'

'Obvious one first. What the fuck's this all about and what's it got to do with us? And second, who's this woman?' He nodded toward where she sat.

'Fair questions, Ray—'

'Oh, 'ello, Treacle. Didn't see you sittin' there. You're quiet,' said Clocks.

The woman raised one eyebrow but said nothing.

Clocks shrugged and turned back toward Morne. 'Guv, seriously. You got any ice? Me knuckle's throbbin' like a virgin's cock in a brothel.'

'What an absolutely charming turn of phrase, John. You've always had a way with words, haven't you?'

'Yep. Ever since I started reading poetry. Some lovely shit there.'

'Would either of you like a drink?' said Morne.

'I could slaughter a cuppa tea,' said Clocks. 'And a few Jammie Dodgers if you've got 'em?'

'Given the morning you've had, I was thinking more of the alcoholic variety, John, but tea is available if you wish.'

'Well, if alcohol is available, then I do not wish for tea, thank you very much. I wish for alcohol.'

'Ray?'

'Little one, please.'

'Don't forget the biscuits if they're goin,' said Clocks. 'Love me a biscuit.'

Morne wrinkled his nose. 'With alcohol? Really?'

Clocks shrugged. 'Yep. Nothin' like a Jammie Dodger dipped in vodka.'

Morne shook his head, rose from his seat and walked over to the filing cabinet that had assisted Clocks in rendering his man unconscious. He pulled open a drawer and removed a full bottle of whisky. 'All I have, I'm afraid. Is this okay?'

Both men nodded and Morne picked up three tumblers with his fingers. 'Would you like one, ma'am?' he said to his other guest.

She held up her finger and waved it slightly.

'Blimey,' said Clocks. 'She's a bit lively, ain't she? All that talking's doin' me 'ead in. I think you've found yerself the perfect woman there, Sam. Sits in the corner an' keeps quiet all day. She any good at makin' the tea?' He grinned at her.

Sam Morne rubbed his face. 'Clocks, this is Louise Fields. I would advise you to be very, very careful how you speak to her.'

Clocks looked over at Morne. 'Why?'

'Because I have the power to keep you out of prison, Mr Clocks,' said Louise Fields. Her voice was flat and even, as if she had learned a long time ago to control her emotions. She looked at Morne. 'Really? This one? He's an idiot.'

'Oi! Steady on,' said Clocks. 'I was just playin' with yer. Jokin'. Who are you, then?'

'A friendly with a lot of clout, and I'm here to offer you both a job. I'm told that you are among the very best the police have to offer. But if you, Mr Clocks, are among the best, then I would say the police are in much worse shape than I know it to be.'

'Oh, that's lovely that, innit? Thanks for that. Makes me feel special.'

Fields stared at him square in the eye. 'The fact that you're here, Mr Clocks, should make you feel special. Sam, explain please.'

'I have an offer for you, gents,' he said. 'You can say no, of course, but it wouldn't be wise.'

# CHAPTER 9

'Drink up, boys, and I'll tell you a story.'

Paterson wasn't happy about the attack on his house and was not in the mood for Morne's minor theatrics. 'Can we just get on with it, Sam?' he said a little testily. 'Please.'

Morne grinned. 'Of course. Do you know why you're here?'

Paterson shrugged. 'Apparently, Tommy Gunn's dead and we're in the frame for it. No surprise there.'

'No, Ray. No surprise there.'

'So what's the score then, guv?' said Clocks. 'Why are we bein' stitched up for it?'

'Well, to be clear, you're not being stitched up. As you know, Mr Gunn had a few issues with you both and your somewhat . . . over-the-top behaviour in achieving your objectives. You may recall what happened a minute ago?'

Clocks shrugged. 'Fair point.'

'He came to me with some story that you were both involved in the murder of that lunatic killer, David Steers.'

'Wait! Hold up, guv. Is Steers dead, then? We got a body now?'

Morne gave Clocks a side-eye glance. He chose to ignore his questions. 'He was of the opinion that you killed Steers out in that field and drove his body away prior to police arrival and that *your* car, Ray, was destroyed to cover up any evidence. He told me that he confronted you both about it and things turned a bit nasty, to the point that you threatened to kill him. Is that correct?'

Paterson shook his head. 'Don't know what he's talking about.'

Morne nodded. 'Hmm. So, he was lying, then?'

'Sounds like it.'

'You wouldn't kill him, would you?'

Paterson shifted in his seat. 'No, I wouldn't. If Tommy had a beef with us, so be it. That's a long list of people he'd have to get behind. Did he have any evidence?'

'No, but there is the matter of your car, Ray. Where is it?'

Paterson sat himself back. 'I sold it.'

Morne stroked his chin. 'Did you now? I take it you have documents supporting that statement?'

'Whatever you need.'

'Well, let me tell you something. You boys are not stupid. Not by a long shot.'

'We know that.'

'We?' said Clocks.

'I'm getting to that, John. Bear with.'

There was tap on the door and a man's head popped in. 'Sorry, sir. You wanted a bag of ice?'

Clocks jumped up and strode to the door. 'Oh, top man. Thank you so much.' He grabbed the bag and slapped it on his bruised hand. 'Ooh! That's 'andsome, that is.' He sat back down.

'As I was saying,' said Morne. 'We are aware of how you boys operate, and we've been keeping an eye on you over the years.'

'Who's "we" again?' said Clocks.

'I'll get to that.'

'Since the time you two paired up, we've watched you closely. Commissioner Young opened a docket on you both and added to it during his tenure. When he retired, that docket remained open and was further added to.'

Paterson and Clocks remained silent. Paterson wasn't sure where this was going but he didn't like it.

'You two have had quite colourful careers, haven't you? People do seem to have a habit of either dying or being seriously injured around you, and you've both had more than your fair share of injuries. Paterson, it makes me wonder how you're still standing. Shot, stabbed and at one point you nearly had your face peeled off. Can't have been pleasant. And just recently you very nearly drowned, thanks to our missing Mr Steers. You've killed, what, three people in the line of duty? Must be. Probably more.'

Paterson said nothing. Just stared at Morne.

'And John. You've been shot . . . by your wife, I believe.'

'Yeah, but she did that in order to save me bein' killed by the baddie. Right through me shoulder, straight into his nut. Judgement call and a fuckin' good shot. An' talkin' of me missus, where is she? She in this buildin' with us?'

Morne shook his head. 'She's been released, John. It was you two we were after, not her.'

Paterson frowned. Given she'd discharged her weapon and shot at police, she should have been arrested for questioning at the very least. Something felt off.

'Anyway,' said Morne, 'you were also doused in petrol and nearly set on fire among other . . . difficulties. You dropped a villain from a building, killing him.'

'To be fair, guv, 'e only died 'cos he landed on 'is 'ead. If 'e'd been sensible about it and landed on 'is feet, then 'e would've just broken both legs and probably been crippled for the rest of 'is life. But, oh no, 'e 'ad to smack 'is 'ead on the pavement, didn't 'e?'

'Hmm,' said Morne. 'You also shot the leg off a man who was buried in a coffin at low tide on the Thames and you did that on live TV.'

'I did do that, yes.'

'From what I understand, it was fifty–fifty as to which way up his head was. You could've blown his head off!'

'Reasonable odds, I thought.'

'No, John. Fifty-one–forty-nine are reasonable odds. Not fifty–fifty.'

'Well, we got 'im out, didn't we? He lived. No 'arm done.'

'Actually, John, I think having a leg blown off rather does constitute harm being done. Would you agree in hindsight?'

'Well, if you frame it like that, then yeah. Harm was done.'

Morne shook his head. 'You've both been under an awful lot of strain over the last few years and it has inevitably taken its toll on you. I think it's fair to say that both of you are fractured. Broken.'

Paterson sighed deeply. 'Is there a point to this? I'm getting hungry.'

'Yeah. Me an' all. Where's me Jammie Dodgers, guv?'

'The point is, we first became really concerned when you went off in Mumbai, Ray, and burned down those clinics. John, you shot one of France's biggest villains in the leg and then you both conspired to murder David Steers.'

Paterson jumped up and jabbed his finger at Morne. 'Enough! Don't keep saying we murdered Steers, all right? If you had evidence, you'd have nicked us by now. If you've got evidence, get on with nicking us, but you don't, do you? So, pack up your fishing rod. You're wasting your time. And as for Gunn, yeah, we had our differences, not disputing that. Yeah, we all fell out, but we had nothing to do with his death.'

Morne nodded. 'I know, you didn't. I did.'

## CHAPTER 10

'What?' said Paterson. 'What did you say?' He stared at Commissioner Morne, not quite sure if he'd heard him correctly. 'Did . . . did you just say you killed Tommy?'

'Well, yes. I didn't actually pull the trigger myself, but I sanctioned his removal.'

'Are you fuckin' jokin'?' Clocks jumped up from his chair. 'Why? What the fuck for?'

'Had to be done.'

'The fuck yer mean?'

'What do you mean, Sam?' said Paterson. 'And you'd best make it a bloody good explanation.'

'Calm down, gentlemen, and allow me to explain.'

Clocks banged his fist on the desk and immediately regretted it. He shook it out. 'Don't tell me to calm down, you sanctimonious prick! Tommy was a copper. One of us. What did 'e do to you to warrant 'aving 'im topped? Jesus! You're the fuckin' commissioner! You can't go 'round 'avin' people killed! Wassamatterwiyer?'

'Have you finished, John?'

Clocks looked at Morne, waiting for him to say something.

'Tommy Gunn was not one of us. Not in the sense that I wanted him to be. That he should have been.'

55

Paterson watched Morne closely, searched his face. It troubled him that he thought he knew Sam Morne and now he was looking at a man who had calmly confessed to arranging for a detective sergeant, *his* detective sergeant, to be murdered and seemed to not give a jot. Certainly, he showed no signs of remorse. Paterson knew that he and Clocks had just stepped into something very big and very dangerous.

'How can I explain? Look, Mr Gunn came to me because he suspected that you both killed David Steers and conspired to cover up his murder. I explained to him that I was uneasy with his allegation and that he was to leave it with me. It became apparent to me that he wasn't satisfied with my position, so I asked him to leave while I made certain arrangements and to await my call. I did make arrangements, but not the kind he thought.

'My hands were tied. Gunn was not going to give this up. Of that, I was certain. Had he taken it further — to the press, perhaps, if he got no satisfaction through the proper channels — then there would be no alternative but to arrest the both of you, and on the basis of the circumstantial evidence, it was likely you would have both stood trial for the murder of Steers. During the course of the investigation, your past misdemeanours and indiscretions would have resurfaced and been tacked onto the investigation and of course, you would have been charged with Gunn's murder.'

'What? You just said you 'ad 'im done in. You can't pin that on us.'

'You and Ray both made it clear to witnesses that you would kill him if he didn't shut his mouth. You both have the motive and the means to have arranged for that, so . . .' Morne shrugged. 'You do the maths.'

Clocks rubbed his face. 'You bastard!'

'I can see why you'd think that, John, but let me continue. You were both marked from the day that you, Ray, murdered DC Walker at the top of Tower Bridge. No need to deny or explain. He was a serial killer and he butchered your wife.' Paterson winced at the memory. 'Any one of us would

56

have done the same. John, your die was cast when you covered for him. It bound you together in blood and your fates were entwined from then on.'

'Fuck me, Ray. Guv'nor's gone all *Game of Thrones* on us.'

Morne smiled. 'You both found something in each other — kindred spirits of a sort. John, you've spent most of your working life being a rowdy yob with a hell of an attitude problem. That's okay. It's fine for our purposes. We knew that you were a solid, dependable copper. Ray, you have skills in the martial arts and are highly intelligent. But it was noted in your papers long before you killed Walker that you exhibited a ruthless streak. It didn't come out in acts of violence or behaviour toward any individual, but it was there, and it was seen. When Walker died on that bridge, it was literally a perfect storm of psychopathy coming together. Two damaged men found each other. Perfect for what we need.'

Paterson sighed deeply. 'Sit down, John. We're gonna be here a while. Let's have the rest of it, Sam. We need to hear this out.'

'What I'm going to tell you is for your ears only. It will change your life whatever you choose to do with the information. Do you understand?'

Paterson nodded.

'Nope!' said Clocks. 'Not yet. Best you get on with the explainin' before I totally lose my shit an' end up lampin' you right on the snot box, you murderin' fucker.'

Again, Morne smiled at Clocks. 'Pot. Kettle. Black, John.'

'What?'

'Leave it, John,' said Paterson. 'Buckle up for me, eh? Let him talk.'

Clocks glared at Morne but sat himself down.

'I have an offer to make to you both. But, and this time I'm serious, it's a one-time offer. No do-overs. You take it or you don't.'

'Wait a minute,' said Paterson. 'You've . . . a few of you have tried before to get us to join your little club or whatever it is and we've said we're not interested. Why d'you keep on?'

'Well,' said Fields, 'your circumstances have changed radically, haven't they? Now you're looking at being investigated for the murder of a fellow officer.'

'Oh, blimey,' said Clocks. 'She's woke up. Thought you'd died, love.'

Louise Fields glared at him, as if she was contemplating how breaking him would be very satisfying.

Sam Morne took a deep breath. 'I'm part of an organisation . . .'

'What organisation?' Clocks blurted.

'UMBRA,' said Fields.

'It's a powerful group, John,' said Morne. 'One that has kept this country safe for over a hundred years. One that is always looking for good help. People it can trust. People who are willing to do things that lesser people would shy from. And that's where you two come in. As I said, you have been watched these past five years and the people I represent feel that you would be a good fit for the work we do.'

'And that work is . . . ?' said Paterson.

'Removing certain elements from our streets and keeping this country that bit safer from all threats, domestic and foreign.'

'Certain elements?'

'Yes. People that live outside the reach of ordinary justice. These people never see the inside of a court. Never have. Never will. They have the resources, the means and the will to avoid being captured and incarcerated. The odd one or two, back in the day, those who did appear before a court, brought mayhem with them. A judge, his entire family and every single juror was slaughtered at the will of one particular criminal and this was on day two of the trial. He did this to send a message. That he ruled. That he was all powerful. That he was not to be touched. And, if he was, well, as I said . . .'

'I don't remember anything about this,' said Paterson. 'Surely that would have been brought up in our trainings as a noted case?'

'Not this one, Ray. It was kept under wraps.'

'So, how long ago was this?' said Paterson.

Morne sighed. 'Eighty-one years ago. Outside the memory of most people. But it was just the start of the rise of the criminal gangs that fought for supremacy in London. However, the government was a different animal back then and the group was set up to ensure that, however many gangs rose, there was a line. And if that line was crossed, then retribution would follow. Not justice. Retribution. This was the government's message to the bosses. There would be no repeat of that day.'

Clocks chuckled. 'So, what? Your mob sent the boys round, did they? 'Ave a good ol' tear-up with the bad boys, eh?'

Morne frowned. 'Indeed, there was a *tear-up*, John. The government put together a team of intelligence officers under the codename *UMBRA* and staffed it with some of the hardest fuckers to have ever crawled out of a trench to walk this planet, whose only brief was to stop the bosses by any means necessary. And then they turned them loose to go hunting. And they were good at hunting.'

'What does UMBRA mean, then?' said Clocks.

'It's a Latin word. It means *shadow*. The darkest shadow that results from a total blockage of light. That's where we operate. Anyway, they found the man who ordered the slaughter of those people, and they took a terrible, terrible revenge. His wife, daughter, thirteen-year-old son, his old father and mother were killed in front of him, and then they hung him on a dockyard gibbet for all to see. They burned every single property and business premises he owned to the ground, sometimes with members of the gang inside, and effectively wiped any record of his having lived from the face of the earth. And then they went after every member of his gang, every known associate, everyone who was in some way criminally connected to him. And they killed them all without mercy.'

Clocks had been listening with ever widening eyes. 'Fuck me! 'Ow many of 'em were there?'

59

'Six. The first recruits. Four men, two women. By the end of the first year, there were forty operatives working up and down the country. However, it wasn't only the British gangs that wanted to build criminal empires. The Americans came here to try their luck. So did the Italians and the Jews. All of them had serious criminal gangs and all were vying for control of London in particular. Of course, the police themselves were no match for this level of criminality and so UMBRA was expanded into groups across the country. It recruited dangerous, callous, intelligent men and women. But most importantly, these people were . . . damaged. All had served in the military, all had seen extreme danger and all had fought on the front line. They were "over the edge" and happy to do what was necessary to continue to protect this country.'

'This all sounds a bit far-fetched, sir,' said Paterson. 'I mean, this isn't the way Britain does things. The CIA and Mossad? I can see that but not us. Not the Brits.'

'You'd think, wouldn't you? But that fight-by-the-rules mentality was a craftily constructed lie to deflect away from some of the things that were done in the shadows. Look, who do you think worked with and trained them? The CIA was formed in 1947. Mossad was formed in 1949. UMBRA was formed in 1943.'

'Yeah but still sounds like bollocks to me, guv,' said Clocks. 'I mean, two women on the frontline? Pretty sure they were nurses and things, weren't they?'

Fields sighed loudly. 'They were. But we had spies. Female spies who undertook dangerous work. *Field* work. And they killed when necessary.'

'Huh. Who knew? So, you're sayin' that the good ol' UK led the way in sanctioned kills against enemies foreign an' domestic, trained some of the 'ardest psychopathic bastards in the world an' let 'em loose to go traipsin' off around the world killin' everyone who was up to naughties?'

'Big naughties, John,' said Morne. 'Big naughties.'

'Fuckin' 'ell.' Clocks shook his head.

'Look at the state of the world today,' said Morne. 'It's bad, yes?'

Paterson and Clocks both nodded.

'Well, it's a helluva lot safer than you think thanks to UMBRA et al. The crime reported on the street is minor stuff, and the police we have on the streets give the illusion of keeping it under control. How, I'm not quite sure.'

'What about all the big drugs busts, then, guv? These guys 'ave been operatin' for years without gettin' their collar felt.'

Morne smiled. 'These people are nothing, John. Yes, they're a problem but not on a big enough scale. We allow them to operate and that gives the papers something to hang their hats on and get excited by. While they're either slagging us off for not being able to catch criminals or patting us on the back when they do go to court, they have no idea that we leave them out in play just to create an illusion. It's a certain level of criminality that the average person can understand and accept. They don't like it, but if they really knew the level of criminality out there, they'd likely all die of fear. While those guys play it out in the public eye, behind the scenes we're hard at work setting things right and using secrecy and manipulation to cover our tracks. Remember this: he who controls the lie, controls the truth. And this world is full of lies.'

'All right, all right, all right . . .' Clocks leaned forward in his chair. 'So, what about people like that dealer, Pablo Escobar, in the states? He made billions, killed 'undreds. 'Ow come 'e got away with it, then?'

'The world needs a villain from time to time, John. Someone being seen to beat the system now and again. Many admired him. Raised him up to legend status. The Americans built him up and then, when the time was right, terminated him.'

'But that fucker was to blame for a shit ton of coke 'ittin' the streets. Killed . . . what? Thousands and thousands.'

'True, but needs must sometimes.'

'Fuckin' *needs must*? Kids died, Sam! Families were ripped apart 'cos of 'im.'

'Again, true. But allowing him to grow unchecked emboldened dozens of other big-time suppliers. Bigger than Escobar by a country mile. And the yanks took them out of the game. Yes, thousands died, but millions more lived. War's a filthy game, John.'

'So, you want us to work for this "UMBRA" unit. You want us to, what, kill the bigger boys? Go to war. Is that right?'

'Exactly right.'

'Why us, sir?' said Paterson.

Louise Fields broke her silence and took a deep breath. 'It's simple, Mr Paterson. We need people who are not afraid to get their hands bloody. And we never send sheep to kill wolves.'

# CHAPTER 11

A sudden sharp rap on the door brought their discussion to a halt.

'Come!' Morne's voice carried a hint of annoyance.

The door opened and a fresh-faced uniformed officer poked his head inside. 'Sir, I have an urgent message for Superintendent Paterson.'

'I thought I gave an instruction that I was not to be disturbed,' said Morne. 'What about that did you not understand?'

'I'm sorry, but I received a call from someone called Monkey. Said that I had to get this message to Mr Paterson or he'd, er, "pull my fucking arms off".'

'What's the message, son?' said Clocks.

'Er . . .' The young officer unfolded a note. '*You need to get your arse back to the nick a bit lively. We've just had four suicides on the manor.*'

Paterson frowned. Four suicides was a definite reason to get their arses back to the nick. 'Sir?' said Paterson. 'Can we go, or are we under arrest, or . . . what?'

Morne sighed and rubbed his face. He looked over at Louise Fields. She nodded. 'Yes, you can go. Of course you can go. But I need you to think about what I've said and when you've thought about it, get yourselves back here with a "Yes, we'd be honoured to join." Today. Understood?'

Paterson gave Morne a wry smile. 'We'll see, sir. We'll see.' Both men headed toward the door.

The PC backed out to let them pass. 'Can I get you anything, sir?'

'Yep,' said Clocks. 'We're gonna need a fuck-off super-duper fast car. We came 'ere by van and I ain't goin' back that way. Go on. Chop-chop! There's a good lad.'

'No need, sir. DC Monkey is downstairs waiting for you.'

'DC Monkey?' said Clocks. 'That's not 'is name, you numpty. That's 'is nickname.'

Paterson grinned as the young man's face flushed, his embarrassment clear to see. 'Don't worry, mate. Easy mistake to make. Did he really say he would tear your arms off?'

The young man nodded rapidly. 'Yes, sir. He was quite adamant about it. Said if you weren't down in ten minutes, he'd come and find me, pull my arms off and stick them back on the wrong way round. Said it would ruin any chance of wanking that I might be thinking of doing in the future.'

Clocks burst out laughing. 'Sounds like Monkey. 'Ow long you got left on the clock, son?'

The PC glanced at his watch. 'About four minutes.'

Clocks slapped him on the back. 'Best you go an' knock one out while you still can. We 'ave to grab a quick cuppa before we leave.'

The two senior men headed off down the corridor laughing and left the young man watching their backs as they went.

'Four suicides,' said Paterson. 'That's a new one. Never heard of that before.'

'Well, it's Monday morning, innit? Probably four people couldn't face yet another commute into the office an' thought to 'emselves, *Fuck this. I'm done. Ta-ta world.*'

'You think?'

'Bound to be.'

'We'll see.'

'We will. I'll bet you a tenner that's what it is.'

'Idiot.'

Clocks grinned. 'No argument there.' He tapped the lift button five or six times in quick succession.

'Right. What was that all about, back there, with Morne?'

'You know,' said Paterson. 'You were there.'

'Yes, I know. Rhetorical question.'

'Rhetorical? Is that you using the app again?'

'Of course. I meant, what do we do?'

'Bastard had Tommy killed. For all his faults, he didn't deserve that. I mean, I can't believe it. Sam, of all people. I thought he was a bit of a snowflake.'

Clocks nodded. 'Yeah, me an' all. So, what's the plan? Do we join or do we nick Morne for murder? I'll go with whatever you say.'

The lift doors opened. Two passengers looked out at them and moved aside as they stepped in.

Paterson pressed the button for the ground floor. 'I don't know yet. This is tricky. He's got us by the bollocks and he knows it.'

'Excuse me,' said the only female in the lift. 'Language.' Paterson and Clocks turned to look at her.

'Mind yer own business, Treacle,' Clocks said. 'Men at work 'ere. If you don't like it, shove yer fingers in yer ears.'

Paterson grinned as he watched the woman's face fall.

'Er, excuse me,' she said. 'Do you know who I am?'

'Nope. You know who I am?'

'No,' said the woman.

'Result!' Clocks declared triumphantly as the lift doors slid open. 'See yer.'

They were out of the lift and heading toward the car park before the woman could utter another word. It wouldn't have mattered if she had. Neither man was in the mood.

As they crossed the car park, Monkey Harris stepped out of his car so they could see him. 'Guv's,' he nodded.

'Morning, Monkey,' said Paterson. 'Sounds like we have another shit storm awaiting us.'

Monkey opened the door and watched his boss slide effortlessly into the seat. He walked back around to his side of the car.

'Oi!' said Clocks. 'What about me, then?'

'Sorry?' said Monkey.

'Whassamatter with my door?'

Monkey shrugged. 'Dunno, guv. Give the handle a tug. Should open.'

'What? No. I meant, why ain'tcha 'eld the door open for me?'

Monkey looked bemused. 'Why would I do that? You're a big boy. You know how to open a car door. Pull the handle.'

'Why'd you open it for Ray, then?'

'Respect.'

'Why don't I get any respect, then?'

'Probably because you're a knob.' Monkey climbed behind the wheel.

Clocks wrenched the door open, slid across the back seat and slammed the door shut. 'I'm your senior officer, Monkey-boy. You show a bit of respect.'

'Yes, sir. Sorry, sir.' Monkey started the car up. 'You'll be all right in the back, Clocksy. The child locks are on.'

Paterson chuckled and looked over his shoulder at Clocks.

'Oh, funny fucker you are, Monkey,' said Clocks. 'Won't be laughin' when I kick you in the dangleberries, will yer?'

'You'll only do it once, guv. Then I'll break you into little bits and post them back to your missus.'

Clocks put his head down and mumbled. 'Do you any day of the week son.'

'What's that?' said Monkey.

'Didn't say anything,' said Clocks. 'I'm just mindin' me own business.'

'Good,' said Monkey. 'Right, Ray, why did I have to come all the way over here to pick you two up? I thought you'd both be tucked up in your pits until the alarm went off. What'd you get up to?'

'Long story,' said Paterson. 'I'll fill you in later but for now, let's just say we had an early morning call from the commissioner.'

'Everything all right?'

'Yeah, everything's fine. Just had to sort out a few things with him. Nothing to worry about. How'd you know we were here?'

Monkey slowed the car as the lights changed from amber to red. 'Got a call from Jackie.'

'Well, 'ow'd she know?'

'Got a call from Lyndsey.'

'Well . . .' Clocks clammed up.

'You bring our guns, by any chance?' said Paterson.

'In the lock box,' said Monkey matter-of-factly.

Paterson was sure he would be wondering what they were up to. He caught Monkey glancing sideways at him and at Clocks in the rear-view mirror. Clocks was staring out into the streets, apparently preoccupied with his own thoughts.

'Tell me about these suicides,' said Paterson.

'Don't know too much at the moment, guv. All I can tell you is, we got a call from traffic management to tell us that they'd captured four people stepping out in front of big vehicles — lorries, buses, that sort of thing — and they've all been pronounced dead at the scene.'

'Fuck. All four of them?'

'Dead as doornails.'

'That's gonna fuck the rush 'our traffic up a treat, innit?' said Clocks. 'One selfish fucker's bad enough, but four? That's bloody chaos, that is.'

'Where's traffic management hide out these days?' said Paterson.

'Kennington,' said Monkey. 'Got the top two floors of a big old office complex.'

'Kennington it is, then,' said Paterson.

'Whack the blues 'n' twos on, Monkey,' said Clocks. 'Traffic's gonna be a right bastard.'

# CHAPTER 12

After wending their way through the slowly building rush-hour traffic, Paterson and Clocks found themselves standing inside a vast, dark room roughly the size of half a football pitch. Monkey had driven back to Tower Bridge Police Station to rally the rest of the squad. This was going to be a long day and Paterson wanted everybody in and ready to graft.

He looked around the room. Three of its walls were covered in screens all exactly the same size, all showing pictures of different points of South East London. In the centre of the room, laid out in a square shape, were two banks of desks containing computer screens. Everybody at their desk was busy, most were talking but it all gelled into a low drone. The room was gently illuminated by ceiling lights, but it was the brightness from the screens that lit up the whole room.

'Shit, Ray,' said Clocks. 'This place is fuckin' mahoosive!'

'What?'

'Mahoosive. Means it's massive?'

Paterson gave Clocks a look. 'Why not just say that, then?'

Clocks shrugged. 'Gives me a chance to ramp up yer word power. Educate yer a bit.'

'Educate me? I don't think so.'

'Whatever. I 'ad no idea this was 'ere. Gi-bleedin'-normous, this is.'

Out the corner of his eye, Paterson saw the silhouette of a man approaching them in a hurry. He held out his hand as he drew closer. 'Gentlemen!' He shook Paterson's hand first, then Clocks's. 'You must be Detectives Paterson and Clocks. Thank you for coming. It's terrible, terrible. I've never seen anything like this in my life. Just terrible.'

Paterson weighed him up. Mid-fifties, short dark hair and a neatly trimmed beard framed a thin, almost skeletal face with cheekbones that could cut a side of beef. He was tall, a good six foot, and smartly dressed. He was also badly shaken up.

'Good morning,' Paterson said. 'You are?'

'What? Oh, yes, yes. Sorry. Er, Simon Fox. I'm the senior officer here.'

'So, you're in charge of this lot?' Clocks's head was still swivelling around the room.

'What? In charge? Er, yes. Yes, I am. That's me. Yes.'

'Are you okay?' said Paterson. 'You seem very agitated.'

The man's eyes darted toward Paterson like a startled animal's.

'What? No. Yes. I'm so sorry. I'm not normally like this. It's . . . It's just . . . In all my years, I've never seen anything like this before. I sat and watched four people kill themselves and I couldn't do a thing about it.'

Paterson nodded. He remembered what it was like to feel remorse. At least, he saw pictures of himself pre Johnny Clocks, when he was just a high-flyer on his way to the top, liberal-minded and full of ideals. Those days were long gone and that Ray Paterson had died some time ago. 'Yes,' he said. 'It's a terrible thing, death. Do you have somewhere we can talk? Your office maybe?'

Fox nodded. 'Yes, yes. Of course. Please. Come with me. I have one or two operators waiting for you in a separate room.

One of them realised what was going on before they killed themselves.'

'What? 'Ow'd 'e do that?' said Clocks. 'Can't know if someone's gonna twat 'emselves by lookin' on a screen, can yer?'

'Er, yes. Sometimes. Most of the officers in the room are quite adept at pre-empting when something is about to happen. They stare at these screens for a total of seven hours a day, five days a week for years. You get to know behaviours. We can predict when an argument is about to develop into a full-blown fight, when a street robber is about to strike, when a drunken man is about to pull a girl into a darkened alley, when a man, a bit too close to a kiddies school, is up to no good.'

'Well, that shut me up, didn't it?' said Clocks.

'That'll be a first.' Paterson gave Clocks a wry grin.

'Tell us about the one who recognised what was about to 'appen,' said Clocks.

Fox opened the door to his office and showed them inside the overly neat interior.

'Take a seat,' he said. 'I'll rustle up some tea if you want?'

'I want,' said Clocks. 'My mouth feels like a camel's flip-flop.'

'Mr Paterson?' said Fox.

'Wouldn't mind a coffee. White, no sugar, please.'

'An' if you've got any knockin' about, I wouldn't say no to a couple of Jammie Dodgers. I was up early this mornin'. Missed me breakfast.'

'I'll see what I can do,' said Fox.

As Fox picked up the phone and ordered their drinks and biscuits, Paterson looked around the office. Nice and roomy. Nothing at all like the old room he had on the top floor of Tower Bridge. That hadn't seen a lick of paint for at least twenty years. This . . . this was class. One wall was entirely glass and overlooked the streets of London and another looked out at the control room. Fox had a standing desk. Paterson's was a lump of old wood that he suspected was left over from

Noah's last big project. All of the files on his desk were neatly stacked, no pages sticking out of their respective folders. His two fountain pens — one red, one black — were exactly the same make and size and both sat on top of an A3-sized blotter precisely half an inch apart, perfectly parallel to each other. His flexi-arm lamp sat bang in the top middle of the top third of the desk.

'Done, gentlemen. Five minutes.'

'Cheers, fellah,' said Clocks. 'Right, fill us in, then. What's the story?'

'The floor duty officer was watching the screens when he noticed a woman acting oddly on Tower Bridge. He immediately sensed something was off and kept a close eye on her. But then, in rapid succession, one after another of my other operatives also spotted someone acting strangely. And all of these sightings were spread out across Bermondsey — your territory, I believe.'

Paterson nodded slowly, his concern growing with each word.

'Well, we were worried enough that we called the police but, by then, it had started.'

'Started?' said Paterson.

'Yes. The woman on Tower Bridge looked at her phone, looked along the road and stepped out on front of a lorry. Terrible. It hit her full on, knocked her for about twenty yards, give or take. The driver slammed his brakes on but it was too big and had too much momentum. It couldn't stop . . .'

'Go on,' said Clocks. 'What 'appened then?'

'It went over her . . . her . . .'

'What? Went over 'er what?'

'Her head. It went over her head.'

'Ooh. Fuck that. I bet it looked like a bottle of dropped jam.'

Simon Fox just looked at Clocks.

'What?' said Clocks. 'Just tryin' to take the 'orror out of it. Thought it might 'elp a bit.'

'Not now, John,' said Paterson. 'Not the best time, mate.'

There was a knock on the door. Tea and biscuits had arrived. Clocks wrinkled his nose at the biscuits. Bourbons. He hated Bourbons. But he was hungry. He picked one up and dunked it in his tea.

'Okay,' said Paterson. 'Where are the staff who witnessed this?'

'Most of them are out there, still working. But I've rounded up the main operators who first noticed the problem. They're all happy to be interviewed whenever you're ready.'

Paterson blew into his coffee cup. 'Good stuff. We might as well get started. John, grab your tea. Let's go to work. We'll need to see the recordings of each suicide, Mr Fox.'

'Simon. Call me Simon.'

'Okay, Simon, where do we go?'

'Right here. They're all ready to view.' He beckoned Paterson around to his side of the desk. Clocks followed behind. Fox pointed to four clips on the desktop of his exceptionally large monitor. 'If you don't mind, I'll be outside. This isn't something I particularly want to watch again. Not just yet.'

72

# CHAPTER 13

'You ready?' said Paterson.

'Born ready, buddy,' said Clocks.

Paterson touched the screen and watched as the first clip played: the woman stood by the kerb. It was clear she was agitated from her movements. He watched her look up and down the road, watched her walk away from the kerb and watched her hug herself once or twice — an almost involuntary, unconscious movement. After another couple of minutes, the woman looked at her phone, shook her head, walked toward the Thames, turned, walked back to the road and stepped out in front of a lorry.

'Oh, shit!' said Clocks as the lorry barrelled into her, sending her flying. 'Oh, Jesus H.' The lorry rolled over her. A few seconds later, it was over. Pedestrians ran across the road in a futile attempt to help. Drivers left their cars to see what they could do. Nothing. A woman threw up.

Paterson remained quiet as the scene unfolded in front of him. So far, everything was just as Fox had said, but Paterson spotted something that he had omitted to tell him.

'You see that?' he said.

'Yep.'

'She dropped her phone in the drink.'

'Hmm.'

Clocks nodded. 'We 'ave to get 'er phone. I'll get on to the flipper squad. Get 'em to start a search of the river. I'll make a call to the nick as well to see if anythin' was found at the scene.'

'Ready for the next one?'

'Told yer. Born ready. Push on.'

Paterson started the second clip. The caption at the top of the screen told him he was looking at the west side of London Bridge. Same scenario. Different sex. A man was giving off similar body signals. Nervous, looking at his watch. Looking at his phone. He walked back toward the parapet of the bridge and this time, both men could clearly see him drop his phone into the water below. He turned, walked back to the road and stepped in front of a bus. 'Ooh! Two for two,' said Clocks. Clip three showed a woman standing outside a mosque. She dropped her phone down a drain before she stepped in front of a fire engine on a blue-light run.

Clip four, and the agitated man they saw was standing on Southwark Bridge. He stepped in front of a bus. His phone had also gone into the Thames seconds before.

Paterson stopped the clip.

'Mr Fox seems to 'ave left out a few bits 'n' pieces he shoulda mentioned,' said Clocks.

'Probably didn't see them?'

'What? Everyone dumping their phones? How could 'e not see that?'

'Easy. His focus was on what he thought was about to happen. He knew they were going to step out. Once the first one did it, he zoned in on that for the other three. You heard of the Gorilla Experiment?'

'No, but I suspect you're about to bore the arse off me.'

'I'll make it brief. I know you were up early and probably used up your allocation of brain power for the day.'

'Oh, you bitch. That's 'urtful.'

'A good few years back, an experiment was conducted on people's attention. Participants were instructed to see how many times a basketball team passed the ball backward and forward to each other. They were instructed to watch very closely and count each pass carefully. When it was over, about 60 percent of participants failed to notice a man wearing a gorilla suit walk behind the players, from left to right. Didn't see it at all. No idea he'd walked through. Fox has probably done the same.'

'Wait a minute. A bloke walks past in a monkey suit an' no one noticed 'im?'

'Some people did, and it was a gorilla, not a monkey. Explains why witnesses to major crimes, or any incident, are shit.'

'Yeah, sounds like they're all too intent on lookin' for this bleedin' monkey. And, yeah, I know. Not just major crimes either. People just don't look properly. I reckon that's why Stevie Wonder fell off the stage a few times.'

'What? He never fell off the stage. Not once.'

'Bloody miracle really.'

'Hmm. Okay, so, getting back to this, it seems to me that someone was directing them to kill themselves. We just need to find out why and who. What did our mysterious phone caller have on the victims that was strong enough to make them kill themselves and how did he know the victims?'

'Maybe he didn't know them? Maybe it's just another mad fucker with a sick game to play and he played it.'

'Maybe. We'll just have to find out, won't we?'

'So, who we startin' with?'

'Might as well start with the . . . what was he? A manager, did Fox say?'

'Yeah. He was the first to notice anything dodgy.'

'I'll go and tell Fox we're going to start talking to his team and you can make a few calls, John. We definitely need someone to fish that phone out of the drain.'

# CHAPTER 14

Fox showed them into a small room. All there was in the way of furniture was a table, six chairs and a water cooler. Seated on four of the chairs were that morning's CCTV operators: Chris Striker, Sean Lown, Sophie Lane and Barry (Baz) McFeine. All four looked up when Paterson and Clocks walked in.

'Good morning. I'm Detective Superintendent Paterson from the Met's Homicide Command Unit and this gentleman is Detective Inspector Clocks.' There were nods from the group.

'I understand you guys have been through a pretty rough morning. Saw some things that were . . . disturbing.' Again, the group nodded as one. 'I'm sorry that happened to you. Death is never nice, and to see that, well, it must have been devastating for you all. Are you being looked after?'

'Best they can, sir,' said Sophie. 'Never needed to put four of us up before.'

Paterson nodded. 'No, I'm sure. This is definitely an unusual case.'

'Weird, I'd say,' said Striker.

'You guy's got any idea why they did this?' Clocks poured a cup of water and handed it to Paterson.

'I haven't,' said Striker. 'Never seen anything like this before and I was in the military. Seen my share of shit.'

Clocks nodded as he poured himself a water.

'Not me,' said Sean. 'I've been doing this for . . . what, fifteen years now? I've seen people kill themselves on the monitors a few times but never four in one go. As the boss says, *weird*.'

'Who's the boss?' said Paterson.

Striker half raised his hand. 'That's me. I'm the supervisor. Part of my job is to evaluate any reports made by my team on things they witness.'

'Hm, hm. I see,' said Paterson. 'But, if I've got it right, you saw the first one, correct?'

'Yeah. A woman. She was acting . . . I dunno, *odd* is the best way I can describe it. I clocked her about five minutes or so before she . . . before I called it in to Mike Delta and then she . . . she stepped out into the road.' He shook his head as if trying to shut out the memory.

'I asked Mike Delta to scramble some troops to see what was up. Mike One showed up, but by then the others were reporting unusual behaviour. The one outside the mosque bothered me for obvious reasons and the thought struck me that this could be a coordinated terror attack. So, when Mike One showed up on Tower Bridge, I got them called off just in case the woman was gonna go bang.'

'Good call,' said Clocks. 'Makes sense, mate.'

Striker nodded. 'But it seems they weren't terrorists, so if I'd let Mike One do their job, she'd still be alive. My fault.' This time Striker rubbed his face with both hands as he let out a huge sigh.

'You made the right call,' said Paterson. 'It's easy to blame yourself after the event but that was knowledge you didn't have at the time. You did it right.'

Striker looked up at Paterson and gave him a nod. 'Thanks. Appreciate that.'

'All right, look . . . DI Clocks and I are going to go back to the nick and fire up an investigation. You guys are obviously prime witnesses, so at some point we'll do a full interview with you. I understand you've all done preliminary witness statements, yes?' Everybody nodded. 'Good. What are you all up to now?'

'Mr Fox say's we're to go home today and come back to work when we're ready,' said Baz. 'The job'll arrange for some emergency counselling if we want it.'

'That's good,' said Paterson. 'Go home and have a stiff drink. It'll do you good. Trust me, I know.'

'We've got yer details,' said Clocks. 'We'll be in touch soon.'

They said their goodbyes and made their way out into the main office.

'What d'you reckon? said Clocks.

'About what?'

'Them as witnesses. Think they're any good?'

Paterson shrugged. 'Not really, John. You know that. But at least what these guys saw was all recorded, so there's not much to dispute.'

'Timex?' A deep male voice stopped Clocks in his thoughts. Paterson detected a note of German in the accent.

'Riz? Fuck me! I ain't seen you for years. 'Ow yer been?'

'Ja, good. Good. You?'

'Yes, mate. All good this end. Oh, sorry. This is me guv'nor, Mr Paterson. Ray, this is Riz. We were at 'endon together back in the day.'

'Good to meet you,' said Paterson. The two men shook hands.

'You ever marry that blonde bird you were knocking about with? Whassername?'

'Norma.'

'That's it. Norma.'

'I did and we are divorced.' Riz shrugged. 'What can you do?'

'Women, mate. Can't live with 'em an' better off without 'em.' The two men laughed. 'Look,' said Clocks, 'I can't stop, mate, we're up to our eyeballs.'

'The jumpers?'

'The jumpers.'

'Understood,' said Riz. 'Look, maybe we'll catch up sometime. Over a beer maybe.'

'Sounds like a plan,' said Clocks. The two men said their goodbyes and Paterson and Clocks went over to inform Simon Fox that his team would be called for more formal interviews later.

'Did I detect a hint of German in his voice, John?' said Paterson as they left the room.

Clocks nodded. 'Yep. Nice lad. His real name's Otto but we always called him Riz.' He grinned to himself.

Paterson nodded. 'Of course you did. Riz Otto. Why wouldn't you?'

'His bird was a right sort. Her last name was Stitz.'

'Norma Stitz?' said Paterson.

'They definitely were. Wasn't a bra built that could 'old 'em.' He shook his head at the memory.

'Hmm,' said Paterson. 'Does everyone you know have unusual names? You seem to know a lot.'

'I know, right? Strange, innit? There was this other bloke in trainin' school. Name of Janus. First name was Hugh. Right arse'ole 'e was.'

Paterson's burst of laughter caused a few people to look up from their screens. He raised his hand as an apology. 'Let's just get to work, eh?'

'Sounds like a plan. Oh, there was another bloke we called Nuggets.'

'Nuggets? Go on, then. Why'd you call him Nuggets?'

'No bottle. Always chickened out of fights.'

'You're a dick,' said Paterson.

'And there was a bird called Anna. She was lovely.'

'What was her surname?'

'It was odd, mate. Falactic.'

'Anna Falactic?'

'Yep. I was shocked.'

Paterson sighed. 'Any more?'

'Yeah. A bloke I knew once 'ad a penis in the middle of 'is face.'

'Oh, yeah? And what was his name?'

'Fuck knows.'

'We've got work to do.' Paterson shook his head and rubbed tears out of his eyes as they walked out the door.

# CHAPTER 15

Paterson and Clocks strolled into the front entrance of Tower Bridge Police Station and made their way up the time-worn stone steps. The sound of Paterson's Guccis echoed around the cream-and-grey-painted stone walls.

'Ray?' said Clocks. 'Innit about time you got us an office on the ground floor? I mean, apart from you, none of us are spring chickens anymore, are we?' He paused for a second to catch his breath.

'Christ sake's, Clocksy. This is the only exercise you get. If it wasn't for coming to work every day, you'd get no cardio at all.'

Clocks sniffed. 'An' the problem is?'

'And the problem is, you'll get even more unfit and won't be able to breathe properly.'

'An' the problem is?'

'Don't be an arse. You know you need to be fitter.'

'Look. Way I see it is, I'm crackin' on toward me fifties now, right?'

'Go on.'

'So, I reckon I might make seventyish with a bit of luck an' a followin' wind, right?'

81

'Right. So?'

'So, after that, it's all down 'ill, innit? Non-stop 'ospital appointments, dodgy illnesses, old people's 'ome and sittin' in me own piss all day. No thank you very much. If I go out early, all I'm doin' is cuttin' out the crusty years where I'll end up lookin' at the wall an' thinkin' an' wonderin' who I am and if the feet I'm lookin' at are mine.'

'Just get up the stairs, will you? Always bloody moaning about something.'

Clocks started up the stairs again. 'I'm not moanin'. I'm pointin' out the inevitability of becomin' an octogenarian.'

Paterson stopped again. 'Was that from the app again?'

'What? No. I know some things, y'know.'

'It was the app, wasn't it?'

'Well, yeah it was, but I do know some things.'

'I know you do, just not *octogenarian*.'

'I know what *fuck-off-an'-do-one* means.'

'I'm sure you do. Nearly there, you old bastard.'

'Fuck off. I'm not even fifty. I told you that.'

'Yeah, you did, but you're huffing and puffing like you're already seventy. I think I might order you to run up and down these stairs ten times a day.'

Clocks nodded. 'Do what you like, son. I'll tell you to go an' do one ten times a day.'

At the top of the stairs, the two men turned left and headed toward the top-floor office they shared with the team of detectives Paterson called his 'troops'. Clocks called them his 'little helpers'.

All heads turned as they walked into the office. The first face Paterson saw was Jackie Steers, a forty-four-year-old, no-nonsense, old-school copper, followed by DS Michael 'Monkey' Harris and DC Ronnie 'Dusty' Doneghan. These three were the nucleus of the team and he trusted each and every one of them with his life. His heart sunk a bit when he remembered that he'd lost two of his team recently: DC Colin Yorkshire, murdered by the serial killer David Steers, and of course, Tommy Gunn. He felt the anger rise in him when he thought of what Sam Morne had ordered. There were a couple of new faces, drafted in to replace the two deceased members. He'd introduce himself to them later. Right now, he needed coffee.

'Morning, all,' he said to his troops.

'Morning, guv,' came the reply from Monkey and Dusty. The rest just nodded.

'Jackie, sweet'eart,' said Clocks. 'Any chance of a lovely ol' cuppa tea, please?'

Jackie sighed. 'Why do I always have to get the tea?'

'Bloody 'ell. Do we 'ave to keep doin' this every time I wanna cuppa tea? You know why I ask you.'

'Because I'm a woman.'

'Because you're a woman. Exactly.'

'That is so sexist, guv.'

'I know. I don't care. You know I don't care. Everyone knows I don't care. So, off yer pop, then. Nice cuppa builders, an' see if you can whip up a whatthefuckisthatachino for the big boss.'

'So sexist,' she mumbled.

'Could be worse, Treacle. I could've slapped yer arse on the way to the kitchen.'

'You could and I'd have smacked you right in the mouth,' she said.

Clocks held his hands up. 'Easy. I'm not like that, love. HR made it abundantly clear that arse slapping women was unacceptable these days.'

'What did they say about getting me to make the teas?'

'They said to tell you to let it brew a bit longer before puttin' the milk in.'

She smiled at him. 'You're an arsehole, guv'nor.'

'Oi! That's offensive.' He closed the door to the office he shared with Paterson.

Paterson was hanging up his jacket as Clocks clicked the door closed. 'Why d'you keep teasing her like that?'

'She loves it, Ray. She's old school, mate. Besides, she knows I'm only tunin' 'er up. So, what's up, Buttercup?'

'Excuse me?'

'Said, what we doin' now?'

Paterson grimaced. 'What we're doing now is we're going to brief the troops and find out what they've got.'

Clocks nodded. 'Better wait for Jackie to get back with the tea. You know what she's like if we start without 'er. Oh, she'll be a moody mare all day.'

'Just pack it in, John.'

Clocks grinned at him. 'Why? It's only a laugh.'

'I know, but we've got things to think about, a lot of things to think about. We've got a shit ton to do and we haven't even started yet.'

'Yeah, good point. Been an eventful day so far, though. Lots goin' on. Coppers in 'ospital, an offer to join an international bunch of nutters.' He looked at his watch. 'Bloody 'ell, Ray. You know what time it is?'

'Go on,' said Paterson.

'Time for me lunch. Where shall we go?'

'We'll have lunch here, mate. Too much to do.'

Clocks fumbled around in his jacket pocket and held up his forefinger to Paterson as he punched a single button on his mobile phone.

'Who you calling?' said Paterson.

'Jackie. If we're not goin' out, I'll ask 'er to nip to the canteen for a couple of sausage sandwiches.'

'Christ . . . you can't . . .'

'It's all right, Ray. The sausage ones are for me. I'll ask 'er to get some poncey sarnie with a coupla quail eggs in it an' a side salad an' the crusts cut off yer mung bean bread for you. Nice an' soft. Like you. I know you don't wanna damage yer fifty grand's worth of false teeth you've got.'

Paterson sighed. He'd given up. 'See if she can get avocado in it.'

Clocks sneered at him. 'A what? Hello! Jack? Be a love an' get me an' the guv a couple of sarnies from the canteen, will yer?'

Paterson could hear her raised voice. Clocks pulled his ear away from the phone and pulled a face at Paterson. He nodded a few times, then a few times more. 'So, look. I know you're not my bitch, Jack. I didn't say you were, but . . . No. She's gone. She's 'ung up. Got the 'ump.'

'So, no?'

'No.'

'Quelle surprise?'

'Is that Japanese?'

'What?'

'What you said. Japanese sayin', ain't it?'

Paterson rolled his eyes. 'Poke your head out of the door and tell everyone to be ready for a briefing in five. Can you do that without winding anybody up?'

Clocks shrugged. 'I'll give it a go. See what 'appens, eh?' He wandered over to the door and poked his head out. 'Oi-oi! Briefing in five! Make sure you bring yer notebooks an' crayons. Try an' stay inside the lines. Monkey, you ol' bugger, don't forget to bring yer ear trumpet. Dusty, go an 'elp Jackie with the drinks, an' you new kids there . . . the grown-ups will be 'avin' a meetin' soon. You can go outside an' play 'til we've finished.'

He closed the door and turned back to Paterson, who sat in his chair shaking his head.

'Turns out I couldn't do it, Ray. Thought I could. I couldn't.'

Five minutes later, Paterson and Clocks emerged from their office. Everybody started to gather up their notes and chairs and arranged them in a semi-circle in front of the large screen that hung on the wall. Clocks grinned as Jackie backed into the main office carrying a tray of drinks for everyone.

'Cheers, Jack,' said Clocks. 'You put sugar in mine?'

'Yes, guv. If spit is the new sugar. I've put in six.'

'Oooh, nice,' said Clocks. 'Always wanted to swap spit with you, babe.'

She shook her head and put the tray down on a table. 'You're filthy, you are.'

'I've 'ad me moments, Jack. An' I do requests if you've got anythin' special in mind.'

'Drink your tea before I pour it all over you.'

Clocks raised his eyebrows. 'Yeah? That'll cost you extra.'

Jackie smirked. 'If I'm going to pay for sex, I'll spend my money wisely. I'm not going to waste it on a two-pumps-and-a-squirt merchant like you.'

'What? Who told you that?' Clocks sounded genuinely hurt.

'Your Lyndsey.'

The office burst into laughter and hoots of derision.

'Can we get on, please?' said Paterson.

The room settled down as Paterson recapped their trip to the CCTV room and dished out a few statement-taking jobs to the newest members of the team. 'So . . . what have you all managed to find out?'

Dusty spoke. 'Okay. I've found out our victim's names. The lady on Tower Bridge is . . . *was* a Mrs Jeanette Colney. Thirty-six years old. Married, one son — Peter, seven years old. The chap on London Bridge was a Mr Oliver Hayes. Forty-six, married, three kids. Late starter apparently. They're all under seven. He got hit by the bus.'

'Ding, ding. Mind the bus,' said Clocks. Monkey spat his tea out and shook his head. Paterson just shook his head.

Dusty continued. 'Then we have a Susan Banks. Unmarried mother of two little girls. She was outside the mosque and she stepped in front of a fire engine.'

'Holy Hoses!' said Clocks. The room sniggered.

'Give it a rest, Clocksy,' said Paterson.

'Thank you, guv,' said Dusty. He cleared his throat. 'And last is a Matt Sullivan. Married, one son. Divorced though. Kid lives with mum. He got done by a car.'

'Okay,' said Paterson. 'Do we have any idea of why they did this?'

Dusty shook his head. 'Too early yet, guv.'

'Is there anything that links them, do we know?'

'Nope,' said Dusty. 'Same thing. Far too early at this stage of the game. Nothing is jumping out at us at the moment.'

'They would've done,' said Clocks. 'But they can't anymore. This is a one-go-at-it game.'

Paterson rolled his eyes. 'Okay. Two things are our priority. Why they did it and what's the link between them. Have the families been informed?'

Monkey jumped in. 'Not as yet. We wanted to see where we stood before we said anything to them.'

Paterson nodded. 'We're going to have to get it done and soon. No doubt our friends in the press are already on this.'

'Of course,' said Monkey. 'Some arseholes sent them footage from their phones — stuck it all over social media too. You know how it is.'

'Fuck!' said Paterson. 'Bloody social media. Nothing's sacred anymore.'

'The Sacred Heart Church down the road is,' said Clocks.

'What?' said Paterson.

'I said, "The Sacred Heart Church down the road is." The clue's in the name. Sacred. Heart.'

'Jesus! You're on fire today, aren't you? Is this what usually happens when you get an early morning call?'

Monkey pulled a face. 'Yeah, what was that all about, boss?'

Paterson looked across the room at him. 'Doesn't matter, Monkey. Nothing to worry about. I'll tell you all later. Let's just say, for now, that John and I were up early this morning through no fault of our own.'

Now Monkey had a puzzled expression on his face. He left it. 'You get anything from the CCTV people?'

'Nah,' said Clocks. 'The operators are all in shock. Not every day you get to see a woman get 'er head flattened by a lorry. Apparently, it "upset" them all. We spoke to 'em an' told 'em we'd be back in touch to get statements from 'em when their little sensitive tummies were feelin' better. That's now. As the guv said, we want statements. Detailed. We're gonna get the shift boss in for a chinwag, bloke by the name of . . .'

'Chris Striker,' Paterson offered.

'That's the fellah. Seems he was the one that spotted our first vic, whassername?' He snapped his fingers as he searched his brain for the answer.

'Jeannette Colney,' said Paterson.

'That's it!' he said with a final click. 'Jam Jar Jeannette. Lovely woman. Jam-coloured hair.'

'John! What the fuck is wrong with you?'

'Sorry, Ray. Sorry, folks,' said Clocks. 'That one fell a bit flat, didn't it? The joke. Not Jeannette. Although . . .'

Dusty and Monkey were struggling to stifle their laughter. Even Jackie was doing her best to hide it. The two new detectives looked both perplexed, amused and a little bit appalled at the same time.

'We'll meet back here at six tonight. New people, in my office, please. We'll have a quick chat now before you go out.' He pointed over to an older officer sitting at the back of his room. He hadn't joined the group for the briefing. Never did. Didn't need to. He could hear everything and he had work to do. Georgie Stokes was the new office manager. Hugely experienced at running squads, Paterson had poached him over to his team when his old office manager retired. The first thing Georgie did on taking up residence was to shift his desk so that it was perfectly positioned within the room. From this position, he heard everything that was said in the office and could see everything that went on, and it was near a window. Georgie was a big fan of the fresh air. Paterson knew that he would clash with Clocks come the wintertime, but that was a problem for later.

'That's Georgie if you haven't already met him. Office manager. Best in the business. Everything that happens on an operation comes from him and goes to him, okay? You feed everything to Georgie.' Clocks gave his friend a sideways look. They were the world's worst at feeding information into the system. 'Has he given you things to do yet?'

DC Alan Watts shook his head. He was early twenties, decent-looking, dark-haired and looked pretty fit. Paterson looked at the female officer, DC Harmony Lee. Like her colleague, she was early twenties, slim to the point of thin, hair short and red. She too shook her head.

'Okay. When we've finished talking, go see him. He'll tell you what your tasks are. Go and wait in my office. I'll be a couple of minutes. Thanks.' Paterson watched them go. 'What do you think, John?'

'About?'

'Those two.'

Clocks looked up at them as the man opened the door. 'Dunno. You got a feelin'?'

Paterson shook his head slightly. 'No, not really. Probably just paranoid these days.'

'Ooh. You don't want to catch that. Nasty.'

'Catch it? You can't catch paranoia.'

'You say that, but I read an article once that said if there's enough people with paranoia in one place at one time and a normal person hangs about with them, that person will get infected with paranoia.'

'Bullshit!'

'I'm tellin' yer. It's true. Unless they were makin' it up. You think they made it up, Ray? They wouldn't make it up, would they? Bastards. See? I've bloody got it from just readin' about it.'

Paterson rubbed his face with both hands before letting out a sigh. 'You're bloody hard work sometimes, you know that?'

'Why? It's not my fault I've got a disease now, is it? Where's your care for me?'

'Haven't got any.'

'Ooh, that hurts.'

'I don't want them knowing too much about us or the rest of the team. Talk to everyone and tell them to be on their guard, just in case. You never know.'

Clocks tapped the side of his nose then pointed at Paterson. 'Right you are, boss.'

'Walls have ears, Clocksy.'

'They do. And ice cream.'

'What?'

'Walls have ice cream. Well known for it.'

'For f . . . leave it. Are you coming in with me?'

'Want me to?'

'Only if you're going to be sensible.'

'I'll 'ang on 'ere, then.'

Paterson nodded and walked off toward his office, quite pleased in some ways. He really wasn't in the mood to have to deal with any more of Clocks's silly jokes at the moment.

He stepped inside to find the two officers standing. He waved them down. 'Sit, sit. Pull your chairs around. We won't be long.'

The two officers did as they were told and settled into their chairs.

'Okay.' Paterson pointed to the woman. 'Tell me about yourself.'

'My name's Harmony Lee. I'm twenty-five, single, detective constable. Six years' service. I joined as a direct entry to the CID from civvy life. Served on the burglary squad, rape squad and, before here, fraud squad over at Leman Street. I have a 98 percent conviction rate and I don't put up with any crap from sexist men. Thought I'd put that out there.'

Paterson grinned. 'Well, that's good to know. Good start. Who interviewed you for this job with us?'

'Commander Reed. He thought I'd be a good fit for the team.'

'You think you will?'

'I'd like to think so.'

'And you?' Paterson turned toward the man.

'DC Alan Watts. Seven years in the job. Mostly CID but I did a stint up at the Palace looking after the Royals. I worked Central Drugs and anti-terrorism. Specialising in intelligence and operation planning.'

'You broke any cells?'

'Four. All battle ready.'

'You firearms trained?'

'Yes, sir.'

'Shot anybody?'

'Yes, sir.'

'Dead?'

'No. Don't particularly want to either.'

Paterson nodded. 'Why are you here?'

'To learn and, without being sycophantic, you and DI Clocks are widely regarded on the ground. To be part of your team would be a huge career boost.'

'You're ambitious?'

'Sir. I want to move up the ladder, of course, but I want to learn.'

'Okay. Well, I don't know what you've heard about us, but we run a tight ship here. Everyone out there has proven themselves to be brave, smart and loyal. I want all three of those qualities from you. I need to know that I can trust you when the chips are down and when the shit hits the fan. And in this department, shit flies faster and further than a Saturn Five space rocket. You will be monitored closely until such time as I'm satisfied that you're a good fit. If you're not, you're out. Clear?'

Both nodded.

'Good. Harmony, what do you know of DI Clocks?'

She shrugged. 'I hear things.'

'And what is it you hear?'

'That he can be a wild card and is somewhat misogynistic and disrespectful to women. That sort of thing. I have to tell you, sir, I'm not going to put up with being treated as an object. I'm not here to be sexualised and treated like a schoolgirl.'

'Hmm, hmm. Well, thank you for laying that out there, but to be clear, DI Clocks is indeed a wild card. First thing I need to clear up is that he is not a misogynist. He doesn't hate women and he isn't prejudiced against them. Far from it. If you're on the team, he'd take a bullet for you without batting an eyelid. He likes to wind people up. It's his way of testing them. He figures if you can't take a bit of winding up, there's a good chance you'll lose it out on the street if you're provoked. Plus, he's a joker by nature, but don't ever make the mistake of thinking that makes him a fool. That man can sniff out a criminal like no one else I've ever known. Nobody gets one over on him. Nobody. Just don't make a mistake in your judgement of him. Understood?'

She nodded.

'Oh, and he'll only tease you if he likes you, so . . .'

'Okay. Understood, sir. Thank you for the heads-up.'

'All right, then.' Paterson stood up. 'Go and see Georgie and I'll see you back here later. Be safe.' Paterson followed them out of his office and back into the main room.

'So,' said Clocks, 'what they like, the pair of 'em?'

Paterson shook his head slightly. 'Well, you're not gonna be a fan of Harmony.'

'Why? What's wrong with 'er?'

'Apart from being a feminist?'

'Oh, she ain't, is she?'

'Oh, she is, and she's not going to be impressed with your old bollocks.'

'Okay, then. Thanks for the heads-up. I better not show 'er me ol' bollocks then, 'ad I?'

Paterson chortled. 'You know what I mean. She's going to want a bit of respect from you.'

'An' she'll get it once she's got the kettle on.'

'Oh, this isn't going to go well at all, is it?'

'Depends what sorta tea she makes. If it's shit, no. Shall I go an' tell 'er 'ow I like it?'

Paterson put his arm on Clocks's shoulder. 'Just hang fire a while.'

Clocks tapped the side of his nose. 'Good idea. Let Jackie square 'er up first. Put 'er right.'

'Yep. That's the spirit. Let the girls sort it out among themselves.' Paterson grinned at Clocks then picked up his desk phone.

# CHAPTER 16

Under an hour later, Paterson and Clocks found themselves back at the CCTV complex. Sat opposite them was Chris Striker, the on-duty supervisor. He looked annoyed that he had been singled out for an interview and wasn't shy about saying so. 'So, why me? I've told you what I know, what I saw. I just want to go home and rest.'

'Perks of being a supervisor,' said Paterson. 'We get all the best jobs.'

Striker scowled at him. 'I've had a shit day, Mr Paterson. I'm upset. Can't this wait a day? I'll be all right tomorrow.'

Clocks shook his head. 'Mate, we're all upset about somethin'. I just found out the new bird in the office is a bloody feminist. You know what that means?'

Striker looked up at him. 'You've gotta make your own tea?'

Clocks splayed his arms wide. 'Thank you! There you go, Ray. This fellah gets it.'

'We've got a couple of them in the office. They're really lovely people until you put them on the tea duty roster, then they get all arsey. I've told them it's not disempowering them, it's a roster. Everyone takes a turn. Even the Indian guy. He doesn't moan about it.'

'Steady there,' said Paterson. 'No need for racism, is there?'

'I'm not being racist! I'm just saying . . .'

'Here, guv. I knew a bloke once. His name, an' I'm not shittin' yer, was Raymond Cyst. Ray Cyst. Truthfully. Couldn't make it up.'

Striker and Paterson broke into a laugh and kept it up until Striker started to cough.

'You're a sod, Clocksy.' Paterson tried to stifle his laughter and recover his professionalism.

'I know. I laughed when me mate told me 'is name. Wanna know who that was?'

Paterson shook his head as he wiped away moisture from his eyes. 'No. No, I don't.' He kept snort-laughing. Striker was shaking his head.

'Warren Peace.' Paterson and Striker lost it. Clocks stood there chuckling and nodding as if really proud that he'd ruined his audience of two.

In between trying to catch his breath, Paterson said, 'Get out! Just . . . get . . . out! Go get me . . .' He laughed again, which started off Striker, who had just begun to get himself under control. 'Go . . . and get us . . . a tea . . . please.'

'Yeah, right,' said Clocks. 'Like I'm your skivvy.' He grinned and opened the office door to see a gaggle of bemused heads looking at him. The office walls were thin and the sound of laughter was the last thing they had expected to hear, given the events of the day.

'All right?' said Clocks. 'Anyone know where I can get a few cups o' tea?'

'Canteen's upstairs,' said a surly looking woman of about fifty.

'No point askin' you to get 'em for us, is there?'

She glared at him.

'Fair enough. Do they do Jammie Dodgers there, d'you know?'

Everybody put their heads down and went back to work. Clocks shook his head and ambled off to the canteen. Ten minutes later, he was back with three polystyrene cups of a pale brown liquid that the man behind the counter swore was tea. Clocks remained unconvinced. Paterson and Striker were fully settled now, laughter gone.

'Mr Striker — Chris . . .' said Paterson. 'This is not a formal interview. We popped back because we wanted to see if you had remembered anything that may help us in figuring this out. You've been doing this a while and have no doubt seen your share of suicides. I think we touched on that earlier.'

Striker nodded as he sipped at his tea. He grimaced as he tasted the hot liquid. 'Jesus. Has he ever used a tea bag before? Why can't he leave it in a bit longer?'

'S'what my wife says,' said Clocks, and Striker snorted.

Paterson turned to Clocks. 'Pack. It. Up. Enough!'

'Sorry,' said Clocks. 'I'll sit 'ere an' drink this hot . . . I wanna say diarrhoea, but I better not.'

Paterson turned to Striker. 'I'm sorry about this. Trouble is, once he gets a laugh, he kicks the arse out of it. Can't stop. Would you prefer it if he left? I'm happy to sling him out.'

Clocks frowned. 'Fuckin' charmin', that is. Right, I know when I'm not wanted. I'll be outside with the civvies. They appreciate me.' With that, Clocks opened the door and stepped out.

Paterson shook his head as Clocks closed the door. 'Sorry about that. Right, let's move on.'

'Why can't we do this tomorrow, sir?' said Striker.

'Best for me to take a fuller note while the events are still fresh in your memory.'

Striker nodded. 'I can see that, but a good night's kip might bring a bit of clarity.' He shrugged. 'You never know.'

'Yeah, maybe. But I'm here, you're here . . .'

'Only because you called ahead and told Mr Fox to hold me back a while.'

'Well, thank you for waiting. Very public spirited of you, I'm sure. Let's go back to what you saw on your screen.'

'You've seen it.'

Paterson took in a sharp breath through his nose. He remained calm. 'I know I've seen it, but I've also seen something on it that you failed to mention.'

Striker looked puzzled. 'Like what?'

'Like, you tell me.'

'Like, I can't tell you if I don't know what you're talking about.'

Paterson felt himself bristle at this man. They'd gone from sharing a laugh to being slightly antagonistic with each other and Paterson didn't know why. He didn't like him.

'You failed to mention that the woman dropped her phone into the Thames just before she stepped out.'

Striker shrugged. 'That'll be because I didn't see her drop her phone.'

'You didn't?'

'I didn't.'

'How come?'

'I don't know. I just didn't.'

'But you're a professional witness, aren't you? You watch, don't you? That's the bulk of your job, isn't it? To watch. You pick up things, you said. I understand that. We all develop a sixth sense of one kind or another, so I'm struggling to see how you missed her drop the phone.'

Striker shrugged again. 'What can I tell you? I didn't see it. I was watching her closely, that's true, but I didn't see her dump her phone.'

'Did you see her walk over toward the river?'

'Yeah. She turned away, looked down, I think, then turned away, walked back to the road and stepped in front of the lorry. Didn't see a phone. Sorry.'

Paterson nodded. 'Clocks!' he called.

Clocks opened the door. 'We all right?'

'Yeah, I think so,' said Paterson.

'Your boss is giving me a hard time because I didn't see the woman dump her phone in the river,' said Striker.

'Yeah?' Clocks stepped inside and closed the door. 'I was wonderin' that an' all. 'Ow come you didn't?'

Striker leaned back in his chair and put his cup down. 'Really? You two came here to give me a hard time on this phone thing? Look, I'm sure you boys have missed stuff in your time. No one's perfect, are they?'

Clocks pointed to Paterson. 'He is. Drives me mental 'ow perfect 'e is.'

'Well, good for you,' Striker said, looking at Paterson. 'Unfortunately, not all of us are. So, let me get this straight . . . because I didn't see her drop the phone, I'm in the shit and I'm the one being put through the mill? Christ . . . You two are pretty desperate, aren't you?'

'Oi! 'Old up, mate,' said Clocks. 'First up, you're not in the shit. Second, you ain't bein' put through the mill. An' third, we ain't desperate, so knock the sudden cockiness off an' play nicely. I know you're shocked an' all that ol' fanny but we've got a job to do an' I don't need any attitude. I don't give out the attitude when I'm talkin' to people, do I, Ray?' Paterson went to answer but Clocks cut him off. 'So don't you start swingin' yer knob about. Capisce?'

Striker nodded. 'Okay. I'm sorry. I'm tired. I'm stressed. But I didn't see her drop the phone. Truly.'

'All right,' said Paterson. 'You can go home. I'm sorry to have kept you. I'll get an officer to call you tomorrow and set up an appointment for a more formal interview.'

Striker stood up and headed to the door. Clocks put his hand on Striker's chest. 'All four of 'em dumped their phones. Did you know that?'

Striker looked down at Clocks's hand on his chest, then looked him in the eye. 'No. How could I? We were kept separate until you both arrived this morning and the others have all gone home to their beds.'

Clocks removed his hand. 'Good man. Just checkin'. Go on, then. Trot off 'ome. See you later.'

Striker left Paterson and Clocks alone in the room. 'What d'you make of 'im, Ray?'

Paterson rubbed his face. 'Well, I don't like him, but that's a personality thing. He got a bit uppity when you were out.'

'Yeah? Didn't 'ave 'im down for that.'

'No. Me neither. Still, as he said, tired and stressed. I don't think he's hiding anything, John. Let's go and get some bloody food.'

Clocks punched the air. 'Yes! About time. I saw a nice Wetherspoons on the way 'ere. We can drop in there for a face-down.'

Paterson closed his eyes, lifted his chin to the ceiling, scrunched up his face and then looked at Clocks. 'They don't do smoked salmon, do they?'

'Do they fuck! They don't even do smoked sausages.'

# CHAPTER 17

Paterson pushed his food around with a fork as Clocks dug into a full English complete with tea and two toast. This was his favourite. All-day breakfast with all the trimmings. Apart from black pudding. He could never understand how eating blood was considered a meal. This from a man who ate jellied eels.

'Whassamatter with you?' he said to Paterson.

'Nothing. Not particularly hungry.'

'Oh, leave off. You must be starvin' like Marvin. When was the last time you ate anything?'

Paterson shrugged. It must have been a good fourteen hours ago, but it wasn't as if that was a problem to him. He regularly practised intermittent fasting. He was hoping for something light from the menu, but nothing appealed to him. He'd ordered a plate of corned beef hash with a side of hash browns, something he would never normally touch. When it was brought to him, he knew he wasn't going to break that particular tradition. There was nothing wrong with the food, it just didn't look like the picture on the menu. Nothing like it. And what was set before him made him feel a bit queasy.

'Don't know, John. Some time ago.'

'So, what's wrong with it?'

'Just don't want it.'

Clocks snorted. 'You're too bleedin' picky, you. Spoiled, that's what it is.'

'Is it?'

'You know it, mate. That's perfectly good food. Get it down yer.'

Paterson stuck his fork into a hash brown, put it into his mouth and chewed.

'S'all right, innit?' said Clocks, as he dropped a bit of fried egg off of his fork.

'If you like your food dripping with fat, then yes. It's lovely.'

'As it 'appens, I do. Can't beat it.'

'No wonder you're piling it on, John.'

Clocks stopped eating and put his knife and fork down. 'What? *Pilin' it on?* That's a bit rude, innit?'

'Truth's truth, mate.'

'I'm not pilin' it on. I'm the same weight I was when I was eighteen.' He picked his utensils back up and cut himself a piece of sausage.

'So, you were a bit tubby when you were a kid, then?'

'Tubby? You can fuck right off, matey. I was a God among men. I was a symbol of manhood, me.'

'So what happened?'

'Shut up an' eat yer grub, you fussy little Mary-Anne.'

Paterson chuckled. 'I'm not fussy. I just like to know what it is I'm eating and this—' he waved the hash brown in Clocks's face — 'is nothing but heavily processed "grub" that isn't going into my body. That's all I'm saying. It's not good for you.'

'Nothing is these days, Mary, so pull up yer big girl's drawers an' eat it. You'll be whinin' later when you're 'ungry.'

Clocks's phone rang. He looked at the screen: *Old Man Clocks.* He pressed a button, rose out of his seat and said to Paterson, 'Gimme a minute. Me dad.'

Paterson tilted his head. Something was wrong. He guessed what had happened straight away and followed Clocks outside.

Clocks had his back to him and was unusually quiet. Paterson stopped and gave him some space.

'All right, mate?' he said, when Clocks had hung up. His friend's face was pinched and there was the beginning of tears forming in his eyes.

'Me mum's just died.'

'Ah, shit,' said Paterson. 'Mate, I'm so sorry.' He leaned in and put his arms around him. For the first time ever, Clocks didn't push him away or call him a 'bloody ol' tart'. He knew Clocks was feeling this. Clocks put his arms around Paterson and let out a quiet sob.

'It's all right, mate. Come on. Whatever you need, understand? Whatever you need. Usual rules apply.' *Usual rules apply* was understood by all police officers and let them know that their colleagues would do whatever was necessary to help them. Clocks nodded.

'Oi! Fuckin' bender boys!' A loud male voice shouted. 'Pack that shit up or I'll kick the fuck out of yer!' Paterson felt Clocks's body stiffen and then he was gone. Clocks flew at the man, overweight, tattooed and in his fifties, standing about fifteen feet away. The man's eyes widened as Clocks descended on him. He held his hands up, face registering panic.

'What'd you say, fat boy?'

The man stuttered as Clocks kept coming. 'No . . . No, nothing, mate, nothing. Sorry!' Clocks smacked him hard on the side of the jaw and watched as the man fell like a tree that had been cut down by an angry lumberjack.

'Mouthy fat bastard,' said Clocks to the fallen man. 'Teach you, won't it, you trappy piece of shit.'

Paterson wrapped his arms around Clocks in a bear hug and swung him away from the man. A small crowd had suddenly formed and was watching intently.

'Y'all lookin' at? Mind yer own business or you'll get a fuckin' clump too.'

He let Clocks go, knowing that his rant at the crowd would keep him away from the man he'd hit. Paterson knelt down to the man and shook him. 'Come on, fellah. Up you get, c'mon.' He slapped his face a few times until the man began to stir. He looked at Paterson with glazed eyes. 'There you go,' he said. 'You're all right.'

The man shook his head as Paterson hauled him into a seated position. 'What . . . happened?' he said, his speech slurred.

'You made a mistake, mate, that's all.'

'A . . . mistake . . . ?'

Paterson could feel Clocks hovering around somewhere behind him. He was worried he'd come for the man again.

'Yeah. My friend just lost his mum. You shot your mouth off at the wrong time.'

'I'm . . . sorry. I didn't . . . didn't know.' The man was recovering now, speech not so slurred, eyes not so glazed.

'How could you?' said Paterson. 'Not exactly public knowledge.'

The man held out one arm to Paterson, looking for a hand to help him stand.

'I haven't lost my mum, but his loss is my loss, you homophobic bucket of scum.' Paterson pushed the hand away and smacked the man into unconsciousness. He stood up, shook his suit straight and turned to Clocks.

'Let's go,' he said. 'Our work here is done.'

# CHAPTER 18

Paterson stood outside in the hallway of King's College Hospital in Denmark Hill. He didn't want to intrude. He could see into the room through the narrow gap in the door jamb. Though Clocks's father — Harry, a man he'd met for the first time just a short while ago — was a career criminal, it was clear that he loved his policeman son and had had to fight hard to keep his credibility among his criminal friends. For his part, Clocks turned a blind eye to his father's activities, working on the basis that if he didn't know what was going on, he didn't have to get involved. And it had worked. Both men had kept their lives separate and one never bothered the other or brought grief to each other's doorstep. There was something about these old-school villains that Paterson found fascinating: they had a certain charm that drew him to them. Perhaps it was the couldn't-give-a-toss attitude most of them displayed. It seemed to gel with his own outlook.

He was also in Clocks Senior's debt. After Paterson murdered the serial killer David Steers, it was Clocks's dad who helped them dispose both of the body and Paterson's DNA-spattered Bentley. And now, here he was, a big man broken. Paterson could see him choking back his tears and bunching his fists at the anger and injustice he felt at losing the only woman he'd ever truly loved. Even though he couldn't see him, he knew Clocks would be struggling. Clocks had a close bond with his family, even though he didn't see them often. But he was always there for them if they needed him and they knew that.

Paterson glanced at his watch. More relatives would be coming soon, and from what he understood, it was a fair-sized family. He turned away and watched the doctors and nurses go about their business, flitting from bed to bed, trolley to trolley. For them, nothing had happened. Nothing had changed. Their world remained the same and always would, until one day it wouldn't. Paterson sighed deeply.

'Ray.' He spun at the sound of Clocks's voice. 'D'you wanna come in?'

He waved his hand. 'I don't want to intrude, John. It's a family time, mate.'

Clocks's dad appeared behind his son. 'You are bleedin' family, mate. If you wanna come in, come in.'

Paterson nodded. 'Of course. I'd like to say goodbye, pay my respects.' He used to joke that Clocks had been raised by wolves, but having met Clocks's mum once and then his dad on a separate occasion, he knew that his friend's upbringing, although rough and ready, had been full of love and loyalty. Unlike his own.

He stepped inside. It took a second or two for his eyes to adjust from the harsh lighting of the corridors to the soft light of the room. June Clocks lay face up on her bed. It jolted him for a second. This was not the woman he knew. Nothing like her. She was always so lively, funny, like her son. This woman was withered, bald and sad to look at.

'I'm so sorry,' he said to both men, but at the same time aimed it at her. He took her hand, felt its coldness, and a wave of sadness came over him. Behind him, Clocks was trying desperately to stifle his sobs. Harry Clocks walked out. Losing his wife and seeing his son lose it was too much for him. Paterson leaned over and kissed Mrs Clocks's head softly before gently laying her hand down back on the bed. He looked at his friend. 'Have you got in touch with Lyndsey?' he said, softly.

Clocks nodded. 'She'll be here in a few hours.'

'Good,' said Paterson. 'You need her now.'

'I need you both.'

'I know, mate. We'll be here for you. Day and night. You know that.'

Clocks sniffed. 'Yeah, I know. Thanks.'

Paterson put his hand on Clocks's back. 'Can I get you a cup of tea or anything?'

Clocks nodded. 'Yeah. Wouldn't mind, mate.'

Paterson gave him a sympathetic smile. 'I'll sort it.'

'Ray.'

'What?'

'What the fuck am I gonna do now, fer Chrissakes?'

# CHAPTER 19

Paterson stepped out into the fresh air, leaving behind the stuffiness of Kings College Hospital. He had never liked hospitals. Something about them set him on edge. It may have had something to do with the fact that, in the last few years, he had spent more than his fair share of time in them. He'd been shot, beaten and almost had his face peeled off by a particularly savage killer. So, hospitals were not his thing. He felt bad about leaving Clocks at this time, but he and his dad needed this time together. He checked his phone. One missed call. Clocks's wife, Lyndsey. She and Clocks had been wed for under a year when she quit the Met and went to join forces with Walter Young, an ex-Commissioner of Police and good friend to Paterson and Clocks.

Young wasn't one to sit on his arse at the best of times and retirement was never going to be a life of pruning roses and playing bowls. He'd set up an elite unit that hired itself out to solve certain 'problems' for certain 'organisations'. Lyndsey Clocks had been an inspector in SCO19, the firearms department of the Metropolitan Police, and was famed for her raw courage, no-nonsense attitude and the ability to shoot the nuts off a housefly at a thousand yards.

From an outsider's perspective, it seemed that the Clockses' marriage was over before it had had a chance to begin, but somehow, they were making a go of it. This would be the acid test. Clocks needed her now, and if she wasn't there for him, that would be the death knell. He knew Clocks wouldn't understand at the best of times let alone now in the midst of grief.

She hadn't left a message. Paterson didn't know if that was a good or bad thing. He chose not to dwell on it and jumped into his car. So much to do. First things first. He drove out of the hospital car park and then for a half-mile before stopping and pulling over in a quiet side street. He was worried. Really worried. Both he and Clocks had been battling their personal demons for a long time now and knew that they were failing. When they first met, Clocks's way of dealing with the pressure was to drink. His was drugs. Cocaine. Both men had kept it under control though. Neither had allowed themselves to fall back down their respective holes, but Paterson knew that it wouldn't take too much more to push them over the edge.

What bothered him the most, what he was truly scared of, was their mental states. He didn't know if it was being teamed with Clocks or whether he would have slipped anyway, but his latest session with the Met's psychiatrist featured the word *sociopath*. The word *borderline* had now been dropped. Nobody wanted to see that on their record and at first he was furious. But the more he thought about it, the more he realised it was true. No wonder UMBRA wanted them.

His wealthy upbringing had sent him to the best schools and he'd learned how to behave well in polite society. He had manners, charm, personality and looks, and until his wife was murdered, he'd had an easy, natural way about him. But now, five years down the line with some of the most sickening crimes a man had ever witnessed, he plainly felt his sanity slipping away from him.

The violence he'd witnessed, the violence he'd endured, was converting into a violent output — an *extremely* violent output. Over the years, his involvement with death grew from sanctioning the killing of criminals to the brutal murder of David Steers, a psychopathic killer of children and policemen, without the slightest hesitation. After callously breaking Steers's leg to prevent him from running, he'd held him down in water until the man drowned. To this day he felt not a shred of remorse nor guilt. This lack of feeling was now becoming a pattern. He knew it and he knew that the Ray Paterson of five years ago would have been appalled. But this Ray Paterson couldn't care less. All he knew was he wanted justice for the victims of this world and he was going to ensure they received it.

A clear image of Clocks appeared in his mind. Clocks was a man he had abhorred when they first met. The two of them were chalk and cheese personified. Everything about them was different, from the way they spoke to the way they behaved. He could never have imagined that Clocks would become the only person in this world he trusted and cared deeply about. He would die for Clocks in an instant and he believed Clocks would do the same for him.

And over the years, he'd watched his friend crumble too. Clocks had always been happy-go-lucky and a bit of a wide boy, but Paterson knew that was more of a front than anything else. Clocks had always been handy, lashing out at anyone who ticked him off, and that was one of the things he had most hated about him, but now his violence had darkened. He too was only interested in rough justice, and woe betide anyone — *anyone* — who stood in his way. He was the bravest man Paterson had ever known, but over the years that bravery had turned into a bravado of epic proportions. Paterson believed that Clocks truly had a death wish, and now that his mum was gone and his marriage was going south, he would have to keep a very close eye on him. He chuckled to himself. A sociopath worrying about another sociopath. What the hell was this world coming to?

His phone pinged — a text from Clocks. *Ray. I'm gonna be here a bit longer. Dad sorting it all out. Sis has turned up. I'll be coming into work later. Chat soon.*

Paterson shook his head then tapped the keys. *Stay as long as you need. Don't come to work. I've put you on compassionate leave.*

He looked out of the window. It was starting to spot with rain. His phone chimed again. *Fuck right off.* X

He smiled. Trying to tell Clocks what to do, even if — *especially* if — it was in his own best interests, was like trying to build a house of paper in the middle of a hurricane. Never gonna happen.

# CHAPTER 20

Chris Striker slugged back his glass of whisky and screwed his face up as the golden liquid burned the back of his throat. 'Happy?'

Forrest, sitting comfortably in an armchair, had been waiting for Striker to come home for the best part of an hour. He knew Striker's routine to a tee: leave the office, walk three hundred yards, catch a number 37 bus, a ten-to-twelve-minute bus ride, get off, stop at a local mini supermarket run by two Albanian brothers, pick up a pint of milk and a ready meal, take a ten-minute walk home, in through the communal door and a forty-five-second walk up the stairs to his flat.

Jack Forrest knew all of this before he'd approached Striker a fortnight ago. He knew everything he needed to know about him. An ex-squaddie. Nothing special. One tour of Iraq. No medals. Nothing about him was remarkable apart from two things: he was extremely patriotic and yet had run away in the face of enemy fire. That cowardice would be his undoing a second time. Forrest had applied pressure and Striker had responded.

'You did well.'

'I'm sure.'

'Do you have the laptop?'

Striker nodded. He stood up and walked over to a small cabinet. He pulled out the laptop and handed it to Forrest.

Forrest placed his drink casually on the small coffee table that sat in the middle of the living room and banged his hands loudly on the chair as he stood up. The sound startled an already jumpy Striker.

'I have to go.'

'Already? Why did you come? I wanted to talk.'

'To the bathroom. We can talk, of course we can. But I need to take a leak first. Where's your bathroom?'

'Sorry.' Striker looked sheepish. 'Down the hall, second on the right.'

'I'll have another of those, if I may?'

Striker nodded.

'Won't be a minute.'

* * *

Striker took a deep breath, fought off the memories of the day and poured out another drink. One for him and another for his guest. His intention was to take it easy with this drink.

'The police have already spoken to me!' he shouted to Forrest. 'Not going to be the end of it, though. The two coppers I spoke to are well known. Right pair of bastards they are, and they're not fools. Got themselves a reputation for being the best in the business.'

There was silence.

'You hear me?' Striker called.

'What?' Forrest called back. 'Sorry. Something's wrong with the toilet.'

Striker sighed. It wasn't unknown for the plumbing to go on the fritz every once in a while. He didn't fancy having to fuck around with it tonight. 'What's the matter with it?'

'Can't flush it.'

'Fuck!' Striker spat out.

'Can you take a look at it for me? I can't get it to work.'

'Just try again in a minute. It'll work.'

'No, it won't. Something's blocking it.'

'I thought you said you wanted to pee,' said Striker. 'I hope you haven't blocked it.'

'Hah! No, not me, but something is.'

Striker put his glass down and resigned himself to having to figure out how to unblock the toilet. He walked down the hall and stood in the doorway, puzzled. His bathroom was covered in plastic sheeting from top to bottom and Forrest wasn't there. 'Fuck!' was the last thing he said.

\* \* \*

Two bullets from Forrest's supressed Ruger punched into the back of Striker's head, spraying blood and bone around the bathroom.

Forrest stepped out from the room across the hall and fixed his gaze on his latest task. Drawing on extensive experience, he got to work swiftly, ensuring Striker's remains were packaged securely. In just fifteen minutes, he had the body wrapped in plastic and sealed with heavy-duty duct tape to prevent any blood or bone fragments from escaping. With the burden slung over his shoulder, Forrest left the flat and moved through the darkness toward his SUV.

Before arriving at Striker's flat, he had meticulously disabled three nearby street lamps to cloak his actions in secrecy. He scanned the area, confident that no one had seen him load Striker's body into the boot and not overly concerned if they did. His thorough research had already assured him that this neighbourhood wasn't one to call the police.

The Range Rover chirped and flashed before Forrest let himself back into the building. Inside Striker's kitchen, he picked up his glass of whisky, drained it and wiped it clean with a tea towel he'd already laid out. On the coffee table, he took out a photograph from a brown envelope: a head-and-shoulders portrait of Striker with a big red X through it and a small note, which he pinned to the back of the door. Turning, he walked over to the TV and kicked it over, the prelude to a two-minute rampage of destruction that left the flat looking like there'd been a fight. He picked up the laptop, stepped into the street and closed the front door behind him.

## CHAPTER 21

By the time he returned to the office, the rest of the team were waiting for him. Two new faces nodded as he walked in. 'Okay, gang. Can you all give me a few minutes? Got a few things to do, then I'll fill you in with what's happening.' Monkey Harris frowned. It wasn't like Paterson to be here without Clocks following behind.

'Hi, there,' said Paterson to the two new faces. 'DCI Carter and DS Winslet, yes?'

Both officers stood and shook Paterson's hand in turn. 'Thank you so much for agreeing to this. I could really use the help. Sorry it's such short notice but it's been a bitch of a day. Sorry!' he said, turning his face to DS Winslet. Grace Winslet was a striking woman and right now she was looking at him in a way that made his stomach flutter. That hadn't happened in a dog's age. He ignored it. Business had to be taken care of. Grace Winslet gave him a smile. She cocked her head to one side. 'No problems, sir. It's a pleasure to be here.'

Harry Carter looked at her as if he'd heard that tone of voice before.

'Give me a few minutes and I'll be with you,' Paterson said and disappeared into his office. He shut the door behind him and fell back against it. He gave a deep sigh as his mind raced. He'd had some days before but this one was taking the biscuit. And to top it all, he'd actually felt something stir in him that he hadn't felt since his wife was murdered five years ago. He pushed Grace Winslet out of his mind and walked over to the small bathroom he had in his office. It had a single-space shower, a sink, a mirror and a toilet. That was it. He looked at himself in the mirror. He looked tired. He splashed his face with a few handfuls of cold water, run his fingers through his hair, sniffed his pits and walked back out. In the middle drawer of his desk, he kept a bottle of Roja and gave himself a few quick sprays before walking back out into the office.

'Okay, folks. Briefing time. Gather round, please.' The office shuffled itself about until everybody was within earshot. 'Thank you.'

'Where's Clocksy, guv?' said Monkey.

'Just getting to that. Clocksy won't be with us for a while. His mum died a little while ago and he's with his family at Kings. Obviously, he's in no fit state to work and has a lot to sort out. To support us, I've been fortunate enough to get some help from the main CID. DI Harry Carter and DS Grace Winslet will be working with us for the duration of this case. Both are well-respected detectives and, Harry, I believe you've run more than a couple of murder investigations. Yes?'

Carter twisted his body around to look at everyone. 'That's right. I've run twenty-six in my time. All but one have been successful, thank God.'

'Didn't you deal with the case of that old pensioner in the care home?' said Jackie Hartnett. 'Jack Knife Bill? The old serial killer?'

'Yes. Both of us worked on that one.'

'Respect,' said Dusty. 'One helluva nick that one was.'

'We got lucky,' said Winslet. 'One of the care home workers, Susan Johnson, she figured it out.'

'That the one that got killed? Shot by SCO19?'

'Yeah,' she said. 'Tragic. Jack had just killed his last. She stood up for some reason, probably shock. Nineteen opened fire and she copped two in the back.'

'Awful,' said Paterson. 'Well, that one didn't have the happiest of endings, but I'm really glad to have you aboard. Do you know much about this case?'

Carter shook his head. 'Only what's been in the news. Four suicides involving traffic.'

'That's it,' said Paterson. 'Obviously, something is very off for four people to do themselves in at the same time, so until we know otherwise, we're running it as a suspected murder case — although, at the moment, we have nothing.' Paterson looked around the room. 'Unless any of you guys are going to tell me different?'

The shaking of heads was disappointing, but Paterson knew the investigation was in the very early stages. There was much more to do. He glanced at Winslet, who seemed to be hanging off his every word. He felt a flush of heat in his cheeks and quickly carried on with the briefing. 'Have the families been informed?'

Georgie, the office manager, spoke. 'Yes, sir. Family liaison have been to all four families and are staying with them for as long as they're needed.'

'Okay, that's good,' said Paterson. 'Have we had any luck recovering the dumped mobile phones?' He looked at Carter and Winslet. 'I'm sorry. Should have briefed you beforehand but . . . it's been a bastard of a day.'

DI Carter held up a hand. 'No worries, sir. We'll catch up.'

Paterson nodded. 'Cheers. Anyone?'

'We're struggling to get the ones out of the river, guv,' said Jackie. 'Obviously, they sink like stones and are probably under a few inches of mud by now. One of the water rats said that the biggest problems was the tide. That'll shove them away from where they landed and, even if they're in the mud, that moves too. So, given that the currents in the Thames are pretty severe and fast moving, they probably won't turn up for another five thousand years or so.'

'Wonderful,' said Paterson. 'Have they looked?'

'Of course. Couple of divers went down in each drop point. Nothing. They're waiting for the tide to go out and they'll try again. They've got special scanning equipment, but they really don't hold out much hope. Sorry.'

'But we have the one from the drain?'

'Yep, but it's damaged. Waterlogged and probably fucked circuitry. Tech boys are on it though, so . . . fingers crossed.'

Paterson rubbed his chin. This he could have done without. 'Okay, so not a good start.'

'Might not be too bad,' said Jackie. 'I got each victim's phone number from the families. I've applied for an urgent show order with the respective phone companies to give us anything they can, but that'll be a waiting game. Nobody hurries themselves these days, do they?'

'Anyone else got anything? Monkey? Dusty?'

Both men shook their heads. 'Sorry, guv,' said Dusty. 'We've been out interviewing shop and office owners but they've not given us anything we didn't already know. I'm going to have a look at the dashcam of the lorry that took out the Tower Bridge girl, so maybe we'll get something useful from that.'

Paterson nodded. 'Have we contacted bus companies for their CCTV? Maybe they picked up something.'

'Yes, sir,' said Monkey. 'They're helpful. Got a couple of buses that were passing in either direction at the relevant time for two of the victims. I've got the CCTV, just gotta go through it.'

'Good stuff,' said Paterson. 'If you need any help, draft in a couple of plods to sit and watch. Make sure they've got a bit of experience under their belt so they know what they're looking for. Okay, we're all done for the day. Monkey and Dusty . . . you're on the overtime for the CCTV, okay?'

Both nodded.

'Find me something, eh?'

'Do our best,' said Dusty. 'Can't promise, though.'

'Guv?' said Jackie. 'What do we do about Clocksy?'

'Well, I'll go back to the hospital if he's still there. Give him some moral support. If I were you, I'd drop him a text to let him know you're all thinking of him. Wouldn't phone him, though. He wasn't in a good way. Give him a day or two. I'll let you know a bit more when I've spoken to him. Go home. Get rest. See you all in the morning.'

'Is Lyndsey with him?' she said.

Paterson shook his head. 'She wasn't when I left. Hopefully she is now.' Jackie nodded slowly. She should be.

'Georgie?' Paterson called, and the office manager looked up. 'Would you be good enough to bring Harry and Grace up to speed, please?'

'Pleasure,' he said.

'Harry? Grace? Can we catch up tomorrow?'

'Not a problem,' said Carter. 'Go and do what you need to do. We'll catch up in the morning. Nine?'

'Nine it is. And I'll spend more time with you both. Promise.' He nodded to them and made his way out of the office.

# CHAPTER 22

Paterson was back behind his desk at 7 a.m. This wasn't the time for resting, even though he was still feeling the effects of the early wake-up call and all the events that followed it. He was never one to sleep late; five or six hours did him usually. On his desk was a black coffee. Not his usual, but he needed this, his third so far. He rubbed his chin and scooted back in his chair.

The office was quiet and this was the main reason he came in so early every day. That little bit of peace and quiet before the day kicked off and everybody wanted a piece of him. *Can you tell me this? Can you tell me that? What shall I do?* was his favourite. Often, he would tell them exactly what to do if he was in one of his ever-increasing bad moods. But for now, at least, it was quiet. That lasted all of five minutes before he heard footfall across the main floor toward his office. Through the glass he saw him. Johnny Clocks. His heart sunk then rose just as quickly. He was glad to see him even though he shouldn't be there.

'Mornin' guv.' Clocksy slipped his jacket off before wandering over to the kettle.

'It's just boiled,' said Paterson.

'Good. Won't 'ave long to wait, will I?'

'Okay, so, what are you doing here?'

Clocks shrugged. 'Well, there was a police sign down the road that said *Help Wanted*. I couldn't get through on the number so I thought I'd nip down in person. What you need 'elp with?'

'I need help with figuring out what you're doing here.'

Clocks poured himself a coffee. He was a tea man but obviously needed something a bit stronger. 'Ok, I can do that. Sounds easy.' He wandered off and sat behind his desk.

'John?' said Paterson. 'What are you doing here?'

'You know what I'm doin' 'ere. I told yer I was comin' in today. It's all right. Family 'ave got it all covered. I'll be there when they need me.'

'They need you now, mate. Go home.'

'Nope.'

'What do you mean, *nope*? I'm your guv'nor and I put you on compassionate leave.'

'And I've took meself offa it. Thank you very much for lovin' me the way you do. But I'm not sittin' at 'ome mopin'. End of.'

'Look, John, it's not that I don't want you here, you know that. It's just that I'm worried about you.'

'What for?' Clocks took a sip of the black liquid and scrunched his face up. 'Ooh! Burned me tongue!'

'Because . . . you know why. Your mum . . .'

'It's fine. Stop bein' an ol' woman, will yer?'

'I'm worried about you mentally.'

Clocks raised his eyebrows. 'You an' the 'ole fuckin' Met, matey boy.' He blew into his cup a few times.

'I'm going to have HR breathing down my neck.'

'Wow! That sounds scary. Good thing I came in as back-up in case they tell you off.'

'You're a pain in the arse, Clocksy.'

Clocks chuckled. 'You wish. Anyway, enough of that ol' fanny. What's the plan, Stan?'

120

Paterson smiled. There was no point trying to get him to leave but he would have to keep an eye on him. 'At the moment, not a lot. We have some information but nothing spectacular. Still a big fat mystery. Oh, because I thought you were going to be off for a while, I recruited a couple of people to help out. DI Carter and his DS, Grace Winslet. You know them, don't you?'

'Yeah, I know 'em both. We've crossed paths a few times. Good coppers, the pair of 'em. Didn't 'e crack that case of the 'undred-year-old serial killer a little while ago. Old boy in an 'ome?'

'Yeah. They both did. Although Grace said it was really down to one of the care workers. Bright girl. Lost her life though.'

'Yeah, I remember it. So, Gracie's with 'im, is she?'

'Yep.'

'She's a sort, ain't she?'

'Yep.'

'You gonna take a run at 'er, then?'

'Excuse me?'

'Are you gonna see if she's gonna succumb to the ol' Paterson charm, y'know?'

'Meaning?'

'Oh, you know what I mean. Are you gonna see if you can play bouncy-bouncy with the nice lady's underclackers.'

Paterson looked at the doorway behind Clocks.

He sniffed. 'She's there, ain't she?'

Paterson nodded.

'How much 'as she 'eard?'

'All of it.'

'Does she look pissed off?'

Paterson nodded.

Clocks spun his chair around and looked straight at DS Winslet. 'Gracie! 'Ow you doin', me ol' treacle? Been a while, innit?'

She stood there with her arms folded, glaring at him.

'Whassamatter, love? I upset you?'

'No, no, not at all, Clocksy. It's always a compliment when you come into work to find out your senior officer is asking his senior officer if he's going to bang me.'

Clocks pondered for a second then nodded. 'To be fair, I didn't actually say that but, in 'indsight, I can see how you'd be a bit narked at that because I'm nothin' if not a new man these days.'

'Yeah, it sounded like an improvement. For you.'

'C'mon, Gracie. You know me.'

'Yep. Ever the dickhead.'

He laughed and got out of his chair. 'C'mon, girl, gimme a big hug.'

'Fuck, no. I've got your measure, Clocks. You just want to feel my tits pressing up against your chest, don't you?'

'It'd cheer me up no end.'

'John, I know you're upset and I'm very sorry for your loss, but you can fuck right off.'

Clocks turned to Paterson. 'Oh, she's good, Ray. Can we keep 'er?'

Paterson shook his head and ignored him. 'Good morning, Grace. Good to see you. You're early. Thought you weren't coming in until nine?'

She glanced at Clocks then back at him. 'That was the plan, but I was lying awake all night touching myself and thinking of you. Couldn't help myself. So, thought I'd come in early and, y'know . . . Where shall we start?'

Clocks wrinkled his nose and cocked his head.

'Er . . .' said Paterson.

'Do you want him to join us?' she said to Paterson.

Clocks's eyes lit up. 'Ask me! Not 'im. He's a bleedin' killjoy. I'm in!'

'Jesus, John. What is wrong with you?' she said. Clocks looked a bit crestfallen. 'Did you really think I was going to do that?'

He shrugged. 'No. Not for a second. I mean, I was 'opin'. That really would 'ave cheered me up.'

She turned back to Paterson. 'I'm sorry, sir. That was inappropriate. I apologise for being a bad girl. You can spank me if you want?' She turned abruptly on her heel and walked out of the office.

Paterson and Clocks never moved.

'A bit strong,' said Paterson. 'She doesn't know anything about me.'

'She knows you're gorgeous. We all do.'

'Was she being serious?'

'She said no, but . . .'

'I mean . . . a spanking . . .' He shuddered. 'John, back to work. See if there are any notes left on people's desks. Let's get a head start.'

# CHAPTER 23

'Why didn't you tell me she was there?' said Clocks. 'Made me look a right lemon.'

'I thought about it,' said Paterson, 'but then I asked myself . . . would Clocksy have bailed me out? Not a chance. So, I thought, sod it. Have a taste of your own medicine. It'll do you good.'

Clocks scoffed. 'If you say so. She loves a bit o' banter.'

'Maybe, but I wouldn't try it with that new girl on the squad . . . Harmony. That will not go well.'

Paterson's phone rang. 'Mr Fox. Good morning. What can I do for you?' Paterson listened and nodded from time to time. 'Is that unusual? Okay. But I don't really have time to go checking up on absent staff. It's not my job. That's yours.'

'Whassup?' said Clocks.

Paterson held up a finger. 'Okay, okay. You're right. We're not far from where he lives. We'll go take a look, but he's probably tucked up in bed. I think the whole thing put the shits up him.' Paterson listened again then nodded. 'All right. I'll get back to you.'

'Well?' asked Clocks.

'That was Simon Fox from the CCTV. He said Striker's not come in today.'

Clocks frowned. 'And?'

'And he asked if we can nip round to his flat and see if he's all right.'

''Scuse me? What are we, 'is bleedin' nursemaids or something?'

'He said that he spoke to Striker at home last night and he sounded worried.'

'What about?'

'Didn't say. But Fox is anxious that he might have done himself in.'

'Oh, leave off! Done 'imself in. Why? 'Cos 'e saw a couple of people kill 'emselves on a screen? Bit extreme, innit?'

'You never know a person's state of mind.'

'True. But I do know you've got be an exceptional pussy to do yourself in over that. I mean, I saw *Equalizer 3* the other night. Massive body count, there was. Blood everywhere. Denzel was givin' it large, mate. Don't see me toppin' meself, do yer?'

'That was a film. You watched it on the telly.'

'Same thing for 'im. Watched it on the telly, didn't 'e?'

'I'm not in the mood for playing, John.'

Clocks chuckled. 'Who knew? So, we going? Probably just forgot to set 'is alarm. Trauma does that.'

'What? Make you forget to set your alarm clock?'

'That and shootin' up shoppin' malls, yeah.'

Paterson sighed. 'Striker lives in a flat in Surrey Quays. Number 959. Top-floor.'

'Oh, good. Why wouldn't 'e? An' I'll bet the bastard lift's not workin'. So that's me up an 'undred flights of stairs, I s'pose.'

Paterson pulled on his jacket and grabbed his notebook from out of his drawer. 'It'll be good for you.'

'Will it bollocks, mate. You tell that to me thighs after the third flight.'

'You always look on the negative side of things, don't you?'

'I try to. Thanks for noticin'.'

'I'll get Monkey to drop us off and hang around until we're done,' said Paterson.

Fifteen minutes later, they arrived on the estate. After a quick drive around, Monkey Harris remembered where Striker's particular block was. Like most council estates, the entrance to the block was secured with a big heavy door controlled by an intercom. Such was the state of crime these days that councils were forced to ensure that all blocks on all council estates were secured.

Paterson pressed the button to Striker's flat and waited. No answer. He pressed again. Nothing. Clocks stepped forward and pressed five random buttons in quick succession. A tinny voice answered. 'Who is it?'

'Post, love. I forgot me pass. Do the 'onours for us, please.'

The door buzzed and Clocks pulled it open. 'Cheers, m'dear,' he said as they stepped inside. The hallway stank of stale piss. Not a big surprise to either of them. Clocks was pleasantly surprised to see that both lifts were working. 'Makes a change,' he mumbled to himself.

'That's a result for you, John. Now you don't have to do anything, stairs or fitness-wise.'

'Good. I'm takin' the lift.'

'You'll regret it.'

They stepped into the lift. 'Christ!' said Clocks. 'Smells worse in 'ere than out there. He turned around to press the button and saw a large turd in the corner. 'Oh, for fuck's sake! Is that human? It better not be human. Dirty bastards.'

Paterson wrinkled his nose. 'Looks human.'

'Whassamatter with people, takin' a squeeze in the lift,' said Clocks. 'The council put in shrubbery for that sort of thing. I don't blame 'im if 'e's done 'imself in for 'avin' to live 'ere. Probably that nodder was the last straw on the end of a bad day.' The door opened and they both left a lot quicker than they got in.

'Glad no one else got in,' said Clocks. 'I'd 'ate for them to think you did that.'

'Oi!' Paterson looked offended.

'Well, they might 'ave done. You hoorahs are the worst for that. Should be ashamed of yerselves.'

'What the hell are you prattling on about now? My being educated ensured that I didn't do things like that, John. That's more your sort of folk.'

'Er, 'scuse me. What d'you mean, my sort of folk? That's a bit racist, innit?'

'What? No. No, it's not racist. I'm just saying—'

'You're just sayin' that poor people shit in lifts.'

'You said that wealthy people shit in lifts.'

Clocks shrugged. 'Well . . . potato, potato.'

'It's potato, potahto. We've had this discussion before.'

Clocks shrugged again. 'Whatever. Lift shitters, the lotta yer.'

Paterson decided to ignore him. It was generally the best strategy when Clocks was in a silly mood. They walked along the balcony until they came to Striker's door.

'Let's see if he's just done it in or done 'imself in.'

Paterson rang the doorbell and waited. No reply. He rang it again. Still no reply.

'Come out the way.' Clocks pushed past Paterson. 'Lemme 'ave a go.' He pressed the bell and kept his finger on it.

'All right, Clocksy. That's enough.' Paterson bent down and peered through the letterbox. In front of him was a hallway leading his eye into the living room. He could only see half of it, but it was enough to make him think there had been some sort of altercation inside. He saw a wooden chair lying on its side, a picture on the wall that was hanging cock-eyed and what looked like bits of broken crockery and cutlery strewn across the floor.

'What d'you see?' said Clocks.

'Looks like the cleaner skipped the living room,' said Paterson. He stood up to let Clocks have a look.

'Bum'oles. Looks like the scene of some fisticuffs. You agree?'

'I agree.'

'An' you can 'ear the sounds of a scuffle comin' from inside the flat?'

'Strangely enough, I can,' said Paterson as he stood back.

'Then we 'ave a duty to preserve life an' limb,' said Clocks. He booted the front door a few times until the lock gave way. The noise echoed around the landing, causing a few curtains to twitch. Neither man was worried. Nobody called the police on this estate. But every once in a while, a neighbour got a bit nosy.

Striker's next-door neighbour, an elderly woman, opened her door. 'Oi! What the fuck are you two doin'?' She looked to be in her seventies but not the sort to knuckle under to anyone. Whatever this was, it was a bit too close to home for her liking.

'Morning,' said Paterson.

Clocks looked at her. 'Avon callin'.'

'Avon? Pull the other one. People don't sell door-to-door cosmetics no more. Who the bleedin' 'ell are you two? I'm callin' the rozzers.'

'Rozzers?' said Paterson.

'Old word for police. Don't 'ear it so much now,' said Clocks.

Paterson nodded as if he understood. He didn't. Nor did he suppose he would ever truly get to grips with Clocks's form of language.

'S'all right, love,' said Clocks. 'We *are* the rozzers. Just come to check up on ol' Chris 'ere.'

The woman looked sceptical. 'You ain't no rozzers. Look at yer.' She pointed an arthritic finger at Paterson. 'He's way too good-lookin' for a start. Ain't never seen no good-lookin' rozzers before. Well, not *that* good-lookin' anyway.'

'Thank you,' said Paterson. 'You're very sweet.'

'Yeah,' she said. 'Sweet? If I was thirty years younger, I'd be on you like a rash, mate.'

'All right!' said Clocks. 'What's with all the flirtin'? Disgustin'.'

128

'I'm not flirting,' said Paterson.

'Well, you're encouragin' 'er. You wanna watch 'im, love. Likes 'em with a bit o' mileage on the clock, this one. He was all over an old churchgoer a little while ago. Worked for the church as well, she did. Didn't bother 'im. Wallop! He 'ad a go at 'er.'

Paterson looked mortified. 'What?'

The elderly woman's face lit up. ''Ope for me, then. You wait there, son. I'll go an' put some lips on an' brush me 'air.'

Now Paterson looked horrified as she went back indoors. 'Clocksy . . .'

Clocks was grinning from ear to ear. 'What can I say? You're now officially a granny magnet.' He chuckled to himself as he stepped into the flat. 'Striker!' he called. 'Police! You in 'ere, son?' Paterson followed him in.

To his right was the kitchen. It was a bit messy but overall looked okay. The living room opened out ahead of him. He stepped forward carefully. The door was half open and from where he was, he could see that it bore all the hallmarks of a fight. Apart from the chair and broken cutlery on the floor, a mirror that had once hung over the fireplace was smashed to pieces. The television was overturned and there was blood smeared on the walls. Not much, but enough to concern him.

'It's empty,' Clocks said noncommittally.

Paterson nodded and turned around. He headed down the hallway carefully. Stealth was never going to be an issue. At the end, he saw two bedrooms and the bathroom. A quick search showed them to be empty.

'We're good,' he said and headed back into the living room to survey the scene. 'Must've made some noise when this all kicked off. Looks like a bomb went off in here.'

'With a bit of luck, your new bird 'ad 'er 'earing aid turned up, eh?'

Paterson sighed. 'Let's hope so. Tell you what . . . you can ask her when we leave.'

'Me? I'm not askin' 'er. She's your bird, you ask 'er.'

'She is not "my bird" and I'm bloody terrified of going anywhere near her. She'll have my trousers off before I can say anything.'

Clocks laughed. 'All right, shy boy. I'll ask 'er.'

'I owe you,' said Paterson.

'What d'you reckon 'appened, then?' said Clocks.

'A fight.'

Clocks tutted. 'Christ! You're bang on it, Sherlock. I know it's a fight. I can see there's been a fight. I'm not blind, am I? What I meant is—'

'I know what you meant. Why was there a fight, who was he fighting with, and here's the real question . . . where the hell is he now?'

'Yep.'

'We need to get a forensic team in here. Get the blood on the wall tested, see whose it is, and we need to get word out that he's on the missing list.'

'I'll give Georgie in the office a bell,' said Clocks. 'He can check the 'ospitals an' the morgue. See if he's turned up at either.'

On the way out, Paterson stepped into the kitchen and looked around. 'John . . .'

'Whassup, Buttercup?'

'I think I've found a clue.'

Clocks stepped into the room. Together, they looked at what was taped to the door: Striker's photograph with a large red cross through it. One word was written on the note beneath it. *Retribution*.

# CHAPTER 24

Monkey Harris dropped the window of his car as he watched Paterson and Clocks approach. 'Anything, guv?'

'Looks like there's been a fight of some kind in there,' said Paterson. 'Also, we found these.' He held up the photo and the note.

'Nasty,' said Monkey. 'So, we looking at a kidnap, d'you think?'

'Maybe. Don't want to jump to conclusions, but yeah, it's looking that way.'

Monkey nodded. 'Where to, then? Back to the nick?'

Paterson took a deep breath, lost in thought for a moment. 'It's all right, Monkey,' said Clocks. 'Changed our minds. We'll walk back.'

'Guv?' said Monkey. 'It'll take ages. It's a good, what, forty-minute walk?'

'Don't matter,' said Clocks. 'We need to walk an' talk. Clear our 'eads.'

Monkey shrugged. 'You sure?'

Paterson nodded. 'It's fine, Monkey. We need to think.'

Monkey started the car. 'Fair enough. I'll see you back there. If you need anything, gimme a bell. Which way you going?'

Clocks shrugged. 'Dunno. Might cut through the Milnbrook Estate.'

'*What?*'

'What now?' said Clocks. 'It's all right. We're big boys.'

'Yeah, I know, but . . .'

'But what?' said Clocks.

'It can be a bit . . . dodgy there.'

'We're a bit dodgy, ain't we? So, what's your point?'

'Just be careful. Some nasty bastards on that estate.'

'Fuck's sake, Monkey. *We're* nasty bastards. We'll be fine. Go on, off you fuck, there's a good lad.'

Monkey shook his head. 'Just be careful,' he said, before he drove off.

'What was he worried about?' said Paterson.

'Nothin'. You know Monkey. Worries like an' ol' woman. We'll be fine.' The two men headed off in the direction of the estate. 'So, what d'you think 'appened to Striker?'

'No idea, mate. I mean, this note could mean anything, couldn't it?'

'S'pose so. 'Ere . . .' Clocks pointed toward the underground garages. 'Let's cut through there.' Paterson nodded and followed him down a ramp to the garages. As soon as they levelled up, Paterson realised that this was not a good place to be. The garages stretched out in darkness, a vast expanse filled with the pungent odour of alcohol and urine that seemed to emanate from every corner. Shadows flickered across the cracked concrete floor, cast by the feeble glow of a flickering overhead light. The air was heavy with the sharp tang of stale beer, and the unmistakable scent of both kinds of human waste assaulted their noses.

Along the grimy walls, rows of garage doors loomed, their once robust frames now twisted and shattered. Some yawned wide open, resembling hungry mouths awaiting their next victim, while others clung precariously to their hinges, threatening to collapse at any moment. Graffiti marred the walls, a chaotic jumble of crude symbols and foul language. Empty beer cans littered the floor, like dead soldiers on a battlefield.

Among them, discarded needles glinted in the dim light, a stark reminder of the dangers lurking in the shadows. The sound of dripping water echoed through the cavernous space, a constant backdrop to the atmosphere of decay and neglect.

Every sound reverberated in the silence. Every shadow seemed to conceal unseen dangers. The air felt thick and suffocating, as if burdened by the weight of the darkness itself.

'We'll stick out an alert for 'im,' said Clocks, oblivious to the scene. 'Bloke'll show up eventually. One way or the other.'

As they walked, Paterson spotted a problem ahead. At the exit, two cars, silhouetted against the light, were blocking the ramp. Standing around the cars were four males. One black, one mixed and two whites. All four were looking in their direction. Paterson saw that the up-and-over door of the garage nearest the exit was raised.

'Heads-up, Clocksy,' he said, interrupting Clocks's rambling.

'What's up?' said Clocks. Paterson nodded toward the youths. 'Oh, bollocks. 'Ere we go.'

The two men never broke their stride and carried on talking until one of the white youths stepped in front of Clocks. 'Where tink you go, ol' man?' He was a skinny kid of about eighteen. Would have been decent-looking if it wasn't for the drugs that left him with dead eyes, dark circles under them and spotty skin. He was tall, with tattoos covering his arms and shoulders. He had some kind of elaborate pattern inked on his neck and three dots under his right eye.

Clocks looked him up and down. 'I tink I is goin' up dat ramp. I is busy man, so fuck right off out of it.'

The group burst out laughing. 'Man tink he can talk street, innit?'

Clocks sniffed and shrugged his head. 'I wasn't tryin' to talk street, son. I was tryin' to communicate with a lower life-form. How'd I do?'

The boy sucked his teeth loudly. Paterson watched the other three. He knew this wasn't going to end well for any of them.

'Who tink you look at man?' said the black man to Paterson. 'I cut out your pussy eyes.' He pulled out a knife with a six-inch blade and held it up. Paterson was far enough away to not be concerned. He said nothing.

The white kid tilted his head cockily at Clocks. 'Pops, if you want to travel troo man's ends, you need to pay us some P's, innit.'

Clocks frowned. 'Ray?'

'What's up?'

'You got any idea what the fuck this little snotgobbler just said?'

Paterson chuckled. 'Not a fucking clue, mate. I have enough trouble understanding you half the time.'

'Kid, what the fuck are you bangin' on about? "Man's ends"? An' why d'you want peas? I mean, lookin' at the state of yer, you do look like you could do with a decent meal in yer belly, but peas? They won't do yer much good. Better off with a McDonald's or somethin'. I mean, yer fuckin' arms look like two strips of linguini.'

'Tch. Nah, man,' said the kid. 'P's. *P's*. You gotta give man P's, a'ight?'

Clocks shook his head. 'Do I look like a branch of Asda, you idiot?'

'I don't arks no more, fool. Gimmi P's, innit!'

Clocks wrinkled his nose. 'What'd you just say?'

'I said, I arksed you for—'

'What the fuck does *arksed* mean?'

The boy looked Clocks up and down like he was the idiot. 'What you mean, fool? I arksed you for P's, innit.'

'P's is pounds, innit,' said the second white youth. Dressed similar to the youth Clocks was tormenting, this one had a buzz cut and a vicious-looking face. He was clearly up for a ruck. 'Pounds, old man. Pounds.'

'Oh, *money*. You want money. I get it now. P is for pound. Like T is for thick. Were you one of the thick kids at school, son? I bet you were. You've got the vacant eyes to go with your vacant head.'

'Fuck dis, man!' The kid waved his arms in the air. 'If you don't give us P's, I'm gonna buss up your ol' white arse.'

'Oi! 'Old up with the racist shit, son. You didn't 'ave to call me arse white. *Old* arse woulda done. An' in case you ain't noticed, you're fuckin' whiter than me — which is no surprise, is it? Fuckin' dwellin' down 'ere in the dark an' damp all day like a weedy vampire. Besides, I can't give you any money because I spent me last one pound fifty bangin' yer mum. She told me to tell you it's all right. You can buy yerself a bag o' sweeties now she's flush.'

'One more word ol' man an' I'm gonna cut you, innit.'

'All right. But before you do that, lemme guess. You little fuckers are the local 'ard nuts, ain'tcha? You an' yer crew 'ere are the ones that spend their days an' nights frightenin' little ol' ladies an' pregnant mums. Well, just so we're clear, you don't fuckin' frighten me in the slightest. Now, I've 'ad a bad coupla days, so I strongly suggest you fuck off outta me way before I smack you right back into yer muvver's womb.'

'Das it! Fuck you, ol' man. You gonna fuckin' die, innit.' The kid reached behind himself and pulled out a small machete from his waistband.

'John,' said Paterson. 'Thank you, my old mate. I need this.'

At the sight of the machete, the other youths became highly agitated and pulled out their weapons. The black kid pulled out a wicked-looking knife with a serrated edge. The mixed-race boy had another machete.

'Hmm. Look at that. They've all got knives, John.'

Clocks smiled. 'Nah. They're not knives.' He reached inside his jacket and pulled out his Glock pistol. 'This is a knife!' Except for the one in front of Clocks, the kids all jumped back at the same time.

'Man got strap!' one of them shouted and backed up against a car.

Clocks pointed the gun at the kid's face. He didn't flinch, nor did he back away. 'Don't know if one of your daddies ever mentioned it to yer, but I'm the *one day, you'll meet someone bigger an' badder than you* bloke.'

135

'You tink me scared, ol' man? You tink me give a fuck? You won't shoot. You is feds, right? Feds tink us scared?'

Clocks sighed. 'First thing you've got right today. Yep, we're feds, an' no, I don't tink you scared. I tink you tick as shit, innit.' Clocks lowered the gun quickly and shot him in the knee. Paterson winced at the sound as the boy screamed and fell to the ground. The shot and the scream echoed around the concrete cavern as the boy rolled around in agony, clutching his knee with both hands. Clocks kicked the boy's machete under the car. The other three boys shouted and screamed, unsure of what to do. Then they ran. Clocks bent down to the boy. 'An' dat's what 'appens to the tick kids who tink they're fuckin' 'ard, innit.' He holstered the gun.

Paterson grinned. 'One down, none to go.'

'Maybe not,' said Clocks. ''Ave a look!' He nodded toward the open garage just as a huge black youth exited it. Clocks ducked. As he walked toward them, the man raised an Uzi sub-machine gun and pointed it straight at Paterson.

'Oh, shit!' Paterson spun and ducked behind a parked car as the youth let off a burst of shots. Clocks stayed down until the man had passed him, then he stood and pointed his gun at the back of his head.

'Oi, oi! Put it down!' Clocks shouted. 'Put. It. Down. Boy. Or I will shoot you right in the fuckin' nut.'

The youth stopped and turned his head. Clocks never flinched as the youth eyeballed him. He was done asking. Without a word, the boy dropped the gun to the floor. Its clatter echoed around the garages.

'Kick it over, son. Do it!' The boy did as he was told.

Paterson stood up and shook himself straight. He walked up to the gunman. 'You're a big lad, aren't you?'

'Fucker's a monster,' said Clocks. 'Looks like a bear in people clothes.'

Paterson looked at the Uzi, now lying in a small puddle. He picked it up. 'That's some serious firepower you've got there, son. Where'd you get it?'

'Fuck are you, man? Come shoot up de mandem in his ends. Lucky I not off you.'

'Oh, fuck me rigid. 'E's doin' it now, Ray. Like 'is skinny little mate. Talkin' gobbledebollocks. Oi! Yogi Bear! What are you bangin' on about? What's *mandem* when it's at 'ome?'

The youth sucked his teeth, a long rasping sound. 'You buss up me fam, you pay. You unnerstand me?'

Clocks looked down at the youth he'd shot in the leg. The kid was whimpering but had stopped screaming.

Paterson smiled. 'Don't know what you said there, big boy, but it sounds like you wanna fight me. Serious?'

'Me tear you up, man. Tell dem ol' man to put down him strap an' we go.'

Paterson gave him a slow nod. 'Put it down, John. Man's made me an invitation I really don't want to refuse.'

Clocks lowered the gun and grinned. 'You've slipped up now, Yogi, me ol' son. This is not gonna go your way.'

'You tink me scared? You two ol' men? Me kill him first, then me come for you.'

'Oh dear.' Clocks leaned back against a car and crossed his arms. 'Where's your little crew gone, son? Is it bedtime in bad boy land?'

The youth ignored him.

'Whenever you're ready,' said Paterson. He stepped casually into a side-on stance, readying himself for an attack. It came fast. The youth lurched forward, right arm drawn back to strike out. As his fist shot forward, Paterson pivoted on his foot and side-stepped the blow. With his left hand he delivered an almighty downward slap to the Bear's face, knocking him sidewards and downwards.

'Oooh!' said Clocks. 'Nice one, Ray.'

'Cheers, John. Naughty boys get little slaps.'

The Bear staggered to his feet. 'Hit like a girl,' he said. 'What man slaps?'

'The man who didn't want to add to your existing brain damage,' said Paterson. 'But if you want to be hit, I'm good.'

He stood side on again. He watched as the Bear pulled a large combat knife out of the back of his trousers. He shook his head at the youth's action.

'Ray?'

'Yes, mate,' said Paterson.

'Want me to shoot him?'

'Nope. No need. Thanks for the offer, though.'

'No worries. Anything for a mate.' Clocks lifted himself onto the bonnet of the car and wriggled about as he made himself comfortable.

Paterson beckoned the Bear forward. 'Are you sure you wanna do this, kid? If you drop it now, I'll just beat you senseless. If you don't . . .'

'Shut up, man. I am kill you now.' He swung the knife wildly in front of Paterson's body.

Paterson grinned. 'You've no fucking clue how to use that, do you? Not a clue.'

The Bear drew closer and swung the knife again, this time toward Paterson's face. Paterson blocked the attempt with his left arm. With his right hand, he punched the Bear straight on the nose. As the boy's head snapped back, Paterson pivoted on his left foot and grabbed the hand that held the knife. He thrust the boy's arm back in toward his body and smiled as the knife slid into the youth's side. The Bear gasped.

'No organ damage, son.' Paterson pulled the boy's arm and knife back out. As the knife left the body a stream of blood came with it, blossoming across the youth's T-shirt. He looked down, disbelief on his face, then looked up at a smiling Paterson. Paterson grabbed the knife out of the youth's hand, dropped to one knee and slammed it into his outer thigh. As the youth dropped to one side, Paterson pulled the knife out, stood up and side-kicked the wound. The Bear screamed as a bolt of pain ripped through his leg. He staggered backward before falling.

'One in the knee, John.'

''Scuse me?'

'You choose which one. Fucker needs to be put out of action. I can't be arsed to kill him. Too much to do.'

Clocks stepped forward, gun ready. He knelt down and pressed it against the boy's knee.

'No, no, no, no, man. Please. No.' The youth had tears in his eyes.

Clocks sniffed. 'Well, aren't you the brave one? Come unstuck today, didn't you, big man? Y'know, I've known people like you all my life. Grown up around you. Bullyin' and intimidatin' decent people. Stabbin' an' robbin'. Wavin' guns around. Shootin' the estate up, fightin' over drugs. Terrorisin' residents. Big man, eh? Except you're not. You're fuckin' nothin', boy. Nothin'.' He pulled the trigger. The Bear's screams rang loud in the garage as his knee exploded. As the boy rolled around on his back, grasping his knee, Clocks blew out the other one.

'Both?' said Paterson, completely unconcerned.

Clocks shrugged. 'Thought it'd be interestin' to see how 'e gets on terrorisin' people from a wheelchair.'

'Good point.' Paterson looked at his watch in the flickering overhead light. 'We need to get on. Say bye-bye, John.'

The youth was on the verge of passing out when Clocks tapped his arm with his foot a few times. 'Listen, big boy. This 'as been fun, but we can't play with you anymore. Places to go, people to see. Listen, though. When you see your little twatlet mates, best you tell 'em to be'ave 'emselves an' go on the straight 'n' narrow or we'll come back for 'em when we get a quiet day. Understood?'

The boy grimaced and groaned.

'Okey-doke, then. I'll take that as a yes. Be good now. See yer, wouldn't wanna be yer.'

Paterson picked up the Uzi that the boy dropped and headed up the ramp toward the daylight. He put his hands behind his back and hid the gun from view.

Clocks followed behind.

'John?' said Paterson.

'What?'

'What's a "twatlet"?'

'A twatlet, Ray, is a young twat. Thought that was obvious.'

'That word's not on the app, is it?'

'No. Made that one up meself.'

As they reached the top of the exit ramp, a gang of youths were waiting for them, all of them armed in some fashion or other. Paterson saw knives, machetes and small-calibre hand-guns. Without breaking his stride, he pulled the Uzi from behind his back, swung it into full view and pulled the trigger. A dozen bullets bit into the concrete close to the gang's feet. Cries of sheer panic went up as the youths scattered in all directions, darting for cover behind cars and jumping over walls to avoid the madman with a sub-machine gun.

'Youngsters today, John. No respect for their betters.'

'Time's 'ave changed, Ray. No discipline anymore. No consequences. They're not frightened of authority like they should be.'

Paterson and Clocks walked on and out of the estate, untroubled by the gang.

## CHAPTER 25

'Sir.'

Paterson had only just set foot inside the station and a young PC was already after his attention. 'Yes, mate,' he said politely. 'What can I do for you?'

'You've got a visitor, sir. I've put him in the waiting room. He wasn't very happy. I got the impression he was a bit . . . unused to being told what to do.'

'Who is he?'

'Says he's from the army. An MP or something. Just told me to get you to see him the moment you arrived back.'

'That's all right. What room's he in?'

'Four,' said the PC.

'How long has he been here?'

'About twenty minutes.'

'And you didn't think to call me?' Paterson sounded mildly irritated. He wasn't digging the kid out, but he would have liked to have been informed.

'Yes, I'm sorry, sir. I was going to call. Things got a bit busy here. Double busy.'

Paterson nodded. 'Okay, no probs. We'll go and see him. Has he got a drink or anything?'

'I made him a coffee.'

'Good man. Can you stick the kettle back on for us in case he wants another.'

'See if you can rustle up a few Jammie Dodgers for us an' all,' said Clocks.

'I offered him some biscuits, sir. Said he wasn't hungry.'

'They ain't for 'im, son. They're for your favourite detective inspector. I'll have a tea as well. Good lad.'

'What d'you think this is about?' said Paterson as the two men made their way along the hallway.

'Dunno. If it's the army, maybe one of our vics was in the military.'

'Maybe, but I think the team would've clocked that by now.'

'S'pose so.' Clocks shrugged. 'Let's go and find out, shall we?'

Paterson briefly tapped the door of interview room four and walked straight in. The man behind the desk was impressively big. He stood up to greet Paterson and Clocks and towered over Paterson by a good seven inches. Nine in Clocks's case. Not only was he tall, he was a wide and muscular with a hard, no-nonsense face. He had a faint scar that stretched from his eyebrow to his receding hairline. The military cut just emphasised the size of him.

The giant held his hand out. Paterson took it and watched his hand get swallowed up like a baby wearing its first woollen mitts.

'Superintendent Paterson?' the giant said.

'Hi. Sorry to have kept you waiting.'

'No worries. I'm sure you're very busy.'

Paterson smiled. 'That I am. I understand you're with the army, yes?'

The man nodded. 'Military police. Name's Jack Forrest.'

'Christ! Big ol' lump, ain't yer?' Clocks was in awe.

The giant chuckled. 'I guess I am, yes. You are?'

'Bloody intimidated, mate. Fuck me, you're huge.'

142

Jack Forrest looked down at Clocks. 'So you said. And don't be intimidated. You only have to worry about me if I'm coming after you.'

'Yeah, well. That's not gonna 'appen, I promise yer. No way I'm upsettin' you, my son.'

There was a rap on the door. Clocks used the interruption to escape from the man and opened the door. The young PC stood there with a tray of drinks. Clocks looked at the tray and frowned. He stood aside to let the young man in, who set the tray down carefully. 'Coffee for you, sir,' he said to Paterson and then turned to Forrest. 'I brought you another coffee, sir, just in case you fancied it — and a cup of tea for you, DI Clocks.'

'Did you forget me Jammie Dodgers, son? I can only see Bourbons.'

'Sorry, sir. They only had these and custard creams.'

'No Jammie Dodgers?'

'No Jammie Dodgers. Sorry.'

'I don't like Bourbon's. Dried dog nodders, they are. Why the fuck can't I get a Jammie Dodger anymore? Is there some sort of shortage of 'em?'

'Would you like me to change them for custard creams?'

'No,' said Paterson. 'He wouldn't.'

'He would,' said Clocks. 'Anything's better than them bleedin' things.'

'Leave it, fellah,' said Paterson. 'Thank you, though. Much appreciated.'

Clocks threw Paterson a look that showed he wasn't very happy about not having his biscuit of choice. In return, Paterson threw Clocks a look that said he wasn't pleased with him complaining about biscuits when they had a military guest in front of them.

'Okay,' said Paterson. 'Sorry about that, Mr Forrest. What is it that we can do for you?'

'I understand that you two officers caught the suicides case. The four people that stepped in front of traffic.'

'Hmm,' said Paterson. 'That's us. What's the military's interest? One of the victims in the army?'

Forrest looked Paterson in the eye. 'Not exactly, no. But there are a couple of people that we have a vested interest in.'

'This is gettin' interestin',' said Clocks. 'Tell us what your interest is, fellah.'

Forrest looked across at Clocks. 'One of the victims worked for the Ministry of Defence. Mr Oliver Hayes. He was involved in some very . . . important work for the country, and obviously we would like to know what you know.'

Clocks shifted in his seat. 'I'm sure you would, but this ain't your case, it's ours.'

Forrest grinned, a tight we'll-see-about-that grin. 'Well, it is for now, Mr Clocks, but we will be taking it over as soon as I serve you the papers I have in my bag. Until then, I'd like to ask you what you have managed to find out so far.'

'Come again?' said Clocks. 'You're tellin' me that you're nickin' our case and we 'ave to tell you everythin'? I don't think so, big boy.'

'John . . .' Paterson could sense Clocks was winding up. 'Let's see where this is going.'

Clocks sat back in his chair.

'Look,' said Forrest. 'I understand how you must be feeling, but Mr Hayes was a government official whose work was above top secret. The Prime Minister herself has instructed the head of the MOD to deal with this case in-house. This is not an investigation for the police.'

Clocks was getting agitated again. 'What about the other victims?'

'Well, we'll have to take them too, I'm afraid. The whole case is mine now. There's no point in you investigating just three victims. Would leave a hole in your investigation, wouldn't it?'

'Or,' said Clocks, 'you can stand up, take your little brief-case, walk out the nick an' fuck off back up whatever bean-stalk you fell down from. Okay?' Clocks stood up. 'Thanks for coming. Mind how you go.'

Forrest had a bemused look on his face as Clocks opened the office door.

'Seems a bit rude,' he said to Paterson.

Paterson scowled at the man.

'Your man seems to be lacking some discipline. I'm surprised you let him get away with it.'

Clocks was at the door, looking back at Forrest. Paterson could see his breathing had changed. Of all the days Forrest could have rolled in, this was not the best.

'Well, fortunately, this isn't the military. We're not overly fond of mindless numbnuts in the Met and we tend to speak our minds and call out bullshit when we see it. Right now, I'm seeing it and smelling it and you're yakking it out of your mouth. So, I think it best you take Mr Clocks's advice and, as he would say, "sling yer bleedin' 'ook". Comprende?'

Forrest grinned. 'Hmm. Can't say I'm not disappointed, Mr Paterson. I would have thought you'd have understood and cooperated. But I can see you're upset. I understand that. I do. However, as I explained a moment ago, I'm here under the highest authority. I will not be leaving here without every single piece of paper, printouts of every piece of information that's gone into your system, and every note your officers have made, whether that be in their notebooks or on Post-its or even on a piece of toilet paper while they took a shit. Now, you can stand your ground but you will lose and you will lose your jobs as a result. Up to you.' Forrest stood and pulled himself up to his full height.

Paterson felt his head spin slightly. Excitement, but not an ounce of fear in him. Forrest was big and no doubt as tough as he looked, but Paterson wasn't concerned. He figured it wouldn't take a lot to put him down. Clocks was clinging onto the doorknob, an attack dog waiting for the word.

'Well,' said Paterson. 'You drawing yourself up like that gives me the impression that you're trying to intimidate me into doing what I'm told. But take a good look into my eyes and see if you can see anywhere in either of them that I give a fuck about you or your size or whatever abilities you have. I promise you, you won't come out unharmed if you want to go down that path.'

Forrest sighed. 'I'm sure you're really tough, Mr Paterson, so here's what I'm going to do.' He reached inside his jacket pocket and pulled out his mobile phone. 'I'm going to make a call, and within thirty seconds of my making this call, ten fully armed soldiers will enter this crumbling little building you call a police station and make their way upstairs to your office. And they will, *they will*, take what I came here for. If anyone tries to stop us, well then, that's on you, but I am taking this case from you, lock, stock and barrel. Now, of course, it doesn't have to be like this. I don't want this . . . unpleasantness at all. But, like you, I have a job to do, and today it just happens to be an extremely important one. Can we be civilised about this, please?'

Clocks tutted. 'Ten fully armed soldiers? Who pops into a local nick with a bunch of troops sittin' outside?'

'Someone that knew he was likely to meet resistance from you two and who really doesn't have the time to play about.'

Paterson never took his eyes off Forrest. 'Tell you what,' he said after a few seconds. 'Let's make this easier on both of us. Why don't we work together, eh? We know the territory. We have informants, people on the ground. I'm not interested in nicking anyone for the glory. You can have that. I just want whoever's behind this caught and punished. So, why don't you get on your phone and put the idea to your boss and see what they say.'

Forrest nodded. 'Would you give me the room, please?'

'Of course,' said Paterson. 'We'll be outside.'

Paterson perched himself on the edge of a desk while Clocks paced around.

'Fuckin' work with 'im? What's that all about? Bloody Little John comes bowlin' in 'ere thinkin' he's the king of our castle an' nickin' our case off us? Cheeky sod. Needs a clump!'

'You going to do that, John?'

146

Clocks stopped pacing. 'You know I would, mate. I'm not scared of 'im. Bigger they come an' all that.'

'How are you going to stick your nut on a bloke that size?'

'Jump? Stand on a desk? I dunno, but he can't come in 'ere givin' it Johnny Big Bollocks.'

'When you're built like that, I should think that's all you can give. Let's see what he comes back with.'

A minute later, Forrest poked his head outside and called them back in.

'What did the boss say?' said Paterson.

Forrest took a deep breath. 'Welcome aboard my team.'

'Welcome aboard ours,' said Clocks. 'You're in charge of the tea and biccies. I like Jammie Dodgers.'

Forrest grinned again. 'You're funny.'

'You said you had a vested interest in a couple of people,' said Paterson. 'Who's the other?'

'Christopher Striker,' said Forrest. 'He's been kidnapped, I understand.'

'Striker?' said Paterson. 'How the hell did you know that?'

'I know lots of things, Mr Paterson. Lots of things. One of those things is . . . Striker's not who you think he is.'

Paterson's phone rang. Simon Fox sounded concerned and asked if Paterson could come to him. 'Hold on,' he said. He pressed the mute button on his phone. 'Mr Forrest. This is a personal call, I'm afraid. I have to take it. Can we pick this conversation up later?'

Forrest looked at him with suspicion. 'Of course. In the meantime, if you could get someone to show me where your office is, please.'

'It's the second star on the right an' straight on 'til mornin', son,' said Clocks. 'Watch out for beanstalks on yer way.'

'Not today, Mr Forrest,' said Paterson. 'Look, this is important. Come back and I promise you can have access. We won't hide anything from you. Mostly because we don't have anything to hide as yet. Early days.'

Forrest looked at Paterson as if trying to work out whether he was being truthful or not. Eventually, he nodded. 'I'll be seeing you both.'

Clocks smiled as Forrest walked away. 'I love this.'

'Love what?'

'When they do as they're told.'

## CHAPTER 26

Paterson unmuted the phone. 'Sorry about that, Mr Fox. I had a very large problem that needed to be dealt with. Done now. Listen, I can't keep coming to see you every two minutes. I've got a ton of stuff to do and I'm up to my eyes. Can it wait?'

'No.' Fox's tinny telephone voice irritated Paterson more than his real voice. 'I have something that you're going to want to see.'

'Can't you tell me what it is?'

'Yes, I can, but you're still going to want to come and see.'

'Maybe. What is it?'

'It's a note.'

'From?'

'I have no idea, but it was addressed to Striker.'

'And . . .'

'It just has one word written on it.'

'Tell me.'

Fox did. Paterson hung up.

'Whassup with 'im, then?' said Clocks.

'We need to get over there. Now.'

'What? Why?'

'He's got a note.'

'What? A note? Who from? 'Is mum?'

'He doesn't know, but it's not his mum.'

'So we've gotta slap all the way over to Kennington again?'

'It's evidence.'

Clocks looked disgruntled. 'We seriously 'ave to join Sam Morne's bandoliers. Won't need any evidence working for 'is little firm. Fannyin' about, drivin' 'alfway across London for "evidence". Got better things to do.'

'Maybe,' said Paterson, 'but this note ties in with what we saw at the flat. Maybe we can get a clue or fingerprints off of it.'

Clocks snorted. 'Got more chance of gettin' 'is finger-prints offa my arse, mate. We both know it an' all. No one leaves dabs anymore, thanks to them bloody CSI programmes on the box. Not like in the ol' days when nobody knew sod all about forensics, eh? Times 'ave changed, for sure.'

'John.'

'What?'

'Shut up, will you? You're like an old woman. You know that?'

'I do. Only 'cos you keep telling me. Otherwise, I wouldn't have a clue.'

'Well, you are. So, shut up a minute.'

'Er, rude,' said Clocks.

It took them the best part of forty-five minutes to make their way through the traffic and park up in the CCTV compound. 'This place is beginning to feel a bit like home,' said Paterson.

'I know what you mean,' said Clocks. 'Nowhere near as posh, though.'

Paterson looked up at the building. Built in 2001, it was somewhat out of place with the rest of the buildings that sat side by side. They were of the 1970s variety and were showing their age. Most of them were in desperate need of a spruce-up. What was once white stonework was now a grimy greyish colour with darker stripes of grey running down in separate streaks, the result of many years of rainfall.

This building was built mostly of glass with panels running floor to ceiling from the foyer to the first floor and onwards.

Inside his office, Fox pointed to the note on his desk, a white envelope slit neatly open lying next to it. Paterson craned his neck around to get a better look at the note. 'Anyone touched it?'

'A few people, yes. The receptionist and message boy touched the envelope and I opened it and took out the note.'

'Message boy?' said Clocks.

'Um-hm.'

'What d'you mean, *message boy*?'

Fox looked confused, unsure how best to answer. 'It's a boy who collects our messages.'

'Seriously? You can't jump in the lift and get it yerself?'

'Well . . .' Fox seemed genuinely unsure what to say. Clearly, no one had ever questioned it before and it was just a generally accepted thing in this building.

'Christ . . .' Clocks seemed more than a little irritated. 'That where we are now? Senior managers are too bleedin' lazy to get off their fat arses to go an' get a message? I thought that sort of shit died out with Charlie?'

'Charlie?' said Fox. 'I'm sorry, I don't—'

'Dickens. Charlie Dickens. Local boy. Lived in Southwark. Wrote a few books. Mostly borin' but *A Christmas Carol* was a stonker. I think that was 'is breakout novel. Can't remember. Anyway, that's the sort of thing 'e wrote about in 'is books and that was back in the sixteen 'undreds.'

Paterson threw him a sharp, sideways glance. 'Eighteen hundreds, John.'

'Was it?' Clocks shrugged. 'Way before my time, anyway. An' 'is books used to 'ave chimney sweeps all singin' an' dancin' on the rooftops, if I remember rightly.'

Paterson shook his head. 'You don't. That was P.L. Travers. She wrote *Mary Poppins*. That had the sweeps in it.'

'Potato, potato,' said Clocks.

Paterson grimaced. Why couldn't he get it? What was so difficult? 'Anyway, all that aside, we're going to have to get elimination fingerprints from both of you, okay?'

Fox nodded.

'When was it delivered, do we know?' Paterson asked.

'About an hour ago.'

'Why did you open it?'

'Policy. We can't use this place as an address for the delivery of mail.'

'It's not mail though, is it?' said Clocks. 'Ain't got no stamp on it.'

'Doesn't matter. We still class it as mail. Policy is to open anything before we pass it on, just in case.'

'In case what?'

'In case there's something in it that may not be in the best interest of the company.'

Clocks frowned. 'Like what?'

'Like someone might be being asked to do something illegal, so we'd need to know about it.'

'Is Striker being asked to do anythin' illegal?' said Clocks.

'Er, no.'

'Then why'd you open it?'

Fox looked confused again. A state of mind that was becoming the norm whenever he spoke to Johnny Clocks. 'If . . . if I didn't open it, then I wouldn't know if it was illegal, would I?'

Clocks tapped the side of his nose a couple of times. 'Exactly. At this point, that is what we in the Met call the Schrodinger's Cat equation.'

Paterson looked at him, bemused.

'I . . . I'm sorry, I don't understand.' Fox looked at Paterson for help. None came.

'There was a professor once who slung a cat in a box an' 'e had this idea that until you looked in the box you couldn't know for sure if it was dead or alive.'

'What about if it meowed?' said Fox. 'Then you'd know.'

Clocks looked at him for a second. 'I must 'ave left some-thin' out. Either that or you just fucked up two 'undred years of theoretical physics. But anyway, this is like that.'

Fox shook his head, clearly bewildered.

'You checked the CCTV downstairs in the foyer?' said Paterson, keen to bring the conversation back to a sensible level.

Fox was glad of the question. 'I've had it sent to my computer. I asked for video from eight this morning until I opened the note.'

Paterson smiled. 'Excellent. We'll have a quick dash through it now. See if there's anyone looking a bit dodgy on it. John?'

'Yeah?'

'Got an evidence bag with you?'

'As it 'appens, no. You?'

Paterson shook his head.

'I'll get one before you leave,' said Fox.

'Ta,' said Clocks, not in the least bit embarrassed that both of them looked unprepared.

Clocks walked around the side of the table and looked at the note again. One word . . . *Retribution*.

# CHAPTER 27

'Oi-oi! What we got 'ere?' Clocks pointed to a figure on the screen. This was the first sighting of anything worthwhile since they started looking at the CCTV of the foyer twenty minutes earlier.

Paterson and Fox leaned in. Walking from the direction of the main doors was what looked like a man. Paterson looked at the top right of the screen. It showed the date and a time of 08:05. The man was dressed in a large black puffer jacket and wore gloves. His hood was pulled up, shielding most of his face and he was careful to keep the rest of it angled down. He didn't appear to be in a hurry when he walked in but wasn't prepared to wait behind the two people, a man and a woman, queuing at the reception desk. He cut past them, and from the way he moved he looked like he was apologising for cutting in. He touched the man lightly on the arm, nodded and dropped the letter on the desk in front of the receptionist. They had a brief conversation before the man turned and left the building.

'Any cameras outside?' said Clocks.

'Um-hm.' Fox pressed a button and the picture changed to show the outside of the main doors. The man exited but still kept his head down. Fox clicked another button. This

154

showed the man cross the main road, but that was the extent of the coverage.

'Any more?' said Paterson.

'Not in the immediate vicinity,' said Fox. 'But if we can say he's our main suspect, I can get someone on it and track his movements via every other camera on the streets. Can't guarantee we can see him all the time, there are still a few dead spots around here, but we might touch lucky. Happy to give it a try.'

'Do that for me. Far as I'm concerned, this guy is our prime suspect. Send me a copy of these clips, please, and call me if you can trace his movements. Double urgent if you manage to house him.'

Fox chortled. 'I don't think we'll get that lucky but I'll certainly give it a try.'

'Nice one,' said Clocks.

'Can I just ask,' said Fox. 'What did you find in Chris's flat?' His face bore the look of a man who was genuinely concerned.

'Can't tell you everything, obviously, but let's just say it looked like there was a fair old punch-up in there.'

Fox nodded. 'Jesus.'

'Probably not 'im,' said Clocks. 'S'posed to be a pacifist, wasn't 'e?'

'Who? Chris?' said Fox.

'Jesus. Not a fighter from what I hear, so I doubt it was him.'

'You're an odd sort for a copper, Mr Clocks,' said Fox.

Clocks grinned. 'Funny you should say that. Others have said the same. Can't think why. I'm an absolute delight.'

'Do you know if he's upset anyone lately?' said Paterson.

Fox shook his head. 'Chris? No. He's a pretty decent sort of a guy, to be honest. Never rude or nasty to anyone. All of his colleagues like him. I've never had to bollock him for anything. He's not perfect, but he's all right, y'know?'

Paterson sighed. 'Is he married? Divorced?'

'Not that I'm aware of. Doesn't have a wife, but as for divorced, he's never made mention if he is. You thinking ex-wife and new lover got upset with him for some reason?'

'I wasn't, no. But now . . . We'll look into it. Will those video clips be on my tablet by the time I get back?'

'Already there,' said Fox.

# CHAPTER 28

'What's the plan, Stan?' said Clocks as he clicked his seat belt into place.

'This bloke looks like he could be a favourite. We'll need to see if the lab techs can knock up some kind of profile for us from what they can see — height, age, gait, that sort of stuff.'

'You'd think we'd 'ave super-duper technology now that can look at that vid and go, "Yeah, that's Bert Fegg of 42 Acacia Avenue, Bermondsey. Got a wife, four kids, two dogs an' a parrot."'

Paterson watched the road ahead of him. He'd spotted a cyclist and knew from old that Clocks wasn't a fan of them. He knew he'd have to try and distract him.

'There's no program that can do that, John. How could it?'

Clocks shrugged. 'I dunno, do I? Got all sorts of whizzbang tech these days, ain't they? Might 'ave something like that. Bet the Chinese 'ave. They're up to all sorts, that firm. Probably listenin' to us now.'

'Doubt it.'

Clocks shrugged again. 'We'll never know, will we? That's the point. Ray?'

'What?'

'Give that little fucker on the bike a nudge for me, will yer?'

'What? No.'

'Go on. Just a little tap. Put the shits up 'im.'

'What's wrong with you? Why do you hate cyclists so much?'

Clocks scrunched up his face. 'I don't 'ate 'em. Just don't like 'em. Think they own the fuckin' road in their poncey little lycra sweat suits dreaming they're at Lemons . . .'

'Lemons?'

'Yeah, Lemons.'

'You mean Le Mans, don't you?'

'Le Mans. Is that what it's called? I thought it was Lemons.'

'It's Le Mans, you div, and why would they want to be there? That's a bloody twenty-four-hour sports car race. Nothing to do with cycles.'

Clocks sniffed. 'Don't matter now. We've passed 'im.'

'Good. Back to work, then. We send a copy to the lab boys and see if they can sort anything out for us and we'll circulate a few stills to all surrounding stations. That'll get the ball rolling for a start.'

'You got any theories yet?' said Clocks.

Paterson shook his head. 'Not yet. From what Fox said back there, it seems our Mr Striker was an all-round good egg. Sounds like he lived a quiet life to me.'

'Musta fucked somebody off in the past, then, and they've come to square 'im up. I mean, you don't stick a picture up an' leave a note like that for shits an' giggles, do yer?'

'Wouldn't have thought so. Strange word to use though, don't you think? *Retribution*. Why not *payback* or *revenge* or *vengeance*, although that last one is just as dramatic as retribution, I suppose.'

'Ray, I think any word with more than three syllables in it is strange and this one's got five in it.'

'Four,' said Paterson.

Clocks frowned and went quiet for a few seconds. 'Oh yeah, you're right. Four.'

'That's what a very expensive education does for you. Only the best, eh?'

Clocks chuckled. 'You're right, though. It's an odd word to use. Think it means anything, apart from revenge and vengeance, like you said? I mean, think it means something specific to him?'

'Time will tell, John. Time will tell.'

'Yep. It will.'

Clocks shot forward in his seat. 'There.'

Paterson jerked on the steering wheel involuntarily.

'What? What is it?'

Clocks pointed out the window. 'There's that bastard cyclist. Must've cut across a couple of lanes to get 'imself there. Let's 'ave 'im.'

'Tch. Let's not. Frightened the crap out of me there, for Chrissakes. I thought you'd seen something important — and don't say you did. You didn't. I think your next session with the shrink best be about your desire to murder cyclists.'

'Should be 'ave 'emselves then an' stop thinking they're the kings of the road.'

'John?'

'Don't start, Ray.'

'What d'you mean?'

'I can tell by the tone of your voice. You're gonna go on about me mum, right?'

'I was going to ask if you're okay. I mean, the joking's shot up a level and I'm worried you're using it as a shield.'

'I am. I'll be fine. Don't worry.'

'John . . .'

'Leave it, Ray! I know you're only tryin' to 'elp, an' I appreciate it, I do. But lemme deal with this in my own way, all right? If I need you, I'll let you know. Okay?'

Paterson nodded. 'Okay. Make sure you do.'

'I will. Thanks, Mum.' Clocks realised what he'd said and chuckled. So did Paterson. 'Ah, what can you do?' He turned to look at Paterson. 'I'll be fine, mate.'

Nothing else was said.

# CHAPTER 29

'Shall we resume our conversation, gentlemen?' Forrest said.

Paterson pulled his chair back out and sat down. Clocks remained standing.

'We got off to a bad start, Mr Paterson. My fault. I can be a tad . . . *authoritative* sometimes. Comes with my particular job.'

Paterson said nothing.

'What do you know about Christopher Striker?' Forrest asked.

'Not a great deal,' said Paterson. 'All I know is that he's a senior supervisor of the CCTV team over at Kennington. Seems to be a quiet guy without too many friends, no family and, as far as we know, no known enemies. I suspect you're about to tell me otherwise, though.'

Forrest gave Paterson a wry little smile and launched into his tale.

'Christopher Striker was a special forces operative for the British government until an injury put him out of the service. He took this job because his training taught him to put his head down and not show out. To you and his team, he's a meek and mild chap who just comes to work, does his job and

160

goes home at the end of his shift. Doesn't cause any bother, doesn't make waves, minds his P's and Q's — a good chap. To us, he's one of the most lethal operatives we ever had. Skilled in hand-to-hand combat, weapons and explosives trained, surveillance instructor level, drone pilot. You name it, he's killed it. Outwardly, you're right about no known enemies, Mr Paterson. But some of us are in the know, and his enemies are in the shitloads. And they are absolutely wicked bastards.'

'What 'appened to 'im, then?' said Clocks.

'Wounded out. Shot in the thigh while on an undercover mission in Iraq. Bullet hit him in the wrong place. Damaged nerves and muscles. You wouldn't know it to look at him — he walks fine — but the injury slowed him down. He lost a lot of his edge while he was in recovery and, as I say, the injury took care of the rest. He just wasn't his old self. We offered him several jobs suitable to his talents but he opted out and called it a day. Bloody shame, really.'

'And his kidnapping?'

'What about it?' said Forrest.

'Couple of things. First, how did you know about it, and second, do you have anyone in mind for it?'

Forrest sat himself back in his chair. 'Because of their background, skills and clearance level, the military keep an eye on certain operatives to make sure they don't do anything naughty with what they know and also to protect them from enemies who may wish to talk to them or simply kill them. The killing . . . well, that's just a part of the life and would be accepted. It's the possibility of them talking that bothers us.'

'You're thinking that's the case here? To get information out of him?'

'Seems a distinct possibility at this stage of the game.'

'So, what's 'e know that's likely to get 'im swagged off?'

'I can't tell you that, Mr Clocks. Classified, I'm afraid.'

'Is it? Well, if you want our 'elp, you better unclassify it and cough up some info a bit lively and stop all the secret squirrel shit.'

'Listen, I really don't need your help at all, Mr Clocks. My superiors told me to work with you as a professional courtesy.'

'Your what?' If there was one thing Clocks couldn't stand it was the notion of one man being superior to another. Different ranks, yes. Different lives, yes, but that didn't make a man superior. 'Oh, you're one of them, eh?'

'One of what?' said Forrest.

'One of those who thinks 'e's better than others 'cos of his rank.'

'That's not what I meant. It's just a term of respect for a higher rank.'

'It's just bullshit if you ask me. We're all the same, mate.'

'Thank you, Comrade Clocks.' Forrest's voice contained more than a hint of sarcasm. 'I appreciate the lecture on communism, brother.'

Clocks bristled. 'Listen up, big boy. I'm no fuckin' commie, but I don't believe anyone is superior to anyone else, so fuck you and fuck your bullshit.'

Forrest banged both hands on the desk so loudly that Paterson and Clocks both jumped. He stood up fast and knocked his chair over in the movement. 'That is enough, Clocks. I'm your superior officer and you—'

Paterson had sprung from his own chair by the time Forrest had uttered his first word. Clocks readied himself.

'Sit down,' Paterson said. 'Before I put you down.'

Forrest turned to face Paterson, eyes blazing with anger. Paterson stood his ground. Clocks backed up against the wall. He'd seen that look on Paterson before.

'What did you say?'

Paterson's voice was quiet, controlled, calm. 'You heard me. Now, listen. It seems like we're all going to have a bit of a tough time getting on with each other. That's just the way it is. But let me tell you now. You are not the senior officer in this room and you don't ever even think of assaulting my officer. If you do, if you try, then trust me when I say I will damage you. D'you understand? Please say you understand

162

because I've had a long couple of days. I'm tired and grumpy and I really don't want to have to educate you on the necessity of being nice to both of us. However, if you wish to continue along your current path, again, I will damage you. Clear?'

Forrest snorted his derision. 'Paterson, it's only because of your rank and the fact that I've been ordered to work with you that I don't snap you in half.'

Paterson nodded and turned his mouth down. 'Well, I appreciate your restraint. Must be hard for you. Let's just get on with the job of finding out who kidnapped Striker and why, shall we? We don't have time for a pissing contest.'

Forrest gave a sharp nod of the head and turned to look at Clocks. 'You, I don't like.'

Clocks shrugged. 'Oh, no. Whatever will I do? The big ol' lump of dopey don't like me.'

Paterson knew he should stop Clocks from goading the big man but there was a part of him that wanted Forrest to kick off.

'Okay, glad that's over,' Paterson said. 'Now, given the picture we found at Striker's flat and the note, do you think that our four suicides have anything to do with Striker being taken?'

'Honestly?' said Forrest. 'I don't have the first clue.'

Paterson nodded and pulled out his phone. He scrolled to the picture from Fox's CCTV. 'Any ideas?'

Forrest looked closely then shook his head.

'This man delivered a note to Striker's place of work,' said Paterson. 'Same word as the one we found in the kitchen . . . *Retribution*.'

Forrest looked again. 'Not going to be easy getting a clear image. Head's down all of the time. Like he knows where the cameras are.'

'Hmm,' said Paterson. 'Could be. Could be someone who works in the office, I suppose.'

'Could be Striker himself,' said Forrest.

Clocks frowned. 'Why would 'e kidnap 'imself?'

Forrest shook his head. 'He hasn't kidnapped himself, has he? But he might have made it look like he'd been kidnapped.'

'You saying he faked it? His own kidnapping?'

'I'm saying it's possible, yes.'

'So, next question is why,' said Paterson.

'Probably because he was involved in the four suicides. While he's got you all running about looking in the wrong direction for a kidnap victim that doesn't exist, there's a good chance he's using that time to get himself out of the country.

'Ooh. Slippery bastard,' said Clocks. 'I'll 'ave 'im for that.'

# CHAPTER 30

Paterson's entire team were gathered together for his briefing. 'Okay,' he said. 'Before we get started, the gentleman at the back of the room is Mr Jack Forrest. He is an MP for the army. He has a vested interest in this case and has given us some much-needed intelligence that will push us forward. Mr Forrest, would you please come up here?' He beckoned the man forward.

Forrest picked up his briefcase, pushed himself off of his seat and headed toward the front of the room. As he walked, all heads turned in his direction. His sheer size gave him a commanding presence. Few would have wanted to go up against him. Even Clocks, if truth be told.

Standing next to Paterson, Forrest nodded in acknowledgement. 'Thank you,' he began in a deep, commanding voice. 'As Mr Paterson mentioned, my name is Jack Forrest and I work for the special investigations unit of the army.' He paused for a moment, his gaze sweeping across the room. 'If you're not yet aware, Christopher Striker was one of our own. He was an exceptional operator until an injury forced him into early retirement.'

Forrest's words hung heavily in the air as he revealed information about Striker's background and involvement in the case. 'Because of his skills and knowledge, the military run a watch program on people like him and we of course knew of his whereabouts and what he did for a living. When we heard about your clutch of suicides, we became deeply concerned. And once we discovered that one of the victims was Oliver Hayes, we knew there was more at play here.

'Christopher Striker was in a relationship with Oliver Hayes for some two years. Hayes worked for the government in a very sensitive capacity and had the highest security clearance. He was a married man who had a peccadillo for younger men. Of course, when he took his own life, we were . . . alarmed. There was no reason to suspect that he would do such a thing, no indicators to suggest he was heading that way. So, it seemed odd. It's possible, of course, that Striker was upset about the relationship. Maybe Hayes wouldn't leave his family, and Striker decided to take his revenge against him and somehow coerce him into taking his own life. Maybe he threatened to tell his wife and maybe the press.'

'Seems a bit strong,' said Monkey Harris. 'And what about the other three? What do they have to do with it?'

Forrest shrugged his shoulders, causing his jacket to rise up. 'As far as we know so far, nothing. It looks like he used them as a cover to divert the blame away from himself.'

'But if he was in a relationship with Hayes, he must have known he'd be found out. All he was doing was delaying the inevitable. Seems a bit unnecessary to me.'

Paterson stepped in. 'I tend to agree with you, Monkey, but we can't rule it out as a possibility yet. However, something else has happened today that has thrown us a bit.'

Everyone in the office was looking intently at Paterson. 'Striker never went to work today, so Clocksy and I went to his home address. We found signs of a struggle and this . . .' He clicked a button on the remote and the picture of Striker flashed up on the screen. 'And this.' The note appeared. 'So, it looks like Striker may have been kidnapped — and I stress the word *may*. Mr Forrest here put forward the idea that the scene may have been staged by Striker himself in order to keep us busy while he buggers off out of the country.'

'There is also this . . .' said Forrest. The CCTV clip played. 'This was taken at Striker's place of work. It's another note that just says *Retribution*. We can't see the face of whoever delivered it, so we don't know who he is. But given the fact that he keeps his head down all the time, it makes me suspicious that he knows exactly where the cameras are. We're not sure, but there's a good chance that's Striker himself, laying down another part of a false trail.'

'Slippery bastard,' said Monkey. Clocks smiled.

'All righty, then,' said Clocks. 'We need someone to go to the LTMS and speak with whoever took that note. Hopefully they can tell us if it was Striker or, if not, what the geezer looked like. Georgie'll sort out who's doin' that before you leave.'

'In the meantime,' said Paterson, 'we're going to need eyes on the street to see if Striker shows up. I want all airports and marine ports checked. Get a picture of Striker circulated to all forces in the county and get them to keep a close eye on ways out of the UK. I want to know of anything suspicious — *anything*. As of now, Christopher Striker is our number-one suspect for the murder of four people. If there are no questions, get to work. Mr Carter, you and Grace . . . a word in my office, please.'

Carter nodded. There was a shuffling and scraping of chairs as Paterson's team made themselves ready to leave.

'Mr Forrest . . .' said Paterson. 'Go and get yourself a cup of tea and we'll meet you in the canteen in about ten minutes. I need to talk to DI Carter.'

Forrest looked suspicious. 'This is the second time you've sent me out of the room, Paterson. Not up to anything, are you? Not cutting me out of intel, by any chance?'

Paterson looked him in the eye. 'No chance at all. I said we'd work with you and we will. DI Carter and DS Winslet were seconded to my team when Clocks needed time off, but as you can see, he's back, so I need to debrief them, thank them for their time and send them back to their normal duties. Ten minutes. That okay?'

Forrest continued to look suspicious, but Paterson knew his story was plausible. 'I'll see you soon, then.'

# CHAPTER 31

'Sir?' said Harry Carter as he and Winslet stepped into Paterson's office. 'Everything all right?'

'Come in, come in. Shut the door please, Grace.' She did so. 'Take a seat, the pair of you.' They pulled out a couple of chairs and sat opposite Paterson. Clocks stood behind Paterson as he dragged out a chair and sat behind his desk.

'What d'you think, then?' said Paterson.

Harry shrugged. 'About?'

'Forrest. What d'you think about what he said?'

Harry took a deep breath. 'Truth?'

'Yes, the truth, Harry. What did you think of his story? Both of you.'

'Personally, sir,' said Grace. 'I think he's full of shit.'

'What she said,' said Harry.

'Told yer,' said Clocks. 'Why d'yer think that?'

'Doesn't feel right,' said Harry. 'Seems a bit like this was all . . . thought out beforehand. As if he was delivering a speech dressed up as a briefing. I've heard that sort of thing before from people like him.'

Paterson drummed his fingers on the desk as he thought. 'Grace, d'you agree?'

'Hundred percent, sir. He was too ready. Didn't look uncertain of himself at any point, and we all know that if we're only working up theories then we're far from certain about anything.'

'Good point,' said Paterson. 'So, if we think he's full of shit, the question is *why*. What's his motive for sending us off on a wander round the houses?'

'Well, and I'm just throwing this out there,' said Grace. 'Maybe Forrest killed him.'

The room was silent for a moment as the thought settled in.

'Why would 'e do that, Gracie?' said Clocks.

'Well, that's the big question, isn't it? Whatever it is, I'll bet it's a whole lot more to do with this Oliver Hayes bloke than it is to do with Striker. I mean, Forrest is military, Hayes was government and Striker was ex-military. Could be Forrest had to do Hayes in for some reason and Forrest is trying to fit Striker up for his death. I mean, if they were in a clandestine relationship . . . I dunno. Just a thought.'

'Okay, good enough for me,' said Paterson. 'John?'

'I think she's on the mark, Ray.'

'Okay. Thank you. We were thinking along the same lines and you've just confirmed it for us. As of now, as far as we're concerned, Forrest is our number-one suspect, not Striker. I'll let my core team know, but for now, we go along with him while we try to figure out what he's up to. We'll keep looking for Striker, of course, but between us, we need to keep an eye on Forrest. Let's bear in mind he's a clever man with an attitude and built like two brick shithouses standing side by side. He's also as paranoid as fuck, which means he's worried. A worried man is a dangerous man.

'I told him you two were off the team now John's back and were going back to normal duties. You're not, of course, but what I want is for you to pack up and make it look like you're going back to normal duties. And stay out of the way; I think this has the potential to turn nasty when we find out what he's up to. If it does, I want at least two people I can trust to pick up the baton if it goes south for us. Harry, can you run deep background checks on Forrest and Striker for me, please?'

Carter nodded. 'Yep. Will do.'

'Sir,' said Grace, a little agitated. 'You will be all right, won't you? I mean, surely it would be better if we were with you. Strength in numbers and all that.'

Paterson smiled at her. 'We'll be fine, Grace. Thank you for your concern. But no. I need you to do as I ask and keep your heads down. I don't want to take a chance on either of you getting hurt.'

'Jesus wept!' said Clocks. 'Get a fuckin' room, you two.'

# CHAPTER 32

'So, how are we going to find out if he's telling us porkies, then?' said Clocks after Carter and Winslet had left the office.

'Well, I think we're going to have to take a look in that briefcase of his. We know he's got a laptop in there, and I think that's gonna tell us everything we need to know.'

'Yeah, that sounds like a plan to me,' said Clocks. 'So 'ow we gonna get 'old of that, then?'

'Dunno yet. I'll think of something.'

'Better do it a bit sharpish, before 'e buggers off into the sunset.'

'I will. Don't rush me.'

'I'm not rushin' yer, but sometimes you gotta move a bit livelier than you do. You're so slow, guv, I'm starting to think you might be French.'

'Don't start. I've got to get this right.'

'What's to get right? We break into 'is gaff when e's out, nick the laptop an' 'ave a little butcher's at what's on it.'

Paterson nodded and smirked at Clocks. 'You're absolutely right. Why didn't I think of that?'

'Dunno, mate. You're the senior man 'ere.'

'There's a flaw in your plan though, John.'

'Where?'

'Every-fucking-where! Break in, nick his laptop and have a look at it! How easy d'you think that'll be? D'you not think his place is going to be belled up to the eyeballs? State-of-the-art system. And what? He's just going to leave his laptop laying around on the sofa so we can find it?'

Clocks sniffed. 'All right. Don't need to show off. I admit that we're gonna 'ave to plan it out a bit, but the principle's sound, innit?'

'Yes. The principle is sound. We're just going to need some help.'

'Who from?'

'Well, who do we know that's any good with computers and doesn't mind bending the law a little bit?'

'Dunno. I don't know any dodgy computer geezers.'

'Think harder,' said Paterson.

Clocks gave it a little bit of thought before the light went on. 'Oh, no. Are you thinkin' about who I'm thinkin' about?'

'Depends who you're thinking about, I suppose.'

'You know exactly who I'm thinkin' about.'

'Alice?' said Paterson.

'That's the very fella,' said Clocks. 'Why 'ave we got to use 'im? 'E freaks me out, y'know? All that dressin' up like a baby an' wearing women's clothes an' all that shit. It's not right. You know it ain't.'

'Couple of things there, John. First, do you know anybody else that might be able to do this?'

'No, but that's not the point.'

'So what is the point?'

'The point is there must be someone else, anybody else we can use. What about Barry out of PC World? Y'know? Spotty kid with a badge an' no fuckin' idea of anythin' when you ask 'im. Let's get 'im. At least Barry's not gonna show up wearin' a fuckin' miniskirt an' a crop top over 'is bleedin' great fat 'airy beer belly.'

'Who the fuck is Barry?'

'Barry's a metaphor.'

'Word app again?'

'Yeah. Been dyin' to use that one.'

'Your trouble is that you have a closed mind and you're not giving Alice his due. He's a technical genius. That's why he's working with Wol and his little band of mercenaries.'

'No. You're wrong. My trouble is 'e frightens the granny out of me. I can't get me 'ead around it, an' it don't matter 'ow many diversity courses you put me on, I never will. Walkin' into that flat an' seein' all them geezers dressed up in nappies did me in fer life.'

'Well, you're going to have to buckle up, mate, because I don't have anyone else on speed dial.'

'All right, all right. Do what you want, but if we 'ave to walk into anywhere an' e's breastfeedin' grown men in nappies again, I'm out of it. Fair enough?'

'Yep. Fair enough,' said Paterson. 'But if you recall rightly, he wasn't breastfeeding anybody.'

Clocks cocked his head. 'No. Thinkin' about it, you're right. It wasn't 'im. It was that freaky bird with the big jubblies he 'ad working for 'im. The one that wanted to give you a squirt of 'er thruppenny-bit milk in yer tea while 'e was tucked up changin' some senior judge's nappy, the fuckin' freakazoid.'

'Oh, yeah, I remember her. I opted for a glass of water in the end. Went right off the idea of tea.'

'Not bleedin' surprised. So, how you gonna get hold of 'im?'

'I'll give Wol a bell. With a bit of luck, she'll be in London somewhere.'

'What? You just said *she*? You said *he* a minute ago.'

'Did I?'

'You did.'

'I meant *she*.'

'All right, look. I 'onestly don't care what 'e wants to be called, I don't. But I'm confused by it all, Ray. Is that what 'e

174

wants to be called, then? She? I mean . . . I don't know what to do, mate.'

'Honestly? I don't know what to call him. We'll just ask. And that's the other point, too, that I wanted to mention. I heard a whisper that Alice is going in for full gender reassignment. Don't know if it's true, but if it is, then it's obviously *she* from now on.'

Clocks shook his head. 'An' that right there . . . that's the bleedin' trouble these days. Nobody knows what the fuck's goin' on anymore. I can't keep up with it. I'm terrified I'll upset someone.'

'Ha!' Paterson exclaimed. 'You? Since when have you ever been terrified of upsetting anyone? You don't give a shit at the best of times. I mean, these days must be a dream for you. Back in the day you only had black and Asian people and the odd gay—'

'Simpler times, mate.'

'And the odd gay person to piss off, but now, now you've got a whole sweetie shop of people to pick from. The future's been good to you, hasn't it?'

Clocks flashed his eyebrows. 'Yeah, I s'pose so. Never thought about it that way before. See, there you go! I learned somethin' from all those race an' diversity punishment classes you sent me on. Turns out I'm an equal-opportunities piss-taker.'

'You're a dick.'

'Thank you. Phone Wol.'

# CHAPTER 33

Paterson pulled over by the kerb, parked up and got out of the car. Johnny Clocks stepped out and looked around.

'So, he's still living in this old block of flats, then? Place is a bloody shit'ole. You think with all the money he's earned out of working with Wol and 'is sideline shenanigans, he'd 'ave got 'imself somewhere decent to live, not the fucking fifth floor of some poxy council flat.'

Paterson looked around and could see that Clocks had a point. This wasn't the most salubrious part of London to live by any means, but Paterson wasn't really sure whether this was Alice's main residence. He knew that Alice had made a lot of money over the years both from his computer skills and the unusual sidelines he had in catering for the certain tastes of certain gentlemen.

'Does it matter?' he said. 'We were lucky to get him.'

'Depends on your definition of lucky, I suppose.'

'Well, he is the only one that can help us, John, and he's certainly the only one that we can call on this time of night.'

Paterson pressed the intercom buzzer and waited. A familiar voice answered. 'Hello, boys! Come on up. I have the kettle on.'

Paterson frowned. The last time Alice offered him tea, the milk delivery system had an altogether too natural source of supply. The buzzer sounded and Clocks leaned his weight against the door. As soon as the door creaked open, a wall of stench hit them. The air was thick with the foul smell of stale urine and sweat, a pungent mix that made him wrinkle his nose. Underneath it all was a sickly sweet scent, lingering in the air like the aftermath of a wild party. Knee tremblers galore. The two men stepped inside the foyer. Paterson looked around.

'Oh, this is eighteen carat, ain't it?' Clocks's nose wrinkled in pure disgust. 'The fuck does 'e live 'ere for? Must 'ave a few quid, I'd a thought.'

'Exactly what I thought when we parked up. I suppose it keeps his clients well away from where he really lives, assuming this isn't where he really lives.'

Clocks pressed the call button for the lift. 'Bit bloody dangerous, though. I mean, 'is clients are all judges, MPs an' soft city boys, ain't they? Must be brickin' it wantin' to come 'ere for their jollies.'

'Perhaps that's all part of the thrill, eh? A little bit more of a frisson to go with what's to come.'

The lift door creaked open slowly and they stepped warily inside. Once more, Paterson wished they'd taken the stairs as the stale scent of urine flooded his nostrils.

'What's a frisson?' said Clocks. 'Is that like a rissole? I like them. Not sure I'd like a frisson.'

Paterson sighed. 'Google it later. I can tell you it's not food though.'

Clocks nodded as the door groaned open on the fifth floor. 'What numbers 'e livin' at?'

'Forty-two. About midway along the balcony. You remember, don't you? Wasn't that long ago that we came here.'

'Tell me about it. There's not enough time in the world for me to forget comin' 'ere, although I 'ad a go at resettin' me memory with a pointy stick jammed into one ear 'ole.'

Paterson laughed. Not too loudly, respectful of the time of night and the neighbours.

'Yeah. You stormed out of there, didn't you?'

'Yep. I 'ad to go and dip me eyes in a bucket of extra-strong bleach. I've never felt so dirty in me life. An' believe me, I've seen an' done some shit in my time that'll make yer 'air curl — but that . . . What was goin' on there, that fucked me 'ead right up. Post traumatic stress disorder, I got. Should've sued the job for that.'

'Christ, John. It was only men dressed up as babies.'

'What? *Only men dressed up as babies.* Can you not 'ear what that sounds like? An' you think that's all right?'

Paterson shrugged as they stood outside Alice's door. 'They're not harming anyone, are they?'

'Fuckin' 'armed me, mate. Never been the same since.'

Paterson tapped on the door. He shook his head at Clocks as they waited. Seconds later, Paterson saw the unforgettable shape of Alice through the frosted pane of glass set in the door. He heard the sound of a security chain being unhooked and the latch opening. Alice stood in the hallway in all his glory. Tonight, he wore a miniskirt over a pair of suspenders. His silk blouse was locked in mortal combat with his enormous gut and was in the late stages of defeat. He had a large number of chains around his neck, one or two of which were caught in fat folds, and he had a heavy application of make-up beneath his bright-red wig.

'Boys! Lovely to see you! Come in, come in!'

Paterson stepped inside. The flat was warm and a welcome relief from the cold night air outside.

'How are you, Ray?' Alice said.

'Yeah, I'm good thanks. How are you doing?'

'Oh, you know, busy.'

Clocks walked in, eyes down.

'Hello, Johnny boy! And how's my favourite copper?'

'Oh yeah. It's all tickety-boo, mate. All tickety-fuckin'-boo.' Clocks edged past him in the hallway.

'Oh! As happy as ever, I see. I forgot how much you liked to joke.'

'Not jokin', weirdo. You worry me, you do.'

'Well, better than being ignored. Go in, loves. Make yourselves comfortable.'

Paterson stood in the hallway. 'No time for that, Alice. Wol tell you what's going on?'

'He did, love, yes. You want me to help you break into someone's flat, find their laptop and take off all their juicy secrets, yes?'

'That's the gist of it, yes.'

'And where is our target?'

'Not too far from the nick.'

Clocks shuffled from foot to foot. 'We think he's in at the moment.'

'So . . . how do we break in and keep him asleep?'

'We're working on a plan to get him out of the flat.'

'At five in the morning?' Alice looked doubtful.

'We'll think of somethin',' said Clocks. 'It's what we do.'

'Well, I hope you're right, dear. I can't be getting into fights at my age and I definitely can't afford to have this face messed up.' Alice walked off toward the bathroom. 'Give me a few minutes to get changed. Make yourselves at home.'

Paterson and Clocks walked into the living room, their footsteps muffled by the plush carpeting that now adorned the floors. As they took in the lavish furnishings and tasteful decorations, Clocks couldn't help but frown. It was a far cry from their last visit. A small fortune had obviously been spent to transform the space into its current state of opulence. As Paterson surveyed the room, he couldn't help but wonder what had brought about this sudden change and whether any of the neighbours knew. He doubted it would remain this way for long if they did.

'Looks like 'e's gone all bourgeois on us,' Clocks muttered.

'That's gotta be the app talking,' said Paterson.

Clocks grinned. 'Strangely enough, it is.'

Paterson agreed with the assessment though. The transformation was jarring, and he couldn't help but feel a sense of slight apprehension. The heavy scent of shit that had been present during the flat's days as an adult nursery had been replaced with the delicate aroma of expensive candles dotted around the place and served to highlight the stark contrast between then and now.

Clocks looked around the room and shook his head. The memories were obviously lodged deep.

'Take a seat, John,' said Paterson. 'Looks like we're gonna be a bit longer than I'd hoped.'

Clocks frowned. 'Like fuck! I dunno what the fucker's been up to on those seats. I'll stand, thank you.'

'Everything's new, John. You can see that.'

'Yeah, I can see that. It's what I can't see that I'm worried about. Gawd knows what 'e's been up to in 'ere. No, I'll stand, thank you very much.'

Paterson knew better than to argue with him. He called out to Alice. 'So, what's the score, Alice? You out of the game now?'

'Sort of, love!' Alice called back. 'I don't entertain anywhere near as much as I used to, and as you can see, no more of the nursery stuff.'

'What happened, then?' said Clocks. 'Ofsted knock a few stars off, did they?'

Alice chuckled. 'I forgot how funny you can be, Clocksy. That was good.'

Clocks rubbed his face then looked at his watch. 'You gonna be much longer?'

'Couple of minutes, love. Be patient, eh? Take's a girl ages to get her face off.'

'Shouldn't 'ave put it on, should yer? You're a big 'airy geezer, not fuckin' Katie Price. Although . . .'

'You're wicked, you are. But I love you.'

'Oi, Alice, I 'ear tell you're goin' in for that gender reassignment. That true?'

'Yes, love. Problem?'

'Nope. Just wanna know for sure. Don't wanna misgender you.' He winked at Paterson. 'See, I'm evolvin'.'

'You won't, I'm sure. But, for the record, I prefer to be called *her/she*, if you want to know.'

Clocks wrinkled his nose and whispered to Paterson. 'That's a fuckin' American chocolate bar, innit? Hershey bars?'

Alice stepped out of the bathroom, but in Alice the sex worker's place stood Alice the mercenary computer hacker. Dressed head to foot in a black boiler suit, she walked into the living room and proceeded to pull on a pair of black trainers. On the floor was a black nylon bag containing a state-of-the-art laptop and a host of other pieces of electronic equipment that were the tools of her particular trade. She unzipped the bag and pushed a few things aside. 'Ah-ha! Got 'em!' She held up a pair of black gloves in one hand and a black balaclava in the other. 'Ready when you are, boys.' She picked up the bag and swung it over her shoulder before picking up her door keys from a china bowl she kept on a sideboard.

'Ray. This is why I'm confused,' said Clocks. 'She's a bloke who wants to be a woman, but she's dressed like a man. My fuckin' 'ead 'urts now.'

Paterson smiled. 'Hang in there, buddy. It's a brave new world we're living in. You'll get the hang of it.'

'You reckon? Oi! Alice! You do know we're only goin' burglin', don'tcha? We're not goin' out to assassinate anyone?'

'I know, Johnny boy, I know. It's just that I've always believed in dressing the part whatever the job. And tonight, I'm a burglar.'

Clocks shrugged as he pulled the street door closed behind him. 'You do know they only wear a striped jumper an' carry a bag marked *swag* over their shoulder. I mean, the black ninja look is so last year.'

Alice sashayed along the balcony looking fabulous. And a bit slimmer too.

# CHAPTER 34

Jack Forrest's rented flat was the total opposite of Alice's. It was nestled in the corner of the top floor of a three-storey block that contained six properties in total. The entrance to the flats was guarded by a keyless security system. As sophisticated as it was, it was never going to be a problem for somebody like Alice.

Paterson pulled out his phone and called Monkey Harris. Clocks looked around the streets. Everything seemed quiet. No curtains were twitching when they gently closed the car doors. This was a respectable part of Bermondsey.

'Monkey?' said Paterson. 'What's the score? Is he in or out?' He nodded a couple of times as Monkey Harris brought him up to speed. 'Cheers, mate. Keep an eye on the street for us and let me know if he comes back.' He hung up and turned to his two friends.

'Well?' said Clocks.

'He's out. Monkey saw him leave about half an hour ago.'

'Where's that little tinker off to at five in the mornin', I wonder?' said Clocks.

Paterson shrugged. 'Don't know, don't care, as long as he stays out until we're finished. Monkey reckons he's gone jogging. Shorts and a T-shirt, bottle of water.'

'Touch!' said Clocks. 'Let's 'ave it, then. Alice, you're up.'

'Oh, darling,' said Alice, 'you'd know if I was up, trust me.'

'Oooh!' said Clocks. 'No need for filth, is there?'

Alice grinned and headed toward the security door. She kept her bag over her shoulder as she stood in front of the keyless pad. Clocks watched as she reached out one hand and pressed a button. Alice pulled out a small, thin electronic device from inside her trouser pocket, switched it on and rubbed it twice on the pad. Paterson saw a little green light flash for a second and Alice pulled the door open. She stepped inside, followed by Paterson and then Clocks.

'That was a bit fast,' said Clocks.

'It wasn't complicated,' said Alice. 'Lots of these places boast security systems that don't deliver, but your average renter doesn't know that. He thinks he's safe. He's not.'

'Where'd you get that little box from?'

'This?' Alice held it up. 'I made it.'

'Yeah?' said Clocks. 'Can you make me one?'

Alice cocked her head. 'It'll cost you.'

'Oh yeah? 'Ow much?'

'Who said anything about money?' A cheeky grin flashed across her lips.

'Fuck that,' said Clocks. 'I'll stick to me sledge'ammer.'

'Up the stairs, folks,' said Paterson. 'You can manage a couple of flights, John, before you start moaning.'

'Wasn't gonna moan,' said Clocks.

'I believe the expression you use is, "my arse is a banjo,"' said Paterson.

Alice's eyes lit up. 'Is it? I know a few tunes we could play on it.'

Clocks pointed a finger at Alice. 'You be'ave yerself. No chance you're gettin' any of this jelly.' He smiled as he turned away. Although Alice had initially freaked him out, he'd got to know her, and despite the jokes and insults, he actually liked her. But he was damned if he was going to jeopardise his image.

The three of them climbed the stairs, Paterson in front. Clocks went last, not trusting Alice to keep her hands to herself. At the top of the stairs, Paterson stood aside to let Alice take a look at the door.

'What d'you think? How long d'you think it'll take you to crack it?'

Alice cocked her head from side to side a few times. 'A minute, maybe less.'

'Jesus,' said Paterson. 'What about an alarm?'

'I have just the thing.' She pulled out a small scanner from inside her backpack and turned it on. She held it at arm's length and watched the small e-ink screen scroll through a repeating set of numbers until it stopped. The screen showed the door number, the name of the block and a seven-digit number. Alice pressed a button and a small green light flashed. 'Disabled and door open,' she said.

Clocks frowned. 'Really?'

'Really.'

'I gotta get me one of them,' said Clocks as he pushed his way to the front.

'Let's go,' said Paterson.

Clocks pushed the door open tentatively. Forrest might have been out but that wasn't to say there was nobody else in. All three entered the flat and bunched themselves up in the hallway. Last in, Paterson closed the door behind him.

'Anyone got a torch?' Clocks whispered.

'No,' said Paterson.

'Didn't think we'd needed one,' said Alice.

'Really? A five-o'clock entry and you never thought to bring a torch?' said Clocks.

'Er, excuse me,' Alice whispered. 'You're the policeman.'

'Use your phones,' said Paterson.

'Fuck this,' said Clocks as he snapped on the hall light. 'Hello!'

Paterson looked mortified. 'The fuck are you doing?'

'Seein' where I'm goin'.'

184

'What if someone sees the light's on?'

'What if someone sees a torch beam flyin' about the room? That's a bit more sus than 'avin' the light on, I'da thought.'

'I'll give you that,' said Paterson.

'Well, there's clearly no one home,' said Alice. 'Let's go find what we're looking for.'

'Hold up,' said Paterson. 'What about CCTV?'

Alice held up the same scanner that allowed them into the flat. She pressed a different button and waited as once again the little box did its thing. The green light lit up.

'We're good,' she said.

The trio made their way along the hallway, opening doors as they came to them. The first one revealed an empty bedroom. The second was a bathroom. At the end of the hallway was the living room. They stepped inside. Paterson was struck by how neat everything was. He knew that Forrest had rented the flat and probably hadn't been there long, but nothing was out of place. Nothing left lying around on any of the surfaces. To him, this said a lot about Forrest, but the one thing that stuck out in his head was the word *meticulous*. Forrest was nothing if not professional.

'Blimey, this place is a lot bigger than it looks from the outside,' said Clocks.

'It's huge,' said Alice. 'Wasn't expecting this.'

'Right then, where do we start lookin'?' said Clocks.

'Could be anywhere,' said Alice.

'I'll try the bedroom,' said Paterson.

'Can't see 'im tuckin' it under the bed, Ray.'

'I know that, John. I'm looking for a safe. He's not going to leave it lying around, is he?'

Clocks shrugged. 'Probably not.'

'Look behind the pictures on the wall or in a cupboard or something.'

'Yes, boss.' Clocks threw Paterson a mock salute.

Paterson walked into the master bedroom. Again, everything was neat and tidy. The bed was made to perfection

— not a crease on the duvet, pillows positioned just so. The cupboards either side of the bed were clear of any unnecessary items. There was nothing on the floor. The whole place was primed for a quick exit. He opened up a wardrobe with a sliding door. One suit, one shirt, one tie, one pair of black shoes. Clearly, Forrest travelled light.

No sign of any safe. Paterson slid the door all the way open. Completely empty but for the suit and the slight smell of wood and dust. He slid the door closed. There wasn't much else in the room apart from a large chest of drawers. Paterson ruled that out as housing a safe immediately. He took a look under the bed. 'Bingo!' he said quietly.

The safe itself was made from steel and was wide rather than high, secured to the floor with bolts. Perfect for a laptop. 'Alice!'

She walked into the room. 'Found it?'

On his knees, Paterson pointed to the bed. 'Under here. Electronic pad.'

'Let's have a look.'

Paterson held the duvet up while Alice dropped low and took a look.

'I don't believe it,' she said.

'Whassup?' Clocks had followed her in. 'Don't tell me it's gonna be a bastard. We ain't got time for it to be a bastard.'

'I wish. This is pathetic. Call that a safe? Ray, would you be a darling and get me my little box, please?'

Paterson handed the black box to her. She held it under the bed until she heard a slight click. 'Got it!'

She rolled herself onto her back and held up the laptop.

'Ooh, you beauty!' said Clocks, as Paterson took the laptop.

Alice tried to sit herself up. Clocks watched with an amused smile on his face as he watched her struggle.

'You all right, chubs? Strugglin' a bit there, ain'tcha?'

'Don't be so ungentlemanly, Clocks. Help a girl up.'

'You're not a girl and, nope, get yerself up. The exercise will do you good.'

186

'You're horrible.' Alice struggled to get herself up but managed to get into a sitting position after holding onto the bedframe.

'C'mon, Shamu. You can do it. Huuup!'

'Don't be a knob, John. Help her up.'

'What? Why? This is a hoot, Ray.' Alice was now red in the face and panting but she got herself onto her knees. The rest was going to be a lot easier.

'There you go, Alice me ol' mate. I knew you could do it. I 'ad every faith in you.' Clocks grinned as Alice pulled herself to her feet.

'You, Johnathan Clocks, are a total prick.'

'An' you, Alice, are a total riot. Funniest thing I've seen in a dog's age, mate.'

'Fuck off,' she said.

'Alice,' said Paterson. 'Can you get into this? It's password protected, obviously.'

Alice looked at the machine. 'Even worse. Fingerprint locked.'

Paterson sighed. 'Great. You got any ideas?'

'Of course I have. I'm not just a pretty face.' She spun around to Clocks and pointed her finger at him. 'And you, shut your mouth.'

'What?' said Clocks. 'I ain't said a word.'

'But you would have, wouldn't you?'

'Maybe. I mean, you just fed me an opener there, didn't you?'

'Well, don't,' said Alice. She turned back to the computer. Behind her back, Paterson shook his head as Clocks grinned, struggling to contain himself.

# CHAPTER 35

'Right, Alice, me old mate,' said Clocks. 'Ow we goin' to get 'old of this fingerprint, then? You may have noticed that the man in question ain't 'ere, so it's not like we can chop 'is finger off, is it?'

'Don't need to,' said Alice. 'This house is smothered in his fingerprints, and I've got the tech that's going to help us. Why don't you take a seat over there, John? Make yourself a cup of tea or something and watch a professional at work.'

Clocks smiled. 'If I do that, Alice, then I'm gonna 'ave to wipe me dabs off of everythin' I've touched when we leave. Just makin' work for meself.'

'You're not making tea, John,' said Paterson. 'We don't have time for that.'

'Wasn't gonna make any tea,' said Clocks, indignant. 'I said I'll end up making work for meself, and knowin' me I'll only balls it up anyway an' leave a couple of fingerprints behind, won't I?'

Paterson wasn't going to disagree with him. Clocks could be somewhat slapdash in his work.

'Right, now that's out the way, what's the plan, Alice? What you gonna do?' said Clocks.

Alice opened up her case and pulled out what looked like a mobile phone of some sort.

'What you got there?' said Paterson.

'This, Ray, is a state-of-the-art fingerprint-reading device along with a few other tricks it has in its bag. This place will have your man's fingerprints all over it. All I need to do is get one good clean one scanned into this and then I can just place it over the fingerprint sensor. And voila! It'll be as if he had pressed it himself.'

Paterson looked impressed. 'Well, I've got to be honest with you Alice, you've certainly opened my eyes tonight. Very, very impressive.'

'Thank you, Ray. You're very kind.'

Sitting on a stool with his arms folded, Clocks wasn't so sure. 'You got any idea 'ow many goes you get at openin' that?'

'What?' said Alice.

''Ow many goes d'yer get? I'm thinkin' . . . our bloke's got eight fingers an' two thumbs, right?'

Alice nodded.

'Right. So, s'pose you only get three goes at it an' the dabs you've picked up in yer little box ain't the right one you need to open it. I'm thinkin' if you don't pick up the right print in the first three goes, say, then it could self-destruct, couldn't it?'

Alice shook her head. 'Why would you say that?'

'What? Perfectly reasonable thing to think — innit, Ray?'

'I suppose so.'

'So, you know, kaboom! Up she goes. Up we go!'

'I very much doubt that'll happen, John.'

'You don't know though, do yer?'

Alice started to look a bit worried.

'Take no notice of him, Alice,' said Paterson. 'He pulls this sort of shit all the time. Loves to get into your head and play about in there.'

Clocks grinned. 'Just sayin'.'

'Well, don't,' said Alice. 'It's a well-known fact that 76 per-cent of people who use this technology use their index finger.'

'An' it's also a well-known fact that 83.7 percent of well-known facts are made up. So—'

'Fuck off, Johnny Clocks. You can be such a bastard.'

'Well, a'right then, Alice . . . say you've cracked the fingerprint scannin' an' we don't all get blown to smithereens . . . whatcha gonna do about the password, because I'm pretty sure that's not gonna be 'is birthday.'

'Well, we use the same piece of equipment, John. Just press a different couple of buttons, different combination, and we'll have his password.'

'Will that not be militarily-grade encrypted?' said Paterson.

'I'd be very disappointed if it wasn't,' said Alice. 'Don't really care though. It's not gonna make much difference one way or the other. We'll get into it. Leave it with me.'

Alice fired up the electronic device and walked around the room. She went to the counters first and ran the scanner along the top. She did this for a couple of minutes until she finally got the machine to beep. She looked at the screen and held it up for the boys to see. A perfect fingerprint.

'Nice,' said Paterson. 'What's next on the agenda?'

'Well, I'll just upload this into our database very quickly and make sure that this fingerprint is actually your man. That way we'll find out if the man who gave you the name, Jack Forrest, is who he says he is. Give me a minute.'

Thirty seconds later, Alice beamed a smile at them. 'Bingo, my lovelies. We have ourselves a hit. He is one Jack Francis Forrest. Forty-two years of age. Worked for the British Army. Served as an officer, moved up the ranks, was recruited by MI5 and moved across to MI6, where he's been involved in matters of the Defence of the Realm for the last eight years. Highly respected, he's been given several awards by the Queen when she was alive, God bless her.'

Clocks stood up and saluted.

'What're you doing?' said Paterson.

'Salutin'. I loved the Queen. Bloody good queen, she was.'

'There's just us here.'

'So? Respect is respect. Gotta show it.'

Alice shook her head and went back to reading.

'Told you 'e was a wrong'un, didn't I?' said Clocks.

'When did you tell me that?' said Paterson.

'When we first met 'im. I said, "Ray, he's a wrong'un. Trust me."'

'No you didn't,' said Paterson.

'What? Yes I did. I'm sure I did.'

'You didn't,' said Paterson as he turned to look at the screen.

'You sure?

'Positive.'

'Huh. I really thought I 'ad. Must've meant to. Anyway, 'im givin' it large about bein' bloody military police. Load of ol' codswallop, that was. I knew it straight away.'

Paterson shrugged. 'Well, yeah. Should always trust your instincts, John. They've never let you down yet, have they?'

'No, they bleedin' ain't,' said Clocks.

'Alice,' said Paterson. 'How long will it take you to copy his hard drive?'

'All of it?'

'Yeah. Might as well have a good look and see what he's up to.'

'You do know that this is all classified?'

'You do know we don't give a toss?' said Clocks. 'Anyway, bit late in the day to throw that one at us, innit? I mean . . .'

'A fair point, John. Ray, I dunno. Five minutes? Tops.'

'Go for it. John, do me a favour and bell Monkey for me, eh? Get an update from him.'

'Yep. Will do.' Clocks pulled out his phone and hit the speed dial. 'Monkey! It's your favourite boss. Any sign of the big fellah comin' back? No? Good stuff. We should be done an' out of 'ere in about ten minutes, I reckon.'

Alice smiled as the laptop screen flashed up a neatly ordered selection of yellow file icons. 'Easier than I thought,' she said to herself. She clicked into one and quickly scanned the document titles. 'I think we've opened a bit of a goldmine here, Ray. There's maps, briefing documents, papers with chemical equations — and look!' She pointed to the screen. 'This map is all in Russian and it's naming some little town.'

'Prokhladny?' said Paterson.

'How d'you spell it?' said Clocks. 'I'll Google it.'

Alice spelled it out while Paterson read out a note attached to the map. '*Situated in the Kabardino-Balkarian Republic, Russia, located on the Malka River, sixty kilometres north of Nalchik.* The hell have we stumbled into?'

'Ray,' said Clocks. 'It's only a little place. Got just over 60,000 people livin' there. Looks cold too. Trip Advisor says to give it a swerve.'

'Trip Advisor?' said Paterson. 'What you doing on there?'

'Just 'avin' a look. You know where it says, *good for*? Y'know, good for couples, good for kids, good for families and so on? Well, it says here *good for fuck all!*'

Paterson chuckled. 'No, it doesn't. You're a bloody wind-up, Clocksy.'

'I'm tellin' yer. It's got one attraction. One. An' that's a museum of — wait for it — *folklore*. Fuck me. Sixty thousand people an' all they've got is one museum between 'em. Must get bleedin' crowded in there at the weekend. Jeeeesus! Wait a minute, 'ave a look. It's only got one restaurant. I mean, leave off. One restaurant. I think I've just found the shittiest shit'ole in the land of shit'oles. Christ. Place must be full of banjo players.' He mimed playing the instrument and hummed the 'Dueling Banjos' tune from the film *Deliverance*.

Alice was laughing now. 'Sounds fabulous, darling. We simply must visit.'

'More chance of kissin' the Queen,' said Clocks. He scrolled down his phone. 'Here you go . . . we can visit for a fortnight, full board. Ten quid an 'ead an' you can 'ave it off with the local goat. Doesn't show you a picture of 'er though. Probably a right minger.'

Paterson rubbed a tear from his eye. 'Give it a rest, John. We need to get all this copied and get out of here before Forrest comes back.'

'Yeah, fair do's. C'mon, Alice. Get yer little stick out an' do the business.'

'Ooh, Johnny Clocks, you naughty boy. Words I've been longing to hear.'

Six minutes later, the laptop had been returned to its safe. Clocks dusted the flat down to eliminate their presence there and Paterson made sure the flat was just as it was before they arrived, knowing Forrest was the type to know immediately if anything had moved even a fraction of an inch.

# CHAPTER 36

Back at the nick, Paterson looked at the plethora of files laid out across his laptop screen. Where to start? He picked the one titled PROKHLADNY and opened it up.

'What's it say, then?' said Clocks.

Paterson sighed. 'I dunno, John. I've only just opened it. There's a lot here to unpack.'

'Unpack? What are you? On yer 'olidays? Unpack? Talk proper.'

'Like what you do?'

'Yep. Like what I do.'

'I don't think so. Look, I'm going to be a while. Go watch the telly or something. *Loose Women* must be on. You like that, don't you?'

'I do, as it 'appens. They always 'ave interestin' topics to talk about an' they act as a supplement to my development as a new man. I'll be next door, then. Call me if you need me.'

'Will do. Alice?'

'Yes, love.'

'Want to keep him company?'

Alice could take a hint and she followed Clocks outside, trying not to be too offended at her dismissal.

Paterson started in on the documents — a quick skim through first to get a feel of what he was looking at. He had documents in English and Russian. That concerned him, although he didn't know why. There were satellite photos of a small town that he presumed was Prokhladny and audio files of several telephone calls, all in Russian. Thanks to his exposure to his father's dubious business contacts when he was young, he could understand some of the conversations. What little he did understand, he didn't like.

Paterson spent over an hour going through the files and making notes on a yellow legal pad before he sat back in his chair, sighed deeply and pushed his hair back tight against his head. He glanced once more at his notes before he stood up to get Clocks and Alice back in the room. 'Fuck' was all he said.

He opened the door to his office and called them back in.

'What's the score, Bobby Moore?' said Clocks.

'Take a seat, both of you. We've got ourselves caught in the middle of something here, folks. This is big. This is a fucking nightmare if I've figured this out correctly.'

Clocks pulled a chair out from under the desk and sat himself down opposite Paterson. Alice perched on the edge of a desk.

'What we have is way above our paygrades. I'm talking conspiracy to murder at the highest levels of government.'

'What?' said Clocks. 'What you talkin' about?'

Paterson took a deep breath. 'Okay, I'll try and explain this best I can from what I've managed to figure out. As we know, Jack Forrest is not an MP. He's a spook.'

'Yep,' said Clocks.

'He's not just a spook, though. He's an assassin. A highly trained and very efficient one.' Clocks frowned. It was bad enough that Forrest was built like half side of a mountain, but he was a deadly operator with specialist skills.

'From what I can make of it, the documents state that our government has been working on a new, highly effective chemical weapon, which they intend to test shortly. Currently undetectable by all known means.'

'Test it where?' said Alice.

'Prokhladny. If it works as they expect, every man, woman, child, rabbit, bird and whatever the fuck is there will be killed and killed horribly.'

'Oh, leave off. You tellin' me the British government are lookin' to test a chemical weapon on Russian soil?' said Clocks.

'Looks that way, mate.'

'Nah. Our government ain't got the balls for that. That'll kickstart a war, an' let's face it, there's no way the Brits are gonna beat the Russians in a bit of fisticuffs, even if they are a bit busy with the Ukrainians.'

'You're right. But the government are ahead of the game here. There's a press release stating that UK drones and satellites have picked up images of a village in Russia where masses of bodies are lying in the street. It's been rigged so that the drones will just happen to fly over the village fifteen minutes after the release of the weapon. The Russians will have no idea of what's happened until the news is released. The Prime Minister will call the Russians to ask what the fuck is going on, the Russians will pick it up, but by then, we'll have released more pre-prepared info. We've got fake audio calls using AI to simulate the voices of certain Russian generals known to be warmongers, and those will tell the world that it was the Russians themselves that released the weapon that killed their own people. And let's face it, we in the west are quite happy to believe that that is exactly the sort of thing the Russians will do.

'The Americans have been briefed and are going along with it, as they'll benefit from the weapon themselves. Once this is all over with, fifty to sixty thousand people will be dead, the Russians will be in the frame for it and we'll have a new, deadly weapon we can flog to the Americans and any other allies with deep pockets.'

'Yeah, that's not gonna play well, Ray. The Russians'll go garrity. They'll know it's a set-up an' they won't be 'appy little vodka sippers, will they? World War Three comin' down the line.'

Paterson shrugged. 'I doubt it, but I suspect we'll go even deeper into a Cold War with them. No one wants to press the button as it's a zero-sum game. Nobody wins, do they? But I've no doubt they'll retaliate big time. Bombs maybe. Poisonings of key government ministers. Who knows?'

'Shit,' said Alice. 'So, what's Forrest doing with all of this information, Ray?'

'Well, his job was to take out a whistleblower. A scientist who worked on the weapon, grew a conscience and decided it wasn't on. The government took umbrage at him threatening to take his ball home and told him so. He in turn stole all of the information on the project, intending to make it public if the government went ahead and detonated the weapon. The very file we have, chaps.'

'What's the name of this geezer, then?' said Clocks. 'The grass?'

'Wait for it. Turns out it's none other than one Oliver Hayes. One of our suicides.'

# CHAPTER 37

'So how does this go down, then?' said Clocks.

'Okay,' said Paterson. 'Oliver Hayes is a highly respected chemical scientist employed by the government as part of a weapons research team. His job is to give us an advantage in warfare. He's high profile, often being interviewed by scientific magazines and doing the odd podcast and radio interview. He's happily married, with two kids and a big house in the country.'

'But?' said Clocks. 'There's a but, isn't there? I can feel a but comin' on.'

'But . . .' said Paterson, 'as Forrest said, he's a closet gay and is known, mostly to his employers, to like a bit on the side, preferably at the rougher end of the market.'

'Does 'is missus know?'

'It would seem not. Somehow he keeps it from her and the kids. Anyway, his being gay turns out to be a plus for Forrest.'

'How so?' said Alice.

'Leaves him vulnerable. And Forrest found out that his current squeeze is a soldier that got kicked out of the army for being of "low moral fibre".'

'What's that mean?' said Alice.

'Mean's e's got no bottle. Cowardy, cowardy custard.'

'Exactly,' said Paterson. 'Apparently, he showed a lack of courage under fire in Afghanistan and was booted out with psyche problems. Got a hard time from his unit and his self-esteem dropped like a stone. Couldn't handle it. And guess who he is?'

Clocks and Alice both shook their heads.

'Christopher Striker,' Paterson announced.

'Fuck off!' Clocks was more than a bit surprised.

'Nope. It's all in here. In Forrest's notes. So, I'm guessing that he's back on civvy street and gets himself into a relationship with Oliver Hayes, who's no doubt seen that our soldier boy is at a low ebb, and he's cruised in and whispered a ton of shit in his ear. So, backing up a bit, Hayes has his bit of rough, our man is feeling lucky in love, and Hayes, being a successful, confident man, fills in the character blank spot in our soldier.

'Except Forrest uses Striker's insecurities to wheedle into him. Tells him that Hayes intends to sell secrets to the Russians and is in possession of a file that the Russians will pay big money for. He tells Striker that Hayes is just using him for sex and will never, ever leave his family, he loves them and doesn't want them hurt. So, this is the one chance our boy has to redeem himself and do right by his country. Vindicate himself, if you like, and help catch a Russian spy into the bargain. The soppy sod goes for it and finds out where Hayes is keeping the laptop with the file. He grabs it and gives it to Forrest, who, by way of thanks, kills him and fucks off with the laptop. So, for the government, happy days are here again. They've plugged a potential leak and can get on with their plan to fit up the Russians.'

'Jesus!' said Clocks. 'So 'e was in on it?'

'Nope. Well, not as such. He was just used as Forrest's eyes and ears. You see, Forrest put together a kill plan for Hayes that kind of disguises the fact that he was murdered. Have you ever heard the expression *mixers* before?'

'It's what you bung in yer drink, ain't it?' said Clocks. Alice nodded.

'Yeah, but in this case, it means something entirely different. It's a code name for innocent victims. These poor bastards get killed along with the mark to muddy the waters. They're *mixed in* with the target. Apparently, it's a tried and tested method.'

''Ang on, 'ang on,' said Clocks. 'I understand that, but I don't understand 'ow Striker fits into the suicides.'

'Coming to that, John. So, Forrest can't just kill Hayes, we know that. Too high profile, perhaps too obvious. So he needs mixers. Forrest does some research on a few high-profile targets. He knows they use public transport and walk to their places of work. Now he needs to get all four to top themselves at the same time. How does he do that? Glad you asked. He has videos faked using state-of-the-art AI technology that shows all four as being involved in a widespread paedophile gang. At the precise same time, he sends the videos to the four and tells them to look at their phones. They see themselves engaged in filthy sex with little kiddies and are completely bewildered. When you're in that state on a Monday morning just bumbling your way to work, you're scared, confused, shocked, frightened and a shitload of other emotions I can't begin to imagine. But most of all, and this is an old trick used by manipulators the world over, you're desperate to escape.

'So, Forrest gives them one way out and he puts an extreme time constraint on it. The only way out is to kill yourself within the next few minutes or this stuff goes viral. He tells them to lose their phones and step out. In their confused, frightened state, they comply. Perfect for Forrest. And to get back to Striker, he gets the satisfaction of watching his treacherous user of a lover die and feels like a hero for saving the country from the dirty Russians. *Fait accompli*, as the French say.'

'Fuck me,' said Clocks. 'Surely a car crash woulda been easier.'

'It would, yes. But it wouldn't have been so well hidden. Forrest's next step was to release info that the four were in a paedo gang, post the AI vids and say that they knew the jig was up and so formed a death pact with each other. Cowards way out.'

'Slippery bastard!' said Clocks.

'John, let me ask you a question.'

'Oh, yeah?'

'If your whole world was about to implode, if everything you had built was about to be taken away from you — your reputation destroyed, everyone you had ever known and loved taken from you, your family turned against you — what would you do? Would you kill yourself?'

'Eh? That's a bit deep, innit? Where's all that coming from?'

'I was listening to an audio recording, the voicemail left on one of the victims' phones. I assume it was the same message played to each of them.'

'Is this what caused them to kill themselves? What was said to them?'

'I'll play it in a sec, but going back to what I said, if all of that stared you in the face, what would you do?'

Paterson watched Clocks think it over, his friend's forehead wrinkling. 'Hard to say, but possibly, I guess.'

'Listen.' Paterson clicked on an audio icon and they were treated to Forrest's voice.

*'Good morning. Who I am doesn't matter. I am about to destroy your life, your reputation, your family. There is only one thing you can do to stop this happening. You will have sixty seconds to decide after you watch the video I have just sent you. Watch it now. I will call you back with instructions on what to do next.'* The audio stopped playing.

'Okay,' said Clocks. 'What's the next part?'

'Watch the video first.' Paterson hit the MOV file on the screen. A crystal-clear image of one of the victims, Susan Banks, burst onto the screen. She was naked and engaged in a sexual act with a group of boys around the age of ten. In the

201

background, two of the other victims could clearly be seen engaged in some very lewd acts with children.

'Oh, fuckin' 'ell, Ray! What the—'

'It's not real, John. It's fucking AI. Good quality, but faked. All of it. This is what Forrest sent to their phones. Now listen to this. Bear in mind what they've just seen. They're shocked. Heavily shocked. And you remember what I said about people who are in an extremely uncomfortable position?'

'Yeah. They wanna get out of it.'

Paterson hit the icon for another audio file.

*'In exactly sixty seconds, the video you have just seen will be posted to all news outlets and the internet. You can stop this happening, but only if you do exactly what I tell you. If you do not comply with my instructions, your family will have to live with what you've done. Throw this phone into the river and step in front of a vehicle. Do this and your secret is safe.'*

*'What?'* Hysteria.

*'Thirty seconds.'*

*'But . . . I haven't . . .'*

*'Twenty-five.'*

*'Er, oh God. God!'*

*'Throw the phone.'* Silence.

Paterson clicked on the stop icon. 'That's it. They followed through. All of them. So, would you have killed yourself?'

Clocks rubbed the back of his neck. 'Jesus, Ray. I dunno. Possibly. Yes. If I had little kids . . . Fuck that. That's a helluva position to be in.'

Paterson pinched the bridge of his nose as he tried to imagine himself in their shoes. He couldn't.

'How do you know it's faked?' said Clocks.

'C'mon, John. I read you the file Forrest knocked up. That's exactly what he said he was going to do, and he did it. Where he got the video of the kids from and the adults in it, I don't know. That's another matter, but we have to find him and expose this.'

Paterson turned to Alice. 'I'm gonna call Wol and we'll launch an assault on Forrest's flat.'

Clocks's phone beeped. He looked at the screen and tutted. 'It's Monkey. Says Forrest's left the flat. Got in a car and shot off.'

'He's running,' said Paterson.

'No 'e's not. I just said 'e's in a car. 'E's drivin'.'

'Jesus. No. He's running. Running from us. He knows.'

Clocks wrinkled his nose. 'Why d'you say that? You can't know that.'

'Just a feeling, John.'

'Oh, well. If it's just a feelin' . . .'

Paterson ignored him and checked his watch. 'Someone like him will have a switch car waiting nearby. Alice, you think you can find him? Can you hack local CCTV, traffic cams?'

Alice looked sceptical. 'I don't know, Ray. I'm more than happy to look, but given what we know about Forrest, he could be anywhere, anyone now.'

'Yeah, could be,' said Clocks. 'Coulda stuck a bandido's moustache an' a fuckin' sombrero on 'imself but he's always gonna be six foot nineteen an' three 'undred pounds of sheer muscle and violence, ain't 'e? Can't change that freaky big frame of 'is, can 'e? Nah. We'll find 'im. An' when we do, what's the plan, boss man?'

Paterson stood up from his seat, closed the laptop lid and nodded to himself.

'We send him bye-byes.'

'Er, if we do that to a government agent, we'll be covered in shit from breakfast to dinner time. I think we'll 'ave used up all of our get out of jail free cards at that point.'

Paterson shrugged as he walked across the room to the door. 'Well, we'll just have to see if we can pick up a few more from the commissioner, won't we? Either way, this fucker doesn't live.'

'Right,' said Clocks. 'We're going up against a cold-blooded, trained assassin who's built like a brick shit'ouse an' probably killed more people than Covid 19 in an ol' people's 'ome on bingo night. An' if we're successful, we're gonna 'ave to go on the trot from all of 'is MI6 mates for the rest of our lives. Not your best plan, Ray, gotta say.'

'You got one?' said Paterson.

'Didn't know I'd need one. Lemme think for a minute.'

Paterson stood in the doorway and waited. And waited. 'How we doing?'

'Ah, fuck it. Let's do 'im.'

# CHAPTER 38

'So, 'ow we gonna do this, then?' said Clocks. 'How are we gonna take down that big ol' Forrest on our lonesome?'

'We're not. I'll give Wol a call and see if he's willing and able to help us bring him down.'

Walter Young, ex-Commissioner of Police and now a private security consultant, had set up his own firm on leaving the Met. From the beginning, Wol had chosen to keep his team small and tightly knit. Only himself, Alice, Clocks's wife, Lyndsey, and an enigmatic operative, Liam Cole, known as the White Ghost, made up their ranks.

The Ghost was a formidable individual. An albino, his stark white skin earned him his nickname. But it wasn't just his appearance that set him apart — it was the ruthlessness with which he completed his missions. He had gained notoriety after going rogue from his army unit in Africa, driven by a personal vendetta against those who used and abused children for voodoo rituals. His most high-profile assassination was that of an African general and his wife, both diplomats visiting the UK for dubious purposes. Paterson, knowing that bringing them to justice through conventional means would be impossible, had given the nod for the White Ghost to continue his lethal mission. With Paterson's assistance in evading the law, the Ghost joined Wol's band of vigilantes, adding another deadly set of skills to their arsenal.

Johnny Clocks had never seen eye to eye with the Ghost, and he was seriously upset when his wife left the Met and went to work alongside him. Not that he thought there would ever be anything between them, but he did worry that she would take on some of his traits. Liam Cole was quiet, moody, suspicious and downright cold-blooded. He would shoot a person in the head as if he was target shooting a melon and think just about the same about it. But, as unhappy as he was, Clocks knew Wol's firm was their best chance of tracking down and getting hold of Jack Forrest.

'Gimme a minute,' said Paterson. 'I'll make the call.' He stepped outside into the cold night air. He watched a stream of warm breath light up from the phone's screen until, after five rings, the familiar voice of his old friend came on the line. He explained the situation and waited for an answer.

'Of course we will, Ray,' said Wol. 'Look, we're still in London at the moment. We don't have anything outstanding, so give us an hour and we'll be with you. Where do you want to meet?'

'Just come to the nick, mate. It's the easiest. You can say hello to a few of the old faces.'

'You still got Monkey, Dusty and Jackie with you?'

'Oh, yeah. Rock-solid little firm, they are. Never letting them go.'

'Excellent. All right. See you soon.' Wol didn't wait for a reply and hung up.

\* \* \*

While they waited, Paterson wandered up and out onto the roof to be alone with his thoughts. He needed to clear his head after fully realising the ramifications of both Forrest's plan and his own. He gripped the handrail that ran the length of the roof of Tower Bridge Police Station and looked across the

River Thames, city lights twinkling in the night. He watched as his warm breath turned to vapour in the cool night air.

The shot ripped the skin between his shoulder and bicep and spun him around, dropping him to the deck. A second shot followed, embedding itself in the brick wall behind him.

Lying on his back, Paterson clutched his wounded arm, feeling the hot trickle of blood seep through his fingers. He cursed loudly, the words sharp and bitter on his tongue. But even as he winced and grimaced in pain, he couldn't help but feel a twisted sense of relief. At least the bone was intact. The bullet had taken out about half an inch of skin and clipped a muscle, leaving a shallow wound that bled profusely.

'Fuck me,' he muttered, shaking his head in disbelief. 'Jesus.'

He gritted his teeth, trying to ignore the throbbing pain in his arm as he moved it gingerly. The red-hot agony shot through his nerves, making him wince. But he knew he was lucky. It could have been much worse. *Silver linings*, he thought bitterly. That seemed to be his life lately. Always searching for a silver lining amid the chaos and darkness.

\* \* \*

Jack Forrest swore at himself. He'd been expecting to pick off all three targets through Paterson's office window but when the man himself walked outside onto the roof, it made his job easier. He cursed himself for rushing and for not taking his time. Anger had clouded his mind.

\* \* \*

Paterson slipped his phone out of his pocket and dialled Clocks.

'What's Wol 'ave to say?' said Clocks.

'John! Hit the deck! Now! Kill all the lights!' He heard Clocks shout at Alice to get down.

'Fuck's going on, Ray?'

'Just had a lump taken out of my shoulder.'

'Come again?'

'You killed the bastard lights?'

'Just done it. What you talkin' about?'

'Sniper. Caught me in the shoulder. Flesh only.'

'Stay down. I'm coming to you.'

'John! No! Wol and the gang are on their way. Leave it to them to secure the place.'

'Where'd the shot come from?'

'No idea, but I was looking over the Thames to the Tower of London, so it's gotta be over there somewhere.' He rotated his shoulder a couple of times. 'Bloody hell, that stings.'

'I'll call SCO19 too. Keep yer nut down 'til I bell you back.'

'No, no! Don't do that, John. Don't want them and Wol's firm meeting up. Questions will be asked.'

'Good point,' said Clocks.

Paterson dropped his head back down on the bitumen roof covering and thought his situation through. Best thing to do was stay down. Whoever had taken a pop at him clearly couldn't get a clean shot while he lay flat, so that was the place to be. His thoughts turned next to who it could have been. He had made plenty of enemies in his time, all good coppers did, but most of those he had dealt with were either dead or, well . . . dead. That just left Jack Forrest, and what bothered him most about that was, they no longer had the advantage.

# CHAPTER 39

For the next five minutes, Paterson lay there pondering their next move when Clocks called to him.

'Oi, Ray! What's 'appenin'?'

'Not much, Clocksy. Just looking up at the stars, keeping out of trouble, y'know?'

'Yeah, yeah. Sensible.'

'What are you doing up here? I told you to wait it out.'

'I know, an' then I thought, *nah*. You know me. I'm not one for creepin' around in the dark. Well, not since I got married. No need to now, is there?'

Paterson chuckled. 'Well, no. I guess not. No more jumping out of bushes at strange women for you, eh? Marriage has definitely changed you.' Clocks started to crawl over on his belly.

'What are you doing? Don't come over here.'

'Shut up, you tart. I'm not leavin' you layin' flat on yer back lookin' at the stars without me.'

'What?'

'I love the stars, me. You know that.'

'No, I don't. How would I know that?'

'Didn't I tell yer?'

'No.'

'Oh, well. I meant to.' He crawled over next to Paterson. 'All right?'

'Yeah, yeah. It's all tickety-boo, thanks. You?'

'Sweet, mate.' Clocks rolled over on his back. 'This is nice, innit?'

Paterson sniffed. 'It's a beautiful moment, John. Thanks for sharing it with me.'

'You're welcome, mate. You owe me a new suit, by the way.'

'What? Why?'

'I'm pretty sure I've just put the knees through on this one. Probably the elbows too.'

'What's that got to do with me?'

'Obvious, innit? If you 'adn't gone an' got yerself shot, I wouldn't be out 'ere crawlin' around on me belly to come an' see you.'

'Hang on. You wouldn't be out here crawling around on your belly if you'd have done as I told you. You ignored me like you always do. That's on you, mate.'

'Hmm. We'll argue about it later.'

'No, we won't. Your suit. Your fault.'

'Ray?'

'What?'

'Me 'air's all wet. As it been rainin', by any chance?'

'Not since I've been up here.'

'Ah. So, er . . . what am—'

'What are you lying in?'

'Yeah, that's it. What am I lyin' in?'

'You're lying in my blood, probably.'

Clocks instinctively went to sit up. Paterson's good hand pressed on Clocks's chest. 'Stay the fuck down, Clocksy.'

Clocks dropped his head back into the sticky pool of blood. 'Jesus, Ray. Why didn't you tell me?'

'I just did.'

'Before I lay in it, you twat.'

'Didn't think of it.'

'Lovely. So, I'm lyin' in a pint of Paterson's best an' it's all congealin' as we speak. That's lovely, that is.'

'It'll wash out. Don't be a baby.'

'Wash out, will it? I don't think 'Ead an' Shoulders do a bottle of Blood Begone. Pretty sure they only do dandruff, not claret. Fuck me . . .'

'I like to choose my own lovers, John, but thanks for the offer.'

'Oh, that's it, mate. You crack out a few jokes while I'm lying 'ere in a ripped suit and doin' the backstroke in your blood juice.'

Paterson chuckled.

'Who do we fancy for this apart from Jack Forrest?'

'Just Jack Forrest,' said Paterson.

'Yeah. Thought that's what you'd say. Fucker knows, don't 'e? An' 'e's comin' for us, ain't 'e?'

'Looks like it, buddy.'

''Appy days, mate.'

# CHAPTER 40

Being a police officer still had a few advantages and one of those was that they usually got seen quite quickly if they had been the victim of an injury of any kind. The staff that saw them as they came in were more worried about Clocks initially. The back of his hair was matted red, blood covered his neck and his suit was in tatters. It took him a good five minutes to convince them that he was fine and that Paterson was the one who had been shot.

'You're lucky, really,' said Dr Armstrong, the consultant on duty. 'An inch further to the left and he could've done some serious damage.'

Paterson nodded. 'Hmm. I guess so.'

Armstrong was a tall man with a slight nervous twitch in the eyes, which made him blink more frequently than usual. Clocks picked up on it and was watching him intently.

'I know how lucky I am, doc,' said Paterson. 'I'm pretty sure the bastard was going for my head.'

'Well, thank God he wasn't very good at his job then, eh?'

Paterson gave the man a wry smile. 'Not overly impressed with God. I'm sure he's a lovely chap and that, but he's not for me.'

'Or chapess,' said Clocks. He stood in the corner of the room, arms folded.

'What?' said Armstrong.

'Chapess. For all we know, God could be a Doris. We 'ave to take that into account these days or we'll get a bollickin' offa someone. Usually a feminist.'

Armstrong blinked wildly as he thought about what Clocks had said.

'You all right, chief?' said Clocks.

'What?' said Armstrong.

'Just that the old, y'know . . .' He imitated the man's blinking.

'What? Oh, yes. Sorry about that.' He put his head down slightly to avoid Clocks's gaze.

'No, look, don't apologise. I'm the one that's sorry, mate. Didn't mean to embarrass yer. That was out of order. Sorry.'

Armstrong nodded. 'It's okay. Some days it's worse than others. Stress usually plays it up.'

'Yeah, well, I am sorry mate.'

Paterson lay on the gurney looking quite amazed at Clocks. In all the years he'd known him, it was unusual for him to apologise for his insensitivities. He had done it before, but it was rare enough to catch Paterson on the hop.

'So, what's the story, doc?' said Clocks. 'Is the soft sod gonna be all right?'

'Should be. It's going to be as sore as hell for a few days but the gunman missed all muscle and bone, so, like I said, lucky. It'll be stiff as well.'

'Hey, hey. There you go, Ray. Silver linings there, eh? Been ages since anything on you's been stiff. That'll cheer Gracie up no end.'

Paterson raised his middle finger then thanked the doctor for his time and attention. He pulled his shirt sleeve back over the large dressing and looked at the hole in it. 'Two hundred and fifty pounds down the Swanee,' he muttered.

"Ow much? Two 'undred an' fifty squids on a bleedin' shirt? I've bought cars for less than that. Whassamatter with yer?'

'You gonna go on about this, John?'

'Course I am. Someone needs to teach you some money sense. If you carry on like that, you'll be down to yer last twenty trillion before you know it.'

'He's joking,' Paterson said to a bemused-looking Dr Armstrong. 'I just like nice things.'

'I'm not jokin', doc. He's a squillionaire and, yes, he does like nice things — 'ouses, boats, cars, supermodels . . . You name it, 'e'll buy it.'

Paterson shook his head. 'C'mon, you. Work to do.' He shook Armstrong's hand and they left the casualty unit. As they reached the exit of the hospital, Wol, Alice, the White Ghost and Lyndsey ran in.

'Ray!' Wol's voice carried genuine concern. 'You okay?'

'Yeah, yeah. Just a scratch. Literally. It just bled like a pig and Clocksy insisted we come. Feel a bit silly, really.'

'Christ, John,' said Lyndsey. 'What happened to you?'

Clocks looked down at his suit. Two big holes in the knees and blood everywhere. He'd had the cheek to wash his hair in a sink while he waited for Paterson to be seen. At least that looked half sensible now.

'Alice filled you in, yes?' said Paterson.

'On the phone, yes. You were lucky. Don't understand why he didn't kill you. Can't be very good at his job.'

'Aw, thanks for that,' said Paterson. 'You're the second person to say that tonight. Perhaps he just fucked up or maybe it was a warning.' He shrugged and winced at the pain in his shoulder.

'All right, Wol?' Clocks gave him a little wave.

'Don't call me Wol, you little shit. It's Walter to you.' He had a big grin on his face. 'And yes, I'm good, thanks. You?'

'Cosmic, matey.' He turned to look at Liam Cole. 'An' 'ow you doin', my dazzlin'ly white friend? Still killin' people?'

'John . . .' said Lyndsey. 'Don't.'

'What?' Me an' the Milky Bar Kid are good, ain't we? Ol' buddies, me an' 'im.'

Liam Cole turned his gaze to Clocks. 'I hate you, Clocks.'

Clocks grinned. 'That's the spirit. I know you 'ate me, but you love me really, don'tcha?'

'No. I hate you.'

'He's just kiddin',' Clocks said to everyone. 'Loves me.' He winked at Cole.

'If it wasn't for the respect I have for your wife I would have turned your head into a puff of red mist a long time ago.'

'Oh, you!' Clocks flapped his wrist at him. 'You say the sweetest things. But not me 'ead. I need it for buttin' the slags with. It's my most effective weapon.'

'That and your mouth,' said Cole.

'That an' me mouth. Correct. Anyway, lovely seein' you again. Although, to be fair, you're so bleedin' white I could see you in the dark. Like 'avin' a talkin' torch, it is.'

'That's enough, ladies,' said Wol. 'We have work to do and we need to be quick off the mark. Forrest will no doubt try again and this time he just might be successful. We can't have that. Ray, back to the nick or . . . ?'

Paterson took a deep breath. 'No. We're staying away from any police premises. Come back to mine. I'm gonna call up the rest of the team and get them to meet me there.'

'All of them?'

'Yeah, why not? It'll be good for the newbies to meet the living legend.' He grinned and slapped Wol on the back.

'They've already met me though,' said Clocks. 'Don't want them to meet 'im. Takes away a bit of me mystique.'

# CHAPTER 41

In less than two hours, the whole team were assembled at Paterson's house. Clocks made tea and coffee for everyone, another sight that astonished Paterson. Not once did he complain, nor did he jibe the girls that it was their job. He'd have to ask him what was going on with him once this case was over. Assuming they both lived.

'Okay, everyone, settle down,' said Paterson. 'Thank you all for coming over at short notice. I thought we'd do the briefing here for a change. Georgie, I know this isn't the usual for you, but we needed to be away from the nick tonight and somewhere safe, so . . . sorry.'

'No worries, guv. I can run an office from here if need be.'

Paterson nodded, grateful for the way the man was happy to adapt. 'There are a few things I need to bring some of you up to speed with. First of all, for my new officers, the four people you see here are old colleagues and good friends: Walter Young, ex-Commissioner of Police; Lyndsey Clocks, John's wife and ex-SCO19 inspector; Alice, absolute tech genius; Liam Cole, ex-military — highly skilled in a number of different fields, he is an invaluable asset.' He turned to face Wol.

'This is Detective Constable Harmony Lee and Detective Constable Alan Watts. They've recently joined our team and I'm told they're both extremely good officers. Not yet battle tested but something tells me that won't be long in coming. Of course, everyone here knows Jackie, Monkey and Dusty.'

'Excuse me,' said Harmony. 'These four people, I know you said they're friends and colleagues, and no offence guys, but why are they here at a briefing and why are we here in your house, sir?'

Paterson smiled at the newbie. She wasn't used to their ways yet and those ways were unconventional at best. He had to be careful with these two. They were unknowns and at this stage could not be trusted.

'I'll tell you who they are,' said Clocks.

Paterson rolled his eyes. 'John . . .'

'It's all right, guv. I'll be'ave meself. Right, Treacle, earlier tonight at the nick, someone took a potshot at the guv when 'e was out on the roof. Clipped 'is shoulder, so we 'ad to lay low for a while until we got some back-up. This firm is our back-up.' Monkey, Jackie and Dusty all swivelled in Paterson's direction at the same time.

'It's all good,' Paterson said. 'No need to worry. Shot just clipped me.'

'What about the firearms unit?' said Harmony 'They're supposed to deal with this type of thing, aren't they?'

'Yes, love. They are. But sometimes, we 'ave to go a bit off the radar, an' believe me, there's no one better than these. Even the stick of chalk over there. He's without a doubt the best of the best.' Paterson saw Liam Cole tense up.

'But they're not police, so what's their role here?'

'Well,' said Paterson. 'We believe that the man who shot me is Jack Forrest. We've found out a bunch of information in the last few hours, which we'll go over later, but Forrest is not what he claimed to be and is without a doubt responsible for the suicides and the murder of Christopher Striker.' Most of Paterson's team looked confused.

217

'Striker's dead?' said Jackie.

'How?' said Monkey.

'You remember the case that Forrest carried everywhere?' Everyone nodded.

'Well, Alice here helped us get our hands on it and inside there was a laptop with a bunch of files on it. We made a copy of everything we could. But, and here's the real biggie, we found out the reason for the four deaths but in doing so we opened up a fucking big can of worms. What we found could — and I stress *could*, nothing's ever certain — lead to war between the UK, America and Russia.'

Everybody sat still, shocked.

'Are you serious?' said Alan Watts.

'I'm known for a lot of things,' said Paterson. 'My sense of humour isn't top of the list. I wish I wasn't being serious, but I am. Forrest knows we know, so he's taking no chances. He wants me, Clocksy and Alice, plus anyone else he thinks we may have told, dead. He'll kill us all to protect this info and retrieve the copy we have. As I said, this is so fucking big.'

Harmony let out a huge breath. 'So, I'm guessing these four are not here for strictly legal purposes?'

Paterson noticed Lyndsey giving Harmony a cold stare. After only ten minutes she seemed to be taking a dislike to the woman.

'Well,' said Clocks, 'the answer to that question depends on the answer you give me. Where do you stand on this?'

Harmony shook her head. 'I've only been with you lot for a day or two but it seems I'm on a squad where a trained killer gets four people to kill themselves. He kills our main suspect, then shoots the guv'nor, who tells us that we're sitting on information that could start World War Three, and I think these four here are a bunch of trained killers themselves who are looking to take out another trained killer. Is that about right, Mr Clocks?'

'Depends on whether you're in or out. If you're in, then yep, you're bang on. If you're out, then nope, dunno what you're talkin' about, love.' He swivelled to the new man. 'DC Watts . . . in or out?'

'Fuck yeah. I'm all in, guv.'

Clocks smiled. 'Good man.' He swivelled back to Harmony Lee. 'So, what's it gonna be, Treacle? In or out. If you're out, no 'ard feelin's, just keep yer flapper shut, let us get on with our job an' don't slam the door on yer way out.'

Harmony frowned. She didn't like the way he spoke to her. 'Okay, first of all, why the hell don't you turn this over to the government? Surely this is their department?'

'If you stay,' said Paterson, gently, 'I'll tell you exactly why we can't turn it over to them.'

She looked shocked. 'Are you saying . . . No! It can't be . . .'

'If you stay, then I'll tell you everything. But you need to know this . . . This will get dirty. *Very* dirty, and the rule book will no longer exist. All of us here will do whatever it takes to ensure that Forrest is stopped and that this information gets into the right hands. *Safe* hands. Up to you. I need an answer in the next twenty seconds.' He pushed a button on his watch.

'I . . . what? This can't be happening. I mean . . . war, for fuck's sake.'

'Fifteen seconds.'

'No . . . wait. There has to be another way. This can't be right.'

'Ten.'

'Oh, Jesus. I'm in!'

'Good girl.' He looked across at Clocks. 'See. Time pressure works, mate.'

'What was the other thing that was botherin' you, love?' said Clocks.

She turned to face him. 'You. Don't ever call me "Treacle" or "love" again, okay? Just don't. I'm a professional police officer, not some sweet little naive girlie you can pat on the arse and force to do everything for you. It's demeaning not only to me, but to all women.'

Wol raised an eyebrow at this little outburst. Clocks grinned. Lyndsey darted across the room, grabbed Harmony by the arm, yanked her out of her seat and dragged her toward the door. The room looked stunned. Harmony screamed and attempted to fight back. She was no match for Lyndsey, who quickly forced her arm up behind her back with one hand and pushed her head forward with the other. Lyndsey marched the doubled-up detective toward the door. 'You boys carry on while us girls have a little chat. Won't be long.' She shoved Harmony into the hallway, still bent up.

# CHAPTER 42

Lyndsey shoved Harmony up against the wall, lifting her high enough that only her toes were touching the ground. She pushed her face in toward Harmony's.

'Get the fuck offa me!' Harmony struggled to break Lyndsey's grip but failed. 'What are you doing? You can't do this!'

'Shut up, child!' Lyndsey spat at her. 'Grown-up about to talk.'

Harmony pursed her lips and scowled. She wasn't happy but couldn't do much about it.

'Do yourself a favour and don't ever talk to my old man that way, you understand? And certainly not in front of his colleagues, all right?'

Harmony struggled again. Pointless. Lyndsey subdued her quickly. 'Those men in there are the best you will ever have the privilege of meeting as long as you live. They give their lives to this job and you, you come in swinging your feminist tits about telling them what they can and can't say and do like you're someone special. Well, you're not. You're a snot-nosed little girlie with a fucking attitude problem, which I'm adjusting for you right now, you understand?'

Harmony's scowl grew deeper.

'I said, *do you understand?*'

'You're all right with this, are you? All this sexist bullshit. Talking to women like they're nothing. Pieces of skirt fit only to serve their men? Is that you, eh?'

Lyndsey scoffed. 'Really? Is that all you've got to worry about? Being called "love"? Jesus, you're an idiot. In this job, in this game and with these boys, you've gotta be tough. They aren't a bunch of baby woodentops that just came out of training. They haven't got the time or inclination to fuck about watching their P's and Q's and worrying about fucking pronouns, and they certainly ain't gonna dance around you all day. You'll be gone before you get your next period. So, lemme tell you this. If you stay — *if* — you'll see and do things that will test you to the limit. Will question your morals. Will make you understand that this world you want to step into doesn't even begin to play by society's rules, and then you'll be a better copper for it, a better human. But if all you want to do is swan around thinking you're going to change the world over pissy little things like being called "love" and "darlin'" then it's best you fuck off back to the main office and get on with writing up crime sheets for the next twenty years.'

Lyndsey dropped her back onto her feet. 'Right now, you get a choice. Make the right one. Oh, and don't make the mistake of thinking you're speaking for me or any other woman ever again.'

# CHAPTER 43

Daniel Bevan, the head of a secret unit within MI6, sat in a plush leather chair, its dark brown colour complementing the mahogany wood of the room. The chair seemed to envelop him, providing a false sense of security that did little to ease his troubled mind. The room was adorned with expensive decor, the walls covered in rich tapestries and the floor lined with a luxurious rug that cost twice Jack Forrest's annual salary.

His piercing eyes, usually full of steely determination, now conveyed a sense of concern as they scrutinised Forrest. The flickering flames of the large open fire cast a warm glow on his face, illuminating the stern lines of his countenance.

Forrest was worried and embarrassed. Never before had he had to go to his boss and tell him he'd been bested. Never before had he lost official top-secret documents and never before had he encountered anyone as determined as Paterson and Clocks.

'Sir, I'm afraid there's a problem. The two policemen assigned to investigate the suicides are proving themselves to be a nuisance.'

Bevan gave a nod. 'In what way, Forrest?'

'They have a copy of the Oliver Hayes file.'

'How in the name of God did they get hold of that?' Bevan's long years of service did a good job of keeping him outwardly calm, but Forrest knew that inside he was raging.

'They are quite formidable, sir. They made use of an outside resource to break into my flat, hack the laptop and copy the files.'

'Okay. First of all. What the hell are you doing leaving those plans lying around, and second, how did they break into your laptop? That's above military-grade encryption. You're telling me they figured out how to break into that and then copy it?'

'Yes sir. They did. I have no excuses, sir. But that is perhaps an explanation for another day. For now, I need to recover the information quickly.'

'Damn right you do! You bloody fool, Forrest. Where are they now?'

'They're holed up in the home of the senior detective in charge of the case. A young man by the name of Ray Paterson. Detective Superintendent Paterson. His sidekick goes by the name of Detective Inspector Johnny Clocks.'

'Do they know what they're looking at?' said Bevan.

'Without a doubt. I've been keeping a listening watch from the woods at the far end of the house. They know exactly what we're up to and they intend to stop us.'

'Do they now?'

'They do, but the good news, if there is any in this, is that they have no intention of approaching the powers that be.'

Bevan cocked his head. 'What? Why not? Do you think they're going to try and blackmail us? Is that their game?'

'No, sir. They're not in it for the money. They want this whole scheme exposed, and from what I can gather, it won't be the proper authority channels they take. I suspect the press or the internet is the way for them. Paterson and Clocks know that I'm on to them and they've recruited the rest of their squad plus a small team of private operatives to assist them.'

'You'll need help, then?'

'No, sir. I can handle this.'

'I hope you're right, Forrest. You have to put a lid on this now. Do you understand?'

'I do, sir.'

'Good. Then you're authorised to use deadly force. Make sure you act quickly.'

'Sir, will it not draw unnecessary attention if a whole bunch of murder squad detectives are . . . removed?'

Bevan thought about it for a moment. 'Of course it will, yes. But right now, I don't care. Call me when it's done and I'll deal with the fallout and the press. You understand me?'

'Sir.' Forrest turned briskly on his heels and walked out of the office, closing the doors behind him.

With each step, Forrest felt the anger boiling inside him, threatening to consume him. He'd been professionally humiliated and he couldn't let that go. He took deep breaths. Anger was not the way to deal with this. Not with these people. He needed to bring his A game to stop them. As he made his way down the long corridor to the main exit, he couldn't help but plot out all the different ways he could destroy Paterson and his team. He envisioned a vicious takedown, dismantling the squad one-by-one. His mind raced with possibilities as he strode forward with determination. It wouldn't be difficult if he acted quickly and decisively. He was ready for battle, ready to take down anyone who stood in his way.

# CHAPTER 44

Paterson sat at the large marble-topped island in his kitchen eating a slice of toast. He and Clocks were squabbling about the state of the counter top. Clocks was busy frying a couple of eggs to slap between two slices of bread and butter and spattering fat about. Being a clean freak, Paterson wasn't happy and was trying to get him to use a splash guard. Lyndsey sat on a chair eating a bowl of Bran Flakes, ignoring them and glancing from time to time at the BBC news. The sound was turned down low and she was just about to spoon in another mouthful when she stopped, her attention fully on the screen.

'Guys,' she said, 'look!'

Paterson and Clocks carried on bickering like an old married couple until they noticed that Lyndsey was transfixed. 'Look!' she shouted. The boys stopped and looked at her, then at the TV.

The newscaster was some way into a report. Lyndsey ramped up the sound. '. . . *The officer, believed to be in his mid-fifties, was shot in the chest late last night in the Bromley area of Kent. Police are not saying much at the moment but believe it to have been a professional contract killing.*'

All three jumped as Paterson's mobile phone rang. He snatched it up and punched the answer button. 'Paterson!' he barked. 'Uh-huh. Uh-huh. Oh fuck . . . no. No!' There was a pause. 'We'll be right over.' He hung up and looked at the expectant faces of Clocks and Lyndsey.

'It was Dusty. Bastard killed Dusty. We need to move.'

Paterson ran upstairs to throw on a suit. John and Lyndsey just sat and looked at each other, dumbstruck. Dusty was one of the original squad, a quiet man liked by everybody. 'Move!' Paterson shouted from the top of the stairs. They snapped out of it and ran upstairs together.

'Fully kitted!' Paterson shouted from his bedroom.

'Gotcha!' Clocks replied.

Paterson wrenched open his wardrobe doors and pushed back an armful of clothes to reveal his gun cabinet secured by a digital pad. Six numbers later, he was in. He snatched his Glock 19 and jammed a magazine into it. He grabbed two spare mags and dropped them into his pockets, one each side. Lyndsey, now behind him, reached into the cabinet and grabbed a pistol and an MP5K sub-machine gun. Clocks opted for the Glock 17, the only weapon left. All three were ready in under five minutes, bashing into each other at the top of the stairs in an effort to get out of the house and into a car.

Paterson chose his custom-made Tesla Model S. He needed speed, and with an acceleration of 0–60 in 2.1 seconds it was the best he was going to get. With all three inside, Paterson pushed the accelerator and headed straight for the iron gates that secured the grounds. He hit a button under the dashboard and turned on the blues and twos before roaring off toward the high street.

Lyndsey, in the back, was struggling to put her seatbelt on. Clocks didn't bother. 'What 'appened, then? Who was that on the blower?'

Paterson weaved in and out of the morning traffic that was beginning to build. 'Jackie. She got the call early this morning.'

'Why the fuck didn't we get it, then?'

'No idea. Doesn't matter. We've got it now. Seems he stopped to get himself some grub when he left mine last night.

Placed an order, waited for five minutes, collected, walked out of the shop and *bam*! Straight in the chest. Didn't have a chance. Plods on scene said there was pandemonium when it happened. No one saw a thing though.'

Clocks shook his head as he looked out of his side window. 'Jesus! Bastard fuckin' Forrest! Where we goin'?'

'Hayes Kebab. Station Approach. Bromley. Put it in the GPS, John.'

Paterson swerved around a line of cars waiting at a red light, tapped his brakes as a stream of commuters drove at him from his right. He pressed on.

'Okay,' said Lyndsey, her head pushed between the two front seats. 'Question is, how the fuck did Forrest know where to find him?' Paterson said nothing. Clocks shook his head.

'He must've been watching your house, Ray,' she said. 'No other way of knowing.'

'Maybe bugged our phones somehow,' said Clocks.

'No, I think Lyndsey's right. I think he was close to us last night and we had no bloody idea.'

'Nah, I don't think so, Ray. Not with your security.'

Paterson jammed on the brakes as a cyclist shot through a junction, narrowly avoiding an accident. Clocks jabbed a button and his window slid open. 'You fuckin' retarded snot-gobblin' son of a toss wipe!' The cyclist wobbled but held up his middle finger. Clocks grimaced as Paterson accelerated calmly away.

'Don't forget who we're dealing with here, Clocksy. This isn't your run-of-the-mill burglar. This is a top-notch operative. No. He was there. I'll bet my life on it.'

# CHAPTER 45

Paterson raced along Pickhurst Lane on the B251 at Hayes. Just before the junction with Hurstdene Avenue, a single shot blew a hole in the Tesla's windscreen. Instinct kicked in. He swerved hard left — too hard. He mounted the kerb, hit the brakes, smashed into a low wall outside a house and rolled it. The car landed on its roof in a shower of sparks and broken glass before coming to a halt in the middle of the road. Inside the car, there was silence save for the spinning of a wheel.

Lying on a carpet of glass that used to be the roof, Paterson raised his head. He blinked several times until he realised blood was streaming into his eyes from a gash on his forehead. He wiped it away, blinked again then looked around the interior. Clocks was in a balled-up heap of blood, his knees almost touching his head, his left arm somehow caught between the door and his seat. Blood was pouring from his mouth. Paterson shook his head. 'John . . .' His own voice was shaky. He reached out and touched Clocks's shoulder and shook it. 'John, you okay?' No answer. Then he remembered. *Lyndsey.* He pulled his frame forward a few inches, across the small pond of broken glass, and looked toward the back of the car. The back window was busted out and he could hear the sounds of people shouting. Someone was on their phone chattering urgently. He began to weep quietly, his body shaking with shock and grief.

He pulled himself toward her, his body aching from the impact of the rolling car, forcing himself between the two front seats. As he reached her, he could see the faint flicker of her eyelids, a sign that she was still alive. With a desperate hope, he whispered her name, praying that she would wake up. 'Lynds . . . It's Ray. Talk to me, sweetie. C'mon.' There was no response. She lay still, her breathing shallow and uneven. Paterson knew that he needed to get help, and fast. He pulled himself closer, oblivious to the cuts he was opening up from the fragmented glass. Someone pushed their head inside the broken window. A man.

'You all right, mate?' His voice was loaded with panic. 'I've called an ambulance.'

Ever the mannered man, Paterson said, 'Thank you. I'm fine. My friends, not.'

'Look, stay still, mate. You might have hurt yourself bad. You'll make it worse.'

Paterson ignored him and reached for Lyndsey. He gently touched her upside-down face. It was covered in blood. Thick wads of it. Gelatinous. He knew that could happen with death approaching. He faced a dilemma. If he undid her seat belt, she would drop on her head. God knows that was in a bad enough state. He couldn't manoeuvre himself properly in the car to catch her. If he left her hanging, she would no doubt bleed out. The Devil and the Deep Blue Sea was where he was at. He decided that release was the best option. He fumbled desperately to try to find the belt release but being upside down with a half-dead body hanging from the seat didn't make it easy. After what felt like an eternity, he found and pushed the button. Lyndsey dropped onto her head with a thump that turned Paterson's stomach. She lay still. 'Mate,' he said to the man outside watching. 'Help me out of here.'

'Stay there, fellah. You could make things worse.'

'Worse than this? I'm a copper, mate. We've been ambushed. Please. Pull me out. Please . . .'

'Shit!' The man ran to the back of the car and lay himself down on the floor. He reached through the back window and grabbed Paterson's outstretched hand. He pulled at it. Paterson grunted as he tried to help his own escape by pushing against one of the seats. He felt a searing pain in his chest as it scraped up splinters of broken glass. The man pulled again until he'd got Paterson close to the back window, then he jumped up into a crouching position and pulled again. A few seconds later, Paterson was out of the window like a baby from the womb. The man stood him on his feet. He wobbled a few times as the man helped to steady him. Others rushed over to help the pair of them. 'Lyndsey . . .' he said. He dropped down and reached in to pull Lyndsey out.

'Mate,' said the man. 'Don't . . .'

'Help me,' said Paterson.'

'Mate . . .'

'Please.' Paterson's voice was small and weak. A pitiful plea for help.

The man shook his head and bent down to help him. Gently, but urgently, Paterson unfolded her and straightened her out the best he could before he and the man pulled her out of the car and into the street.

'Oh, Jesus!' said the man as he took in Lyndsey's broken head and face. A few bystanders turned away. Oddly, nobody was filming it on their phones. Older generation. Concern and respect for the injured.

Paterson's eyes welled up when he saw the hole in her chest. High. Below the collar bone. He sat himself on the floor and cradled her broken body, wiped blood away from her face and kissed her gently on the forehead several times. In between, he sobbed like a mother that had lost a child.

\* \* \*

Three floors up and four hundred yards away, Jack Forrest had guessed Paterson's route correctly. He took his time as he lined up Paterson's head in the sight of his trusted Remington 700 rifle.

# CHAPTER 46

When Johnny Clocks opened his eyes, it was to a searing pain in his head. A bright light shone into his face, blinding him to the figures standing around him. He pushed his tongue out between his lips, feeling the dryness of both. Slowly, he moved his fingers and jerked his legs. He could feel them. Good sign.

'John! It's Ray. How you doing, buddy?'

Clocks could feel himself mumble something, but what it was, he had no idea. Damn, his head hurt.

'It's okay, mate. We're in hospital. You had a helluva bang to the head. Doctors say you're fine other than a concussion.'

'Lynd . . . Lyndseeeee . . .' he mumbled.

Paterson patted his hand. 'She took a bit of a bang too, mate, but—'

Clocks tried to force himself up from the bed. 'Where . . . she . . .'

Paterson took his shoulders. 'Take it easy, John. Let's get you fixed up first and then I'll get you to her, eh? Don't try and stand.'

Clocks dropped back, his head sinking into the pillows. 'My head . . .' He swatted at it with one hand. 'Hurts . . .'

'I know, mate. You clumped it in the accident. You'll be fine. Doctor said it won't affect your previous brain injuries.'

It was a poor attempt at humour that made him wince at what he'd said as the image of an upside-down Lyndsey with part of her brain exposed flashed into his memory. 'You'll be fine. You'll be fine. The doctor's here now. He's gonna give you a once-over, okay?'

Clocks nodded.

A man in his early forties stepped forward. 'Mr Clocks. I'm Dr Bide. Nasty accident you were in. Hit your head and cut it open quite badly. We've already stitched it while you were unconscious, saves on the anaesthetic.' He chuckled at his own joke. Everyone's a comedian. Clocks forced a smile. 'Gonna shine a torch into your eyes now. It'll be very bright but it's only for a few seconds.' Clocks felt his right eyelid being forced open and a brilliant light floodlit his brain. 'Okay,' said the doctor. 'Other one now.' The same thing happened.

'Jesus!' said Clocks. 'My fuckin' 'ead's splittin'. You got any Anadins or summin'?'

Paterson breathed deeply as he watched his friend come back to life.

'I'll get you something stronger,' said the doctor. 'And then we're going to send you for an urgent brain scan.'

Clocks watched as the doctor's white coat flashed out of his peripheral vision and was gone. 'Ray?'

'What?'

'Where the fuck . . . did you learn . . . to drive?'

Paterson smiled. 'I know, right? Nearly as shit as you at it.'

Clocks suddenly went rigid. 'Where's Lyndsey, Ray? Where's my wife?' This time, Clocks sat himself bolt upright. 'Where . . . is she? I've gotta find her.' He swung his legs around to the edge of the bed.

'Whoa, whoa, whoa! Slow down, John. Slow down.'

'You know where . . . she is?' He looked into Paterson's face for some hope. Paterson nodded. A small, sharp nod.

'Yeah. She's upstairs.'

'What? Where upstairs?'

Paterson took a deep breath. He didn't want to tell him this. 'She's in the ICU, John. She got banged up quite bad.'

Clocks launched himself into an upright position and wobbled on his legs as he tried to make for the doorway out of the ward. Paterson caught him. 'Easy, mate. C'mon. Back to bed.'

Clocks pushed him away with what little strength he had. It was then that he noticed the two armed police officers keeping guard outside the doorway. 'The fuck . . . ?'

'Sit down, John and I'll explain. Lyndsey's being taken care of. She's in good hands. Sit down now. Let me talk to you.' He hooked himself underneath Clocks's arm and guided him back to bed.

'What happened, Ray?'

'You remember anything?'

Clocks shook his head. 'I remember a bang and then the car was tumblin'. I 'eard crunchin' metal, I think, scrapin' sounds and then . . . sod all until I woke up with this king-size nut ache.'

'Forrest took a pot shot at us. Hit the window, I swerved. Must've hit a kerb. Rolled the car. I managed to get you both out and onto the pavement. Some of the public helped me. A few minutes after that, an ambulance arrived.'

'What 'appened to Lyndsey?'

Paterson went quiet and looked down.

'Ray? What the fuck? Tell me, for Chrissake's. What's 'appened to her?'

'She's in a coma, John.'

Clocks nearly slid off the side of the bed. 'Coma?'

'Yeah. She hit her head, mate. Badly. When I came to, she was still strapped in her seat. I managed to get her down and out and then came back for you. She's in a bad way, John.'

Clocks felt the bile rise and burn his throat as he fought to stop himself throwing up. He recognised the signs in Paterson. He was holding something else back. 'Go on . . .'

'The bullet hit her, John. Caught her high, below the collarbone. Went straight through her. I'm sorry, mate. I'm so sorry.'

In that moment, all of Clocks's senses shut down. Time seemed to stand still as he processed the news, unable to fully comprehend the magnitude of his loss. The world around him faded into nothingness as he struggled to come to terms with the reality of his wife's condition. She was probably going to die.

Clocks and Lyndsey had both known the risks when they signed up for the job, and they had both taken monumental risks throughout their careers, but nothing could have prepared him for this. Grief settled over him like a heavy blanket, suffocating and consuming him, leaving nothing but emptiness in its wake. He was now a man without a purpose, without a future, and it looked like without the love of his life. He tried to wrestle that in with the fact that he'd just lost his mother too. All he could do was stare into space. Paterson let him be.

Eventually Clocks came back from his thoughts. He heard Paterson talking to him but couldn't determine a single word. He felt cold. Physically cold. Mentally, he finally died right there. 'Take me to her,' he said.

'What?'

'Take me to her.'

'I'm . . . I'm not sure . . . not sure that's . . .'

Clocks looked at him, his eyes dead. 'I wasn't asking.'

Paterson grabbed a nearby wheelchair and helped his friend into it. 'Two floors up. Lift's at the end of the corridor.' As he pushed him out of the room, Dr Bide came rushing back in holding a small white paper cup containing two white tablets in one hand and a paper cup of water in the other. 'Hey! Where d'you think you're going to?'

Paterson kept moving. 'To see his wife. We'll be back.'

'No, no. He's badly concussed. He needs a scan. Come back!'

Paterson kept going, got to the lift and pushed the button to the ICU.

As the doors opened, Clocks could see the hallway stretching endlessly before him. The walls seemed to move and close in on him, as if they were alive, and he could sense their malice. The hallway seemed dark, the kind of dark you saw in a dream, a half-dark.

He didn't hear Paterson tell him that hers was the second bed on the left. He heard nothing until the wheelchair jerked to a halt at the foot of Lyndsey's bed. Her appearance was terrifying, her face mottled with deep, angry bruises, swollen and distorted beyond recognition. A tightly wrapped bandage covered her head, hiding the true extent of her injuries. A ventilator protruded from her mouth, making her look like a mutilated doll. Paterson took in the sight of her then looked at Clocks. What he saw broke his cold heart. The Clocks he knew was gone. The lairy and cocky man now appeared frail and broken, as if he had aged decades in just a few short hours.

'What the hell are you two doing here?' a female doctor in her mid-fifties barked at them. 'You're not supposed to be here. This is a clean area.'

'She's his wife,' said Paterson. 'We're the police officers that were in the crash with her.'

The doctor backed up a step. 'Oh. Oh, I see. I'm sorry. I'm really sorry, but you can't stay here dressed like that. You'll have to put gowns on and then only for a few minutes.'

'Will she live?' said Clocks without taking his eyes off Lyndsey.

The doctor started for a second. 'What? Er . . . er . . .'

'Will she live?' Clocks said again.

'Look, to be honest, we don't know. She's suffered two very severe injuries. We're keeping her in a coma for now while we monitor the pressure on her brain. She's already been in for an operation and that has helped, but we can't be sure just yet. She has a way to go, I'm afraid.'

'How long will she be in a coma for?' Clocks said.

'Can't say for sure. Too early. But we'll keep her this way until we can be sure she's out of danger. We're doing our best, I promise.'

Clocks nodded. 'I know. Make sure she lives.' He pushed himself up out of the wheelchair and, with some effort, stood up straight.

'John, what are you doing?' said Paterson, concern etched on his face.

'Leavin',' he said.

'What?' said the doctor. 'I was told you had a severe concussion. You can't leave yet! You could collapse and die.'

Clocks turned and faced her. 'Doc, I just lost my mum. If my wife dies, I have nothing to live for, so . . .' He shrugged.

Paterson shook his head slowly. 'So, where we going, John?'

'To chop down a fuckin' big Forrest.'

## CHAPTER 47

They sat themselves in the back of an armed response vehicle with the instruction to take them back to Tower Bridge nick.

'John?' said Paterson.

'What?'

'We need to think this through.'

'I already 'ave.'

'No, mate, you haven't. You have a concussion. You've reacted.'

Clocks noticed the driver of the police car glance in his rear-view mirror. Paterson was clearly trying to be tactful around the other officers in the car.

'We can't give in to anger, John. Forrest is banking on it. You know that.'

'Yeah. So what?'

'So, if we want to catch him, we need to be shrewd.'

'I'm not interested in shrewd, Ray. Not after what 'e's done. 'E's killed Dusty and now probably Lyndsey. 'E wants a fight, 'e can 'ave it.'

Paterson went quiet, trying to pick his words carefully.

'Sir,' said the driver. 'If I may?'

'What is it?' said Paterson.

'Look, we know what's happened, all right? We know what this bastard's done to you and your team and the guv'nor's wife. I can sense you're being a bit wary about what you say. Don't be, okay? If that was my wife, I would find this fucker and shoot his face off, so you just work out what you've got to do and don't worry about us. We both knew Mrs Clocks. She trained me and I have a ton of respect for her. Mr Clocks, I'm so sorry. Look, if you need anything, anything at all, just ask. If this fucker's declared war on the Met, then we have to stick together, right?'

'Right,' said Paterson.

The second firearms officer nodded. 'I'm all in too.'

'Cheers, boys,' said Clocks. 'Appreciate that, but I won't need your 'elp an' 'e's dancin' around the bush because 'e's more subtle than me. I don't wanna drop you in it if push comes to shove. Plan's simple. Find 'im. Kill 'im. Job done.'

'Sir?' said the officer.

'I said no. Thank you, but no.'

Paterson's phone rang. 'Monkey. What's up?'

Clocks turned to look at Paterson for the first time since their ride began. Paterson sat in silence as Clocks strained to hear what Monkey was saying.

'Oh God . . . no.'

Clocks frowned.

'Okay. Listen, we're heading back to the Bridge. Get everyone to meet us there. First one back, kill all the lights and meet in the kitchen.' Monkey said something in response. 'Yes, the kitchen. The shutters are down on the counter and the office is dead centre of the building. Hard for anyone to get a bead on us in there.' Paterson hung up and shook his head.

'Go on. What's that fucker done now?' said Clocks.

Paterson hesitated for a second. 'There's been a car bomb.'

'Oh fuck.'

'Initial reports from officers are saying that it's cops. One dead. One in a bad way.'

'Who, for fuck's sake?'

'They've found Wol's wallet on the pavement.' Paterson looked away. 'And someone matching Alice's description.'

'Wol? No. No. No. Ah, Jesus.' Clocks banged his fist on the back of the headrest, startling the officer in front. 'Please, not Wol as well.'

'Sirs,' said the driver, 'the offer still stands.'

Neither man answered, both lost in their own thoughts, both unravelling fast, both raging, desperate for revenge.

Clocks looked out the window. They were coming along Tooley Street. 'Just get us in safely, mate. That's all I want.'

'Will do, sir.'

The car pulled up outside the station and both gunmen bailed out then stood in front of the respective back doors, guns drawn, held high as they scanned the street and surrounding buildings. Paterson and Clocks opened their doors and stepped out. The officers kept them close as they swivelled about low and high and escorted them inside the building. Once inside, Paterson and Clocks thanked both men and jumped the counter. The station officer looked confused as the scene unfolded in front of him. It was an officer Clocks knew. 'Jim. Kill the lights. Lock the doors and go home. I'm givin' you the night off.'

'What's goin' on, guv?'

'Just do as I say, mate. Get home an' be safe. Go on, step lively, son.'

As Paterson and Clocks headed for the darkened stairwell, Paterson saw the ambient light behind him go out. Jim was doing as he was told.

When they reached the canteen, Paterson entered carefully, weapon drawn. Clocks stood behind him, Glock held high.

The canteen was in darkness. They made their way toward the kitchen area. The shutter was down and they were safe from any clean shots through the windows. For a moment, neither man said a word, just stood in silence. Clocks dragged out the canteen manager's chair and plonked himself down.

He sighed heavily. 'The fucker's got Wol. I can't believe it. I just . . . he's tearin' us to fuckin' pieces, Ray. Jesus.'

'Is there a radio in here?'

'What? You mean a job radio?'

'No, no. A radio, I wanna put the news on. See if I can find out what's happened.'

'Could always phone Morne. Fuckin' commissioner should know what's 'appenin', shouldn't 'e?'

'He should, yes. But can we trust him, Clocksy? Right now, I only trust you.'

'Good point. Where's the others? Thought at least one of 'em would've been 'ere by now.' Clocks struggled to see his watch in the dark. 'Knew I should 'ave bought a digital.'

Paterson's phone rang.

'Who's that?' said Clocks.

Paterson looked at the screen. 'Jackie.'

'Put it on speaker.'

Paterson did. 'Jack? Where are you? Are you gonna be long?'

'Sadly, Mr Paterson, she won't be able to make it.'

Clocks stood bolt upright, grabbed the phone and screamed into it. 'Forrest! I'm gonna fuckin' tear your cuntin' 'ead off an' shit down the 'ole, you bastard! You fuckin' 'ear me? I'm gonna kill you!'

'Hello, Clocks. Lovely to hear your voice. Elegant as usual.'

'Tell me where you're 'iding yerself an' I'll come an' do yer right now, you two-bob piece of shit!'

'You seem upset. I'll talk to Paterson. Much more civilised.'

'Where is she, Forrest?' said Paterson.

'With me. And Detective Harris. Monkey, you call him, I believe? Jackie and the young female detective. Bad start for her.'

'What do you want?'

'The USB with the Hayes files and all of my reports.'

'Don't know what you're talking about.'

'Yes, you do, Paterson. You made a copy from my laptop. I watched you.'

'No, you didn't. Wasn't there.'

'Ray, you don't have time to play silly games. You, Clocks and the one in dress-up, the fat person in black. Good with computers and electronics, except not as good as you all thought. The security services are well ahead of the game when it comes to surveillance technology. Further ahead than you, for sure. So, ready to stop playing games, eh?'

'Go on.'

'Tell us where you are, shit'ead, an' I'll deliver it meself!' yelled Clocks. 'I'll shove it right in your fuckin' eyeball an' stamp it out the other side of your fat, ugly thick-as-shit 'ead.'

'John! Shut it! Just shut up!'

'He's hurting, Paterson,' Forrest sneered.

'Not as much as you when I get me 'ands on you, you circus freak!'

'John!' Paterson scowled at his friend. 'Look, Forrest, leave them alone and I'll bring it to you.'

'Both of you.'

'Both of us. Just leave the others alone.'

'Can't do that, Ray. They know of the plan and that cannot be allowed.'

'So what? You're gonna kill them?'

'Yes. Just like the others. I can't leave witnesses, Ray. This is too big. Bigger than a few coppers. You've no doubt read the files. You know how important it is that news of this doesn't leak out.'

'So, if you're going to kill them, why the fuck would I bring you the USB? Might as well just release it and fuck you up.'

'Well, it comes down to two things really. First, how quickly you want them to die. I can make it quick or I can make it excruciatingly painful over a period of time. A *long* period of time — and they can watch each other die.' Paterson went quiet. He had no answer. 'And second, you both want a piece of me. You won't be able to resist. And believe me, I will not be running away.

'Paterson, There's no way out of this for any of you. I've killed Dusty, Young, the fat one who was with you, Clocks's wife—'

'Don't you mention my wife, you cowardly piece of filth. I'll fuckin' kill you! Hear me? I'll. Fuckin'. Kill. You.' Paterson had seen Johnny Clocks enraged many a time but not like this. Never like this.

Forrest ignored him. 'I killed the soldier too. White Ghost, wasn't it? One shot, clean as a whistle, right in the chest. And you two . . . you should be dead.'

'Why did you leave us alive?'

'It wasn't intentional, believe me. After you rolled the car, I had you in my sight when, wouldn't you know it, a bus stopped to help. A bus! Completely blocked any shot I had. You can never usually find one when you want one, can you? There you are . . . luck!'

'Okay,' said Paterson. 'When and where?'

'One more thing, Paterson. I've just sent you a video. Have a quick look. I'll stay on the line.'

Paterson opened the video and watched in horror. The film was grainy, not too clear, but it was obvious it was him and Clocks. They were in an office somewhere, impossible to tell where. The footage looked like it had come from a spy cam, the type concealed in a briefcase. Paterson and Clocks were boasting. Boasting about all the crimes they'd gotten away with . . . murder . . . fraud . . . rape. As the video went on, the two policemen talked about how they'd had to kill their own squad and the outside team of investigators because they were under yet another investigation. The net was tightening, and they had to run. Killing everyone ensured that they couldn't give evidence against them.

'Finished it, Paterson?'

Paterson rubbed the knot of tension in the back of his neck. 'You bastard.'

'Isn't technology wonderful? The things AI can do now.'

'Have you released this?'

'Just before I called you.'

'No one will believe this.'

'You don't think so? Of course they will, Paterson. People believe what they want to believe, and when they see and hear this . . . That's you two in the video for all intents and purposes, and people know you're a pair of dodgy operators. They'll want to believe it. Two rogue cops murdering people to save their own skins. You're dead in the water. You're finished, both of you. The whole country will be hunting you down now. Chances are a few trigger-happy cops will shoot you on sight. I understand they were rather fond of Commissioner Young. Many of them anyway. And you two evil bastards killed him.'

'It's so obviously a lie.'

Forrest chuckled. 'Well, you know how it goes. You control the lie, you control the truth. So, I'll text you the address and you bring me the USB. I'll kill your team quickly, then I'll kill you and release a story that you and Clocks had these ones as hostages, and you'd just killed them when the security services arrived. They engaged you in a firefight, and you both lost your lives. So sad.'

'You know what, Forrest?'

'Go on.'

'You're dead.'

# CHAPTER 48

'Gentlemen. I have a plan.' The voice came out of the darkness.

'What the fuck?' Paterson whirled around, gun in hand and raised to shoot. Clocks followed suit.

'Easy, boys,' said the voice.

'Liam?' Paterson lowered his gun.

'Casper?' Clocks kept his gun at the ready.

The White Ghost stepped out of the darkness.

'Jesus!' said Paterson. 'He said you were dead. How long have you been standing back there?'

'Long enough to prove a point.'

'What bloody point?' said Clocks.

'That you can't see me in the dark, Clocksy.'

Clocks cocked his head slightly. 'Fair point, son. No more ribbin' yer about being glow in the dark then, eh?'

'If you wouldn't mind,' said Cole.

'Forrest said he'd shot you. What happened?'

'Oh, he shot me all right. Hit me straight in the chest. Like being hit by a bloody train. Knocked me clean off my feet and sent me flying. If it hadn't been for a brick wall that conveniently stopped me, I'd probably still be rolling.'

'How'd you survive that, then?' said Clocks.

'That was thanks to a double layer of Kevlar and plates. Since this whole thing started and I knew what we were up against, I doubled up on protection. Heavy as hell, but it worked. That said, the force of impact has left a huge bruise and has no doubt done some serious internal damage. But I can breathe and I can function . . . just. I'm lucky to be here. I'm surprised the shock alone didn't finish me off.'

'Thank gawd it didn't,' said Clocks. 'I'da missed your smiley face and witty banter.'

'Well, lucky for you, you don't have to.'

Clocks patted the man on the shoulder, saw him wince and realised he was in a lot more pain than he was letting on. 'You sure you're okay?'

'Yeah. Even if I wasn't, I'd still be coming with you. I can't believe what this bastard's done to us all. Clocksy, John, I'm so sorry for what he's done to Lyndsey. I'll kill him for that alone.'

Clocks gave him a little half-smile. 'I know you would, mate, but this fucker's on me, okay? He's mine. You two copy?'

Cole sighed deeply. 'Copy that.'

Paterson shrugged. 'Yeah, why not? But Clocksy—'

'I know you're worried about me,' said Clocks, 'but don't be. I'm a big boy an' I can 'old me 'ands up. You know that.'

'Yeah, I do know that, but I'm worried they won't be big enough to knock this fucker down.'

'Well, they might not be, but 'e can 'ave a Millwall kiss as an opener. That'll soften 'im up a bit.'

'A headbutt? He's six foot, double plus.' Paterson pulled a milk crate off the top of a freezer chest. 'Best you take this to stand on, then.'

'Listen,' said Cole, 'we have a real advantage here, you know that, eh?'

'He thinks you're dead,' said Paterson.

'Yep. So, when he texts you the address, we're gonna find me a vantage point.'

'You are not shootin' 'im,' said Clocks. 'I said 'e's mine an' I meant it, you understand me?'

'I wasn't going to shoot him, Clocksy. I was going to take an overwatch position on the flat just in case you do somehow get into trouble, even though you're a scrappy sod. He's a fricking monster-sized killing machine. All you've got is a big set of balls, a couldn't-give-a-toss attitude and a milk crate. I just wanna look out for you.'

'Ah. You love me, don't you?' said Clocks.

Cole smiled. 'Don't push it or I'll take the milk crate off of you — see if I don't.'

Paterson's phone pinged. The light from the screen illuminated his face. 'Got it,' he said. 'It's not that far from here. John, fire up the computer there. We need to Google Map this place first. Find you somewhere to go, Liam.'

'Where is it, then?' said Clocks.

'Rotherhithe New Road. What's that, a couple of miles from here?'

'Yeah, not far.' Clocks had logged in and was looking at Google Maps. 'Doesn't look like anything special. Casp . . . sorry . . . Liam, can you find a spot somewhere?'

Cole leaned over Clocks and scrutinised the map. 'Put the little man on the street for me. I want to have a street-level look around.'

Clocks clicked and dragged the little yellow figure and dropped it onto the street. 'Oh, shit. Where am I? This bloody thing never goes right first time.'

'Turn it around,' said Cole.

'Wait a minute. I'm tryin'. Bleedin' thing's all over the place, innit?'

'Well, just click on one of the arrows.'

'Arrows?'

'Yes, the arrows! Can't you see them? There!' Cole stabbed the map with his finger. 'It looks like an ordinary two-up two-down.'

'Except I've got a nasty feeling this is an MI6 safe house,' said Paterson. 'That means it's got all sorts of safe rooms in it. If he's using them to hold the team, we're gonna have a rough old time getting to them. Liam, I think you'll find the windows are bulletproof.'

'Maybe,' he said. 'But they're gonna have to be seriously, seriously bulletproof to stop the firepower I have. We'll see, won't we?'

'So, if it goes tits up and by some slim chance the man mountain starts to get the better of me, you can't guarantee you can shoot him?'

'That's about it.'

Clocks sniffed. 'Better not lose then, had I?'

'We ready to get going?' said Paterson.

Both men nodded. 'Okay, Liam. You can't come with us, obviously. Nip up to my office and take one of the pool cars or there's a motorbike. Whatever suits you, okay? Keys are on the board in the main office. Keep the lights off.'

'Take these.' Cole handed them two small radio transmitters and earpieces. 'I'll let you know when I'm in position and have eyes on the property. Do not go in until I give you the nod. Understand?'

'Okay,' said Paterson. 'John, let's go kill this piece of crap.'

Paterson and Clocks made for the stairs while Cole headed upwards.

'John, when we go in, I get the feeling this is going to go bad very quickly. He's not going to waste time with us.'

'I know. I don't intend to waste time either.'

'Just . . . Look, I know this is a silly thing to say given the circumstances, but don't lose your rag, okay? You know what I've told you. You lose your temper, you lose clarity. You lose clarity, you lose the fight.'

'Blah, blah, blah, Ray. I know what you've said, but I'm goin' for the surprise. The last thing 'e'll expect is for me to go straight at 'im. 'E'll be thinkin' we're gonna wanna see proof of life an' all that. Way I see it is, when we go in, 'e'll do one of us straight away. Not both, 'cos if we ain't got the key on us, 'e won't know what we've done with it. So, 'e'll do one of us, beat an' torture the shit out of the other. Fact.'

'Oh, lovely. Well, let's see where the night takes us.'

'I know where I'm goin'.'

Paterson frowned as he opened the car door.

Clocks pulled the other door open. 'Straight to 'ell, mate. Straight to 'ell.'

Paterson nodded and chuckled. 'See you there, mate.'

# CHAPTER 49

'Shit!' Paterson's voice cracked as he gripped the steering wheel, his knuckles turning white. 'Do we know where Carter and Winslet are?'

Clocks shook his head, fear etched across his face.

'I'll give them a call,' Paterson said through gritted teeth. He waited anxiously for someone to answer on the other end of the line. Finally, after what felt like an eternity, Carter picked up.

'Guv! What the hell is going on?' Harry's panicked voice came through the phone.

'You seen the news? It's Forrest. He's a bad fucker and he's been found out. We searched his flat and copied all the files off of his laptop. It's on a USB in a folder called "The Hayes File". Harry, its contents are unbelievably scary. He knows we've got it and he's taking out anyone who knows about it.' Paterson's voice trembled with anger. 'Is Grace with you?'

'Yeah, we're together.'

'Good. Keep it that way. Listen to me, Harry. Do not go anywhere near the nick under any circumstances. Hopefully, I'll let you know when it's safe to do so. Understood?'

'Hopefully? Guv—'

'It's not up for debate. That's a direct order. Do you understand me?'

'Yes, sir.'

'I'm not risking any more casualties.' Paterson took a deep breath, trying to remain calm. 'Clocks and I are with the Ghost now. Forrest's taken three of the team hostage to lure us out.'

'Shit! Guv, I don't want to leave you alone,' Harry said hesitantly.

'I'm not alone,' Paterson reassured him. 'There's three of us, and this is our fight. We'll finish it one way or another.'

'Do you have a plan?' Desperation was creeping into Harry's voice.

'Of sorts,' Paterson said. 'We're just gonna confront him. He said he's going to kill all the team if me and Clocksy don't show up and bring him the copy. It's on, Harry.'

'That doesn't sound like much of a plan!'

Paterson wrenched the steering wheel as he took a sharp left. 'It's all we've got. But listen, there is one thing you can do to help.' Paterson's voice took on a serious tone. 'Alice also backed up the Hayes file on a private server.'

'Alice? Alice? Who the fuck is Alice?' Harry asked, confused.

'This isn't a fucking joke, Harry!' Paterson snapped.

Harry stuttered, trying to explain himself. 'I didn't mean it as a joke, sir. I genuinely have no idea who Alice is.'

'I'll explain later,' Paterson said impatiently. 'Listen, John said he's left the location of the server, password and account details with someone you both met when you first encountered each other. D'you remember that?'

Harry wracked his brain, trying to remember. 'Er, no. I can't recall off the top of my head.'

Paterson became agitated. 'I need you to think! He looked across at Clocks, who mouthed something at him. 'He said to tell you that it stunk to high heaven. Does that help?'

'Yep. It does.' Harry knew exactly where he and Clocks had first met. Southwark morgue.

# CHAPTER 50

Paterson and Clocks stood at the end of the driveway looking at the safe house. There was nothing special about it. Typical cookie-cutter box house in a row of thirty. Two had balconies at the top, two didn't. A repeating pattern until the end of the row. All of them had a one-car drive.

The garden was neat and tidy with the obligatory three waste bins lined up neatly like scruffy plastic soldiers. Other than those, an upturned cracked pot lying near the street door was the only thing that wasn't in pristine condition. It looked oddly out of place somehow. From somewhere upstairs, a dim light radiated through the window and out into the street. The front door was slightly ajar, beckoning them to enter. Clocks steamed forward until Paterson put a hand on his chest. 'Just hang fire, John. We don't know if he's rigged the door.'

Clocks looked down at the hand and then up at Paterson. The look left nothing to the imagination. Paterson removed it. 'Why would he do that? No value in it for 'im, is there? No us, no key.' He gave a little nonchalant shrug. 'Come on.'

'Wait. Let me speak to Liam.' He tapped the earpiece. 'Liam, where are you?'

The White Ghost's voice crackled in his ear. 'Six minutes.'

'You got somewhere in mind?'

'Yep. Buy me six minutes, total. Then I'll be ready.'

'I'll leave the channel open,' said Paterson.

'Copy that,' said Cole.

Clocks pushed the door open. 'Forrest!' he called. 'The fuck you 'iding yerself, son? Come on, then. let's 'ave yer.'

Forrest's voice boomed out. 'Up here, Clocks! When you're ready.'

Clocks marched over to the stairs and started up them, Paterson close behind. At the top, there was only one room with a light in it, the door half open. Like a moth, Clocks headed straight toward it. With no hesitation, he kicked it open the rest of the way. His heart sank. Sitting at Forrest's feet was DC Harmony Lee. Her face was battered and bruised, her hair matted with blood. Tears streaked her bruised face and blood lined her teeth. She was handcuffed to a radiator. Forrest had a gun pointed at the top of her skull.

Clocks glared at him, fists bunched, teeth gritted.

'Ah, there you are. The Met's finest.' Forrest looked down at the girl. 'She was a bit more feisty than I anticipated. Don't normally hit women.'

'Let 'er go, you evil cunt, an' me an' you can go dancin' together. What d'you say?'

'I say it's a good idea, but first off, I need to know if you have the USB.'

Paterson reached inside his jacket pocket and fished it out. He said nothing, surprised that Clocks's prediction hadn't come true about him killing one of them straight off the bat.

'Put it on the table over there,' said Forrest.

'No.'

'No? What do you mean *no*?'

'Shouldn't take a lot of workin' out, you arse,' said Clocks. 'It's like when yer mum said no to yer dad, but here you are . . .'

Forrest smiled. 'C'mon, Paterson. It's not like you know I won't kill her.'

Paterson stepped a bit closer. Forrest pulled the hammer back on the gun. Both men understood each other perfectly.

'Well, you're going to do it anyway, but I'm going to ask that you don't. She's not done anything. She's brand spanking new to the team. So new, she doesn't even know what the fuck's going on. So, do at least one decent thing in your vile life and let her go.'

Forrest pulled a face that said he was thinking about it, but Paterson knew a mickey take when he saw it. 'Where are the others?' Paterson said.

'In a room off of the hallway back there. They're all alive. For now.'

Clocks turned to look along the hallway. 'So, when are we goin' at it then, numbnuts? I'm bored with all this jibber-jabber.'

'Oh, Clocks. I'm going to make you pay for all your piss-taking and insults.'

'Yeah, yeah, course you are. Just shut up bunnyin' about it and get on with it, will yer? Yer like an ol' woman with yer *yap-yap*. Man up, you fuckin' murderin' coward.'

Forrest bit his lip and dug the gun into the girl's skull. Neither Paterson nor Clocks flinched. Harmony moaned softly and sobbed.

'How's the missus, Clocks. Any better?'

Clocks glared at him, murder in his heart. 'You're just gonna make this worse for yerself. I'll 'urt you a thousand fuckin' ways before I kill you. D'you 'ear me?'

'Why, Forrest?' said Paterson. 'Why are you going along with this?'

'It's my job, Paterson. King and country and all that.'

'Your job? Murdering people left, right and centre and helping some shiny-arsed bigwigs tune up the Russians. Helping to kill thousands in a fucking chemical attack so that your bosses can demonstrate how powerful we are now. Fucking innocent people, Forrest! Families, children. Christ, I'm not sure your king nor your country would thank you for that.'

'Well, luckily, I don't worry too much about that. I have a job to do. It's dirty but I do it.'

'So, 'ow long 'ave the British government been employin' yakkity ol' women with a desire to murder dozens of people? I'm guessin' you're not the first.'

'Good guess, Clocks. Good guess. Not as stupid as you look.'

'Oh, I'm not stupid, Forrest. I've been tested. What they found out is that I'm a high-functionin' sociopath with 'omicidal rage and a tendency to keep windin' people up until they snap an' come at me, then I get to kick the granny out of 'em for doin' so. Winner, winner.'

Forrest took a key off the counter next to him and threw it at Clocks. He caught it without looking at it. 'That's to the room down the hall. Lock Paterson in there with the others and then we get to dance.' Clocks turned his back and walked toward the hall.

'C'mon, Ray. Let's go.'

'What? No. I'm not leaving you here.'

'You are. I told you 'e's mine an' I meant it. Now, move!' Paterson followed him to the door. Clocks unlocked and opened it. Inside, chained to a safe rail, were Jackie and Monkey. Clocks knew he was standing in an interrogation room where prisoners were secured and most likely tortured for information. Both of them had a two-inch strip of gaffer tape over their mouths and eyes.

'I'm gonna need to hear that lock click, Clocks,' Forrest called. 'Get him in there.'

'Don't do this, John,' said Paterson.

Clocks smiled at his friend. 'Look, mate. We've 'ad a blindin' run, ain't we? If it ends 'ere, so be it. If he does me, you're the only one that's not secured. Make it count, mate. Go on . . . best you start settin' the troops free instead of yammerin' on, mate.'

'John . . .'

Clocks pushed him inside, locked the door and threw the key along the hallway toward Forrest. He followed it and stood back in the room. 'Ready, fuckwit?'

Forrest gently released the hammer on the gun and took it from Harmony's head. He placed it on the counter before removing his jacket. Clocks saw his chance. Forrest had shrugged his jacket off, leaving his arms caught for a second or two. In that time, Clocks had crossed the floor and thrown himself at him. Forrest crashed into the wall, grunting as his head hit brick. Clocks followed it up with a headbutt, which stunned the big man for a moment. He knew that once Forrest got the jacket off, his odds were severely diminished. He kicked Forrest's left leg away, dropping him onto one knee, following it up with a push-kick to the chest, sending Forrest sprawling. He jumped on him, aware that despite the beating he was getting, Forrest had almost squirmed his way out of his jacket. Clocks sent a flurry of punches to Forrest's face again and again, spurred on by the sight of the blood that appeared in Forrest's mouth.

'You fuckin' no-good piece of shit! I'll kill you, you 'ear me? I'm gonna kill you!' Clocks stood up and raised his foot to stamp down on Forrest's face, but the man rolled out from under it before it could be delivered. Seeing Forrest scrabble to his feet made Clocks angrier and he ran at him again, knocking him back down. Forrest, now free of his self-imposed restraints, was ready. He rolled backward and stood in a half-crouch like a monstrous Marvel superhero. Clocks kept coming. Forrest stood up quickly and side-stepped Clocks, punching him on the side of the head as he went past. Clocks's legs gave way and he stumbled into the sink, knocking a pile of crockery all across the draining board. He reeled about as Forrest moved in.

* * *

Inside the holding room, Paterson spoke into his radio, his voice urgent. 'Liam! Do you have eyes?'

He waited. 'Stand by. Yep. Got 'em. No shot. No shot.'

Paterson took a quick look around the room. Windows. He looked out. Small window ledge. He flattened his face against the cold glass of the double glazing and could just about see the room next door where Clocks and Forrest were fighting. He stepped back and looked at the locks on the window. Not your ordinary. He stepped aside. 'Can you take out my window lock? We're in a secure interrogation room. There's a metal enforcement rod running from top to bottom.'

'Not easily.' Cole fired a shot anyway. The sound of metal hitting metal made Paterson jerk back. 'I reckon it'll take four or five shots. Stay well away until I say go.'

\* \* \*

Clocks felt a sharp, searing pain in his ribs as Forrest hit him with a blow so powerful that it took him an inch off his feet. He stumbled back, struggling to keep upright. He knew that if Forrest got him off his feet it was all over bar the shouting. He swung out wildly, missing Forrest's head by a good foot. He swung again — air. Forrest smacked Clocks in the face, opening up his nose. Blood gushed out and ran into his mouth. The taste seemed to galvanise Clocks and he pulled himself straight. Next to him was a stack of plates. He swung his arm into them and sent all but one flying toward Forrest. As Forrest covered his face, Clocks moved toward him, bent down and snatched up a viciously pointed piece of broken china. He grabbed it like a dagger, cutting his own fingers in the process. He drove it downward jamming it into Forrest's forearm. The man yelped in pain and dodged away, moving quickly to the other side of the room.

'That's the boy,' said Clocks. 'Run, Forrest, run!' He stepped toward the wounded giant, cornering him. Holding out the makeshift dagger, Clocks looked straight into Forrest's eye. 'I'm gonna gut you like the fat fuckin' whale you are, you understand me?' He raised the china dagger, ready to bring it down, when Forrest sprang forward, hitting Clocks in the stomach with his full weight, locking his arms around his back in a rugby tackle. Clocks managed to plunge the dagger into Forrest's back before he was squashed against the

258

wall. His head jerked back and banged loudly on the bricks before Forrest's weight dragged him down and buried him underneath. Forrest dragged himself up, grabbed Clocks by the collar and punched him twice in the face. Clocks's head lolled backward as his senses left him.

'Enough of this, Clocks. It's your time.' Forrest walked over to the kitchen counter and from the butcher's block drew out a large meat cleaver and walked back to Clocks, slipping in his blood as he got closer. Harmony Lee, trussed up and with gaffer tape covering her mouth, made a muffled screaming sound.

Forrest stood over Clocks, who could barely comprehend what was happening. 'You're a fucking idiot, Clocks. No other word for it.' He raised the cleaver over his head then stopped as warm sticky blood sprayed his face. There was a clatter on the kitchen tiles as the cleaver hit the floor. Forrest, bewildered, looked up at his hand and saw nothing. He turned and saw a small hole in the window. Forrest roared in pain as he doubled up, trying to hold his stump with his other hand. There was a small tinkling sound and he fell to the floor, a hole in his upper thigh. A bullet had gone through and through, collecting a bit of bone on the way out.

* * *

Liam Cole had delivered his message to play fair. He could've killed Forrest, *wanted* to kill Forrest, but he would keep his promise to Clocks.

From his vantage point, Cole watched Forrest drop then calmly went back to shooting at the metal bar that was holding Ray Paterson back. 'Ray! So you know, I've levelled the playing field.'

* * *

Johnny Clocks painfully pulled himself to a lying position, resting on his elbows. He spat blood onto the tiles and wriggled his tongue around his mouth, counting teeth. He forced himself onto his knees before straightening his arms. He turned slowly to sit himself down, his upper body swaying as he looked around the room. Forrest was groaning and grunting in pain. Clocks had no idea what had caused it, but he saw the meat cleaver lying on the floor. He flopped forward onto his hands and knees and made his way toward it. Forrest was closer to it but struggled to move at all. Blood was pouring down his leg. He groaned in pain as he dragged his way toward the chopper as well.

# CHAPTER 51

Clocks got to the chopper first. He wrapped his bloody fingers around it and swung it around behind him. Pain shot through his twisted torso, a reminder of Forrest's rib punch. The chopper found flesh. Forrest's good hand. He yelled out as it sliced into the palm, nearly severing it at an angle. Forrest moved toward the radiator where the girl was secured. He pressed himself up against the wall and watched as Clocks pulled himself up to a staggered stand. He swayed about a bit before moving toward Forrest. Harmony's eyes were wide with fright as the bloodied and beaten Johnny Clocks lurched toward them.

* * *

Four shots was all it took for Cole to shoot out the metal bar that secured the windows to Paterson's prison. *Cutbacks*, he thought. MI6 must be using cheaper materials.

With the window now free to open, Cole turned his attention back to Clocks. 'You better get in there, Ray. Clocksy's got him down. He's gonna do a number on him.'

261

Paterson pushed the window open and hauled himself out and onto the precariously thin ledge that ran the length of the house.

* * *

Clocks knelt down in front of Forrest. 'Said I'd kill yer, didn't I?'
'Fuck off, Clocks!'
He swung the cleaver at Forrest, embedding it deep into his upper arm. Forrest roared as Clocks wriggled it out. 'That one's for Dusty. A fuckin' good man, 'e was.' He changed hands and swung it again, opening up an ugly gash along Forrest's chest. 'That's for Alice. She was my friend. She was a good . . . girl.' He nodded to himself. Covered in Forrest's blood, Harmony was screaming against her bonds, tears blinding her as she scrabbled about, trying to get any distance she could, away from Clocks.
Clocks slashed the blade across both of Forrest's upper thighs half a dozen times. Forrest screamed with the agony of it. 'These are for Wol. I bloody loved that ol' sod. I loved 'im! You 'ear me? I loved 'im! An' this . . . this, you no-good dirty piece of low-life fuckin' shit, is for my wife. You shot my wife!' Clocks swung the chopper and sliced open Forrest's stomach. He watched with a numb fascination as a small pile of organs started to peep through the opening.
A banging noise at the window made him stop for a moment. He saw Paterson behind the glass trying to force the window open. Clocks got onto his knees. He raised the chopper over his head with both hands. Forrest looked up at him, defiant.

* * *

The frame gave way as Paterson launched himself into the room. 'John! No!' He slipped on the blood that was washing across the floorboards, banging his head when he landed.

'Lyndsey sends 'er best.' Clocks swung the chopper down on Forrest's skull, splitting it down to the eyebrows. Paterson was up. He saw Clocks fall onto his backside. He looked at Harmony and his heart sank. She was a twisted, broken doll, her face and body covered in blood and bits of Jack Forrest, her screams swallowed by thick, suffocating tape as she stared in horror at the carnage before her.

Her eyes were locked onto Clocks and the cleaver he held.

Clocks turned to her. 'All right, Treacle? S'pect you're gonna want a bit of a cuddle after all this?' He tried to pull himself upright, but his legs had gone.

Paterson managed to hook an arm under each shoulder and held Clocks gently as he slipped back down into a sitting position.

'You're all right, mate. Just wait here. Rest up, y'hear? Rest up.'

Paterson grimaced at the state of his friend. 'Ambulance!' he shouted. 'Get an ambulance. Now!' Monkey Harris, having entered the room the same way as Paterson, turned on his heel and ran for the door. Jackie just stood there, shocked. Forrest had taken their phones from them, so a knock on a neighbour's door was the way forward.

'Made a bit of a mess of 'im, didn't I?' said Clocks.

'Yeah,' said Paterson. 'He deserved it, though.'

'Yeah . . .' Clocks's eyes started to glaze over.

'John. John! Look at me, mate. Look at me!'

Clocks grimaced as he moved his body slightly. 'Fuckin' 'urt's, Ray.'

'What hurts?'

'Everythin'. Me 'ead's killin' me again.'

'I'm not surprised. Tell me you didn't headbutt him, John. You've got a fucking concussion, for fuck's sake!'

'I didn't 'eadbutt 'im, Ray. Swear to yer.' His voice grew weaker.

Paterson looked across at Jackie. Tears streamed down her face, anguish etched across it. He altered his position, shuffled about a bit so that Jackie could get closer. She took Clocks's hand and stroked the back of it with her thumb.

'C'mon, guv,' she said. 'Don't fuck about like this. You're scaring me.'

Clocks rolled his eyes toward her as he licked away the blood from his bottom lip. ''Ello, babe. You doin' all right? Safe now . . .' His voice was fading.

She gave a little sob and a painful, desperate smile. 'I am, yeah. You, not so much, eh?'

'Me? Nah. I'm good . . . good as gold.' He coughed, his face wracked with pain. 'You wanna see the other fellah.'

She looked over at Forrest's butchered body and quickly looked away again. 'I have, thank you. Nearly chucked up.'

Clocks nodded weakly. 'Good. You could do with droppin' a few pounds. Been meanin' to say . . .'

She laughed, spittle leaving her lips. 'You bastard, Clocksy.'

'Ray. I've got . . . a killer . . . 'eadache. Any aspirins floatin' about?'

'Monkey!' Paterson shouted. 'Where's that fucking ambulance?'

Clocks screwed his face up. 'Mate . . .'

Paterson looked at him. 'What?'

'Said I've got an 'eadache. Don't shout.'

'Shit. Sorry. It's just that . . .' Paterson could feel Clocks slipping. He shuffled around again, moved them both so that he could support Clocks's weight better.

'Ray . . . There's a light. A . . . bright light.'

Paterson gripped him tighter. 'John, listen to me . . . stay away from it. Do not go toward it. Come back here.'

'What?'

'Stay away from it.'

Clocks screwed his eyes up. 'It's so fuckin' bright . . . 'urtin' me eyes.'

'John! No! Stay away from it.'

'I will . . . if one of you . . . turns it off.' He pointed to the ceiling with a nod of his chin. Paterson and Jackie looked up.

The ceiling was dotted with LED lights. Paterson had shifted Clocks directly underneath them.

'For fucks sake. I thought . . .'

Clocks smiled. 'Gotcha.'

'Yeah, you fucker.'

'Ray?'

'What?'

'I'm tired, mate. It all 'urts. I just need a kip . . . a little kip. Ten minutes, eh?' Clocks closed and opened his eyes a few times.

'Can't go to sleep yet, buddy. Can't let you do that.'

'Tired . . . coupla minutes . . . tha's all . . .' His speech was slurring now. 'Coupla . . . coupla minutes . . . rest . . .'

Paterson grabbed him by the jaw and squeezed him as he shook his head from side to side. 'Not now, John! C'mon. Wake up, mate!'

'I'm . . . sorry . . . I'm . . . just . . . tired.'

Paterson looked across at Jackie, helpless and frightened, tears streaming. 'Clocksy. C'mon, mate. Stay with me, eh? Don't do this.' He started to sob but fought it down, not wanting his friend to know he was losing his battle.

Clocks's head lolled back, his eyes closed. Paterson felt his body become instantly heavier. He pulled his body into his, held him tighter. 'Oh, John. John, John, John, John, John! Please, mate. Please don't go. Please . . .'

Jackie fell onto her backside, still holding Clocks's hand. She was as much a ball of tears and snot as Paterson. She shook her head. Denial. Paterson cradled Clocks's head on his shoulder, dropped his face onto the top of his head and gently stroked one cheek, wiping away blood. 'It's all right, mate. It's all right.' He kissed him gently on the top of the head and laid him down before he let out the most painful howl. Johnny Clocks died thirty seconds before two paramedics burst through the door.

'Jesus!' one of them said as he quickly took in the scene. One on the floor tied up, two sitting, smothered in blood, and a pile of sliced-up meat propped up against a wall.

'The one on the floor!' Monkey screamed at them. 'Help him!'

Monkey took Paterson's arm and pulled him away. He didn't want to go and threw a look of pure rage at Monkey.

'Guv. You're in the way. C'mon. Jackie, you too!'

'I'm staying with him,' said Paterson.

Monkey grabbed him by the collar. 'Come here, guv. You're in the way.'

Paterson sprang to his feet, wracked with grief, not even sure who he was looking at now. Behind him, he could hear the paramedics working frantically on a dead man. He heard Clocks's shirt being ripped open, buttons pinging on the hardwood floor, packets of bandages being torn open, the sudden sharp tang of antiseptic, the high-pitched whine of a portable defibrillator winding itself up. Paterson stood in the middle of the room having an out-of-body-experience. He saw everything and felt nothing.

# CHAPTER 52

Two months later, Daniel Bevan was sitting in his drawing room completely absorbed in his book, one of John Grisham's earlier novels, the words transporting him to another world. Reading was one of the few things that brought him true joy these days.

Bevan had lived a life full of intrigue and danger, recruited to MI5 straight out of Oxford University. His intelligence and cunning propelled him quickly up the ranks until he made the daring move to MI6 after a decade of service. With his natural talents and keen mind, he became the youngest head of MI6 at only forty-two years old. And for nearly two decades he had held on to that position with an iron grip, earning both respect and fear from enemies and colleagues alike.

A sudden noise caught his attention. It was faint but distinct, not like any sound he had heard in his house before. Built centuries before, it was no stranger to creaks and groans, but this was different. Bevan knew every single sound it made. This one was new and unfamiliar. It stirred a sense of unease within him as he put down his book and listened intently for any other signs of disturbance. There was a creak outside the door.

'Please, come in,' he said, keeping his voice even.

The door to the room creaked open.

'Thanks for that. We were wonderin' 'ow we were gonna get in without you noticin'.'

Bevan peeked around the high wing of the Chesterfield. He instantly spotted the suppressed pistols that both men held. 'Paterson and Clocks,' he said. 'No doubt that explains why Forrest has been dark for the last two months. Where is he?'

'I chopped 'im down,' said Clocks. 'It was always gonna be 'is fate with a name like that, wasn't it? Big fucker, that one. Took some work.'

'Why did it take you so long to come and see me?'

'I was lyin' around in 'ospital. The big lump broke two of me ribs, one of which punctured me 'eart. Fucker actually killed me. Can you believe it? I bloody died for a little while, but thanks to the good ol' London Ambulance Service at the scene an' their little box of tricks and magic, 'ere I am.'

Bevan picked up a bookmark, placed it in his last page and put the book on the table.

'Any good?' said Paterson.

'Not his best, but I like it.'

'I've read it,' said Clocks. 'Want me to tell you the endin'?'

'I presume it doesn't end well?'

Clocks grinned. 'It does not.'

'What's happened to my security team?'

'They're all having a little lie down,' said Paterson. 'Not as good as you were led to believe, that lot.'

'Are they dead?'

Paterson shook his head. 'No. They're just guards. They didn't get in our way.'

Bevan made to stand.

'Woah, old fellah,' said Clocks. 'Where you off to?'

'Nowhere. Just wanted to look you both in the eye and express my admiration for you both. It's not just anyone who could have killed Forrest and then get past my team. Yet two

268

good old-fashioned coppers did. I really did underestimate you both. I must be slipping in my old age.'

'I reckon,' said Clocks.

'What have you done with the information you took from him?'

'Oh, that's safe,' said Paterson. 'We'll out it if it becomes necessary.'

'And what would make it necessary?' Bevan peered at Paterson. He really did admire them.

'If you went ahead and executed the plan, and . . .'

'And?'

'And if either or both of us gets taken out,' said Paterson. 'You must have known we'd topped Forrest when you hadn't heard from him for so long. So I'd be surprised if you haven't mustered up all your clandestine operatives to come look for us.'

Bevan nodded then shrugged his shoulders. 'Of course. But I can stop it. I could use people like you.'

'Oh yeah?' said Clocks. 'Is this you offerin' us a job?'

'Not the usual way of doing things, Mr Clocks, but this is an unusual night and you two are both very unusual men.'

'Think so?' said Clocks. 'Thought we were just a pair of old-fashioned coppers.'

Bevan nodded. 'Clearly not. So . . . interested?'

'Are you serious?' said Paterson. 'You want to murder thousands of innocent people and provoke a war. You have my friends killed and you think we'd join you?'

'Well, it was worth a shot.'

Clocks put one in his leg. Bevan screamed as the bullet tore through his flesh, dropping him to the floor.

'That's a shot worth takin'.'

Paterson looked over at his friend and grinned.

'What the fuuuckkk!' Bevan hissed. 'What are you doing? Do you know who I am? What resources I have?'

'Well, as my ol' wank mate Shania Twain once said, "That don't impress me much."'

269

'You idiots! I'll have you wiped out for this. Do you understand?'

'Yeah, right you are. You tried that once before, didn't you, an' look 'ow that worked out for you. You rollin' around on the floor wonderin' if you'll ever walk again. Short answer is . . . no.'

'For God's sake, man. I'm all that stands between us and anarchy. I have to do things that others won't. I have to pull the trigger.'

'Like this?' Clocks shot him in the other leg, just below the knee, smashing through bone on its way out. Bevan screamed again. 'I can see the appeal,' said Clocks.

Bevan groaned through gritted teeth. 'You'll be hunted down like dogs. Nowhere will be safe for you. We'll find you and we'll kill you.'

'Others, maybe, but you won't,' said Clocks. 'You had my friends killed. You wanted us dead. You had my wife shot. She's in a coma, might never come out of it. That's on you.'

Bevan looked up helplessly, tears in his eyes and dribble on his chin. 'That's a tragedy, Clocks. She wasn't the target.'

'Who was?'

'You and Paterson.'

'That's charmin', innit, Ray? Me an' you. Two of the nicest guys you could ever wish to meet an' he wanted us dead.' He flashed a grin at Paterson before turning back to Bevan with a snarl. 'Instead, you shot my wife. You know how that makes me feel?'

The man rolled around on the floor, suffering the agony of two broken bones and the velocity pain that comes from being shot. 'Feel? What do you mean, *feel*? I'm not in the feeling game, man. I can't afford that luxury. I have to keep the country safe.'

'Do you have family?' said Clocks.

He nodded. 'Yes, yes. Of course. A wife, two daughters, three grandchildren.'

'I wonder if they'll feel.' He pulled the trigger and shot Bevan in the head. A small explosion of blood splatted across the floorboards in the instant he died. Paterson and Clocks stepped forward. Paterson put another four into his head, Clocks put six into his face. It all added up to a pile of mush on the floor where once there was a head.

'Do you think they'll be upset, John? His family?'

'Couldn't give a fuck, Ray. Not a single flyin' fuck.'

# CHAPTER 53

From his fifth-floor office, Commissioner Sam Morne looked out of the window over the city of London. The sky was a calm blue with a few cotton wool clouds that settled themselves on the horizon. He was quiet for a full minute as Paterson and Clocks sat impatiently for him to say something.

'I was sorry to hear about Mr Young . . . Wol,' he said finally. 'He was a good man. A very good man. Did he happen to mention he was one of us?'

That got Paterson's attention. 'What d'you mean?'

'Wol had been a member of UMBRA for, ooh, best part of twenty years, I guess. He didn't mention it?'

'No,' said Paterson. 'Never.'

Morne gave a nod and went back to gazing out of the window. 'He headed up one of the main command units. Oversaw numerous operations. A calm, measured man who never once made a mistake. A fine man. When he retired, he was told to take it easy. God knows he'd earned a break but that wasn't his way. Watching the world go to shit wasn't for him, I'm sure you knew that.'

Paterson and Clocks stayed silent.

'He'd had his eye on you for years. Did you know that? Thought you two would make a good team. Solid, dependable, tenacious, capable.'

'Any chance you could turn around, guv?' said Clocks, his agitation more palpable than Paterson's. 'Only, I don't do too well talking to people's backs. Rude, innit?'

Morne turned, a thin smile on his lips. 'My apologies, John. I was just reminiscing.'

'You crack on then, just turn around an' do it.'

'Are you surprised that Wol was one of us?'

Paterson shrugged. 'Considering we had no idea that you even existed until a couple of months ago. But then once I found out, no, not at all. He had approached us a number of times before about working with him but he never discussed UMBRA. Doesn't surprise me though. Wol was all about doing right even if it meant doing wrong.'

Morne's smile grew larger. 'Ah. Your motto, isn't it? The two of you, hmm? Sometimes you have to do wrong to do right. It's how you justify your behaviour.'

Paterson watched him closely. Sam Morne appeared to be a decent man. Smartly dressed in a sharp navy-blue suit and tie with black brogues, he looked every inch the senior officer and careful politician.

'Get to the point, Sam,' said Paterson.

'You know the point, Ray. I was going to ask you again whether you were going to join us, but John's act of barbaric revenge has, I think, taken away your options somewhat. I have the chief of the intelligence service crawling up my arse wanting to know where his operative is. Jack Forrest, yes? What do I tell him?'

Clocks grinned. 'Tell 'im 'e failed to kill us an' 'e's all cut up about it. Tell 'im that.' Paterson stifled a laugh.

'Very funny, John. Hilarious.'

'Yeah, I know. Thing is, you can't tell 'im anythin' anyway.'

Morne's brow creased deeply. 'Meaning?'

273

'Meanin' I sorted 'im out an' all.'

'What?'

'Yep. Popped round to 'is gaff this mornin to tell 'im the good news that 'is number-one assassin 'ad been relegated when 'e started gobbin' off at us. I wasn't in the mood for it, so I shot 'im in the swede.' He looked at Paterson and gave him a wink.

Morne froze as if not sure if he was hearing right. 'You shot him? You fucking shot the one man who has more power than the Prime Minister? Why?'

'Really? I 'ave to explain it to you? It's because of 'im me missus is lying in a coma an' some of my best friends are dead, and in case you forget, he killed me. Actually fuckin' killed me, so, in the words of the famous poet, fuck 'im.'

Morne shook his head. 'How the hell do you expect me to cover this up?'

'Dunno. Sure you'll figure it out. What with all your sneaky-deaky ways of doin' things.'

'Christ!'

'Him? Oh, 'e's next on me list. I understand 'e's due to come back soon. I can tell you, 'e'll wish 'e 'adn't bothered if 'e does.'

Morne sat himself heavily into his chair, his hands on his knees and shaking his head. 'If you don't join us now, I can't protect you, you know that. In fact . . .'

Paterson eyed him. 'In fact, what?'

Morne looked away. 'In fact, I'll . . .'

''Ave to 'ave us bumped off, yeah?' Clocks sat opposite him, defiant. 'Well, good luck with that.'

'Don't be an arse, John.'

'We're in,' said Paterson. 'We know we've gone way too far this time. Forrest fucked us big time with the AI videos so—' he gave a small shrug — 'where do we sign?'

'You understand what this means, don't you?'

Paterson said nothing.

'You are never going to see your loved ones again. Any of them. Ever.'

'Well, if my Lyndsey don't make it, I don't give a tuppenny toss,' said Clocks.

Morne looked at Clocks carefully. 'Are you sure, John? You have family now. A grandchild on the way.'

Clocks nodded. 'I 'ave a son who's havin' a child. A son I never knew existed, an' to be honest, I 'ave no relationship with whatsoever. 'E's a wrong'un, so I don't want a relationship with 'im. As for me grandkid, well . . . that is unfortunate, but the more I think about it, I don't want anyone to ever give me the nickname Grandfather Clocks.'

'We'll make sure your lifestyles don't change. Your incomes will be routed through a number of electronic accounts and eventually land where they can be easily accessed under a false identity. Alice will take care of that for you.'

Paterson was startled. 'Alice? I thought Alice died with Wol?'

'Technically, that's correct, but the paramedics were able to revive her. She lost one leg completely and one below the knee. She lost part of her lower intestine, two fingers on her left hand and is waiting for an operation on her right eye.'

'S'pose we'll 'ave to change 'er name to "Lucky" then,' said Clocks.

Paterson ignored him. 'What's happening with the Hayes file?'

'It's been put on the back burner for now,' said Morne.

'Not good enough, Sam. It needs to be abandoned completely. I'm not having fifty thousand people die for a test.'

'Ray, I know you're upset—'

'Ray's not upset, Sam,' said Clocks. 'You'd know if 'e was, believe me.'

Morne glanced at Clocks then turned back to Paterson. 'Look, Ray. You know how bloody complex this world is. Nothing stays the same. The world turns and we come and go, but the security of the free world is paramount.'

Clocks shook his head. This might go bad.

'I kept copies of it, Sam. Just so you know. If this program doesn't shut down, they'll be released into the wider world.'

'Let's not do this, Ray. This isn't the time.'

'No? Oh, I think it is.'

'Okay, Ray. Look, I'm more than happy to discuss it with the pair of you, I am, but we have a lot to do for you both. I need you to rest, I need to get you trained in all manner of things. I need to get Alice out of hospital and up and running so she can work with you, and I need to recruit Jackie and Monkey too. I assumed you'd want them in some capacity. I need you to take over from Wol to head up a team. Nothing will happen with the Hayes file for some time, and if it ever rears its ugly head again, we'll deal with it. And we will. But for now, please just go home or go to see Lyndsey, whatever you want to do. Will you do that for me?'

Both men nodded sharply. 'I'll talk to Jackie and Monkey, not you,' said Paterson. 'I want to make sure they have a way out if they want it. I don't want them being stitched into anything.'

'Of course. Not a problem.'

'With regard to the AI vids out there about us, what can be done about it? I don't want our legacy to be that we were cop killers, you understand?'

'Understood. I have to be honest though and say I don't know. We'll work through it and see what we can do but, unfortunately, he who controls the lie controls the truth, and I'm afraid that, for all intents and purposes, Forrest controlled the lie.'

Paterson stared at Morne. Cold. 'Come on, John. We need to speak to what's left of our team.'

# CHAPTER 54

'Can we slow down a bit?' Clocks limped along the corridor, trying to keep up with Paterson. 'I still 'ave a dodgy leg.'

Paterson slowed. 'Sorry, John. Thinking.'

'Thought so. What's up?'

'Did you hear it?'

'What? Your thought? Nope.'

'No, not my thought. What Sam said?'

'Course I did. I got punched in me 'ead, not me ears. What d'you reckon?'

Paterson stabbed the button on the lift console. 'Dunno, but when the Commissioner of Police and the current head of a secret organisation recites almost word for word what Forrest, an enemy assassin, says, it bothers me greatly.'

Clocks winced as he felt a sharp pain in his leg. It passed.

'*You control the lie, you control the truth,*' said Paterson. 'That's what Forrest said, didn't he? That's not something you randomly say, is it? No one says that. It's not a saying, either. It's a fucking motto.'

The lift dinged and the doors slid open. They stepped inside. 'So, these fuckers are all tied in together some'ow?' said Clocks.

'Must be. I just don't know how yet.'

'Why did you agree to join UMBRA, then?'

'What choice do we have really, John? Morne's already got us on a shitload of charges that'll see us in the nick for the next God knows how many years if we don't, and you cutting down the Forrest kind of cemented the deal.'

Clocks glanced down at his shoes. 'Yeah. Sorry about that.'

'Don't be. Fucker had it coming. Glad you did it, mate. If it hadn't been you, it'd have been me. Good riddance to the piece of shit.'

The doors slid open, and they stepped out into the lobby. Paterson nodded to the security guard behind the desk as he signed them both out.

Clocks threw a friendly salute to the guard then turned to Paterson. 'One thing at a time, mate. First thing on the agenda, brekkie. Fry-up at a café. Fancy it?'

'About as much as I fancy you.'

'Not a good analogy, is it? We all know 'ow much you love me.'

'Don't kid yourself.'

They pushed through the revolving door and stepped out into the sunlight.

'Which café you want to go to?' said Paterson.

'Don't care, mate. Long as I can get a fry-up, I'm good.'

'Lead the way, then. You know all the best places to get a heart attack in London.' They headed off down the steps, slower than normal, Clocks limping slightly.

'Can I ask yer something, Ray?'

'Yeah, course.'

'When I was busy turnin' me toes up, I had a vision. A dream. I dunno what it was, but I saw a wolf on a mountain top and it was 'owlin' like a good'un. What d'you reckon that was?'

Paterson glanced sideways at him. He knew exactly what that was. Him. Clocks's death had wounded him.

'You remember you used to say I was raised by wolves?'

Paterson nodded.

'I wonder if me dream 'ad anythin' to do with that?'

'Dunno. Maybe.'

They reached the bottom of the steps. Clocks stopped for a minute and held on to Paterson's shoulder.

'You all right, John?'

'Yeah. Leg's givin' me a bit of gyp, that's all. I'll be all right in a sec.'

'Take your time. No rush.'

'Ta. An' another thing . . . Did you kiss me on the 'ead, by any chance?'

Paterson shuffled about and looked away. 'What's that now?'

'Did yer kiss me? On the 'ead.'

Paterson started to feel uncomfortable. 'No. You wish.'

'Jackie said you did. Said it was the saddest thing she's ever seen. Worse than when Lassie died.'

'Well, Jackie's full of it, mate. She was upset.'

'So were you. You kissed me.'

'I didn't.'

'You love me.'

'Fuck off.'

'Don't be ashamed, mate. I love you.'

'Tch. Look, all right. I gave you a little peck. I was in shock. I thought I'd lost you. It's how it was. Don't make a big thing of it.'

'I'm not. You love me though, don't yer?'

'Christ. You're milking this, you needy fucker. Yes, I love you, but like a brother. Nothing else. All right? Is that it?'

Clocks shrugged. 'Well, that's not very romantic, is it?'

'Romantic? What's wrong with you?' Paterson shook his head. 'When's your next brain scan due? I swear you're worse than before.'

Clocks gave a sharp nod. 'I'm all right now. Come on.' The two men set off again.

'Listen. Serious now, Ray. I saw God.'

'No you didn't.'

'Yes I did.'

'You don't believe in God.'

'I know, but as it says in the Bible, 'e believes in me.'

'That's nice. Did he have anything to say to you, his newest recruit?'

'Yep. Says to me, "All right, Clocksy, my son? What you doin' up 'ere with all the decents? You get on the wrong bus or summin'?"'

'*Did you get on the wrong bus?* So, what? God's from South London, is he?'

'Must be. Who knew, eh? God's probably a Millwall fan. Wonders'll never cease, will they?'

Clocks stumbled as he stepped off the kerb. Paterson's arm shot across his chest. 'John!'

The roar of a motorbike shattered the air as it screeched to a halt, barely missing Clocks by inches. He glared at the reckless rider, rage boiling inside him. But as he raised his hand to signal his anger, he froze in shock. The rider slowly lifted his visor and revealed the face of Detective Tommy Gunn.

Clocks stumbled back in disbelief, unable to comprehend what was happening. Gunn was supposed to be dead. And then the nightmare became reality as Gunn pulled out a pistol and pointed it directly at Clocks. Panic surged through him as screams erupted from bystanders, but before he could react, two shots hit him in the chest. Paterson was rooted to the spot. The first shot caught him high on the leg. He dropped, turned and looked into Gunn's face. A bolt of pain hit him in the chest, followed by a second one. By the time the third one hit him, he was already out of the game.

People were screaming and running in all directions as the two detectives fell. Clocks on his back, Paterson on his side. Neither man moved as their shirts bloomed red.

\* \* \*

From his office on the fifth floor, Commissioner Sam Morne looked down at the street. He made another call. 'It's done, ma'am,' he said. 'They're gone.'

# CHAPTER 55

The press room in Scotland Yard was full to capacity. The noise made it difficult for anyone to hear anyone else as they all speculated as to the identity of the men killed and the possible reasons for why they were murdered. The room was awash with theories and rumours but they wanted, *needed* to hear it from Metropolitan Police Commissioner Sam Morne. As he entered, flanked by his senior press officer and a legal advisor, the room quickly settled down into a tangible silence.

'Good afternoon,' Morne said. 'As you all know, two men were shot and killed outside New Scotland Yard earlier today by a man who made good his escape on a motorcycle. It is with deep sorrow that I now confirm that the victims of these horrific killings were Detective Superintendent Raymond Paterson and Detective Inspector John Clocks. Despite the best efforts of the London Ambulance Service to revive them, both men were pronounced dead at the scene. Their families have been informed and are receiving help and counselling in coming to terms with this senseless loss. At the moment, we have no suspect, but a large number of the public were witness to the killings and are now helping us with our enquiries.'

Morne took a deep breath before looking directly into the camera and continuing. 'Whoever did this needs to know that the full might of the Metropolitan Police will be levelled at finding them. We will not rest. We will not stop. You will be caught. And you will be brought to justice.' Morne suddenly stood. 'I will not be taking questions. Thank you.' As the room broke into a riot of shouts, he turned abruptly and walked out.

## THE END

# THE JOFFE BOOKS STORY

We began in 2014 when Jasper agreed to publish his mum's much-rejected romance novel and it became a bestseller.

Since then we've grown into the largest independent publisher in the UK. We're extremely proud to publish some of the very best writers in the world, including Joy Ellis, Faith Martin, Caro Ramsay, Helen Forrester, Simon Brett and Robert Goddard. Everyone at Joffe Books loves reading and we never forget that it all begins with the magic of an author telling a story.

We are proud to publish talented first-time authors, as well as established writers whose books we love introducing to a new generation of readers.

We won Trade Publisher of the Year at the Independent Publishing Awards in 2023 and Best Publisher Award in 2024 at the People's Book Prize. We have been shortlisted for Independent Publisher of the Year at the British Book Awards for the last five years, and were shortlisted for the Diversity and Inclusivity Award at the 2022 Independent Publishing Awards. In 2023 we were shortlisted for Publisher of the Year at the RNA Industry Awards, and in 2024 we were shortlisted at the CWA Daggers for the Best Crime and Mystery Publisher.

We built this company with your help, and we love to hear from you, so please email us about absolutely anything bookish at feedback@joffebooks.com.

If you want to receive free books every Friday and hear about all our new releases, join our mailing list here: www.joffebooks.com/freebooks.

And when you tell your friends about us, just remember: it's pronounced Joffe as in coffee or toffee!